DOWN THE RABBIT HOLE

Peter Abrahams, described by Stephen King as his "favourite American suspense novelist", is a bestselling author of adult crime thrillers. His novels include *A Perfect Crime*; *The Fan*, which was adapted into a major Hollywood movie starring Robert De Niro; and *Lights Out*, which was nominated for an Edgar Award for best novel. *An Echo Falls Mystery: Down the Rabbit Hole*, so-called because it features the play of *Alice's Adventures in Wonderland* in the novel, is Peter's first book for young readers and is a 2006 Agatha Award Winner. *Behind the Curtain*, "a deliciously plotted, highly satisfying adventure" (*Kirkus Reviews*), is the second book in the series. He lives in Cape Cod, Massachusetts, USA with his wife and children.

Another Echo Falls Mystery

Behind the Curtain

DOWN THE RABBIT HOLE

An Echo Falls Mystery

PETER ABRAHAMS

WALKER
BOOKS

Published by arrangement with HarperCollins Children's Books,
a division of HarperCollins, Inc.

First published in Great Britain 2006 by Walker Books Ltd
87 Vauxhall Walk, London SE11 5HJ

4 6 8 10 9 7 5 3

© 2005 Pas de Deux

The right of Peter Abrahams to be identified as author of this
work has been asserted by him in accordance with the
Copyright, Designs and Patents Act 1988

This book has been typeset in Sabon

Printed and bound in Great Britain by J. H. Haynes & Co. Ltd

British Library Cataloguing in Publication Data:
a catalogue record for this book is available from the British Library

ISBN 978-1-4063-0028-4

www.walkerbooks.co.uk

For my children,

Seth, Ben, Lily and Rosie,

with love

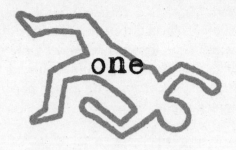

ingrid Levin-Hill, three weeks past her thirteenth birthday, sat thinking in her orthodontist's waiting room. You're born cute. Babies are cute. Not hard to guess why – it's so everyone will forgive them for being such a pain. You grow a little older, and people say, "What beautiful hair," or "Get a load of those baby blues," or something nice that keeps you thinking you're still on the cuteness track. Then you hit twelve or thirteen and boom, they tell you that everything needs fixing. Waiting in the wings are the orthodontist, the dermatologist, the contact lens guy, the hair-tinting guy, maybe even the nose-job guy. You look at yourself in the mirror, really look at yourself, for the first time. And what do you see? Oh my God.

Two orthodontists divided the business in Echo Falls: Dr. Lassiter, who didn't mind pulling a tooth or two to speed things along, and Dr. Binkerman, who liked to say he'd turn in his badge before sacrificing a single tooth. One kind of parents sent their kids to Dr.

Lassiter. Ingrid, whose parents were of the other kind, was well into her second year with Dr. Binkerman, and behind her braces lurked the same jumble of teeth she'd come in with in the first place. And by the way, what stupid badge was he talking about? Ingrid flipped to another page of *Seventeen*. The glossy paper made an angry snapping sound.

FLIRTING TIPS:
WHERE THE HOTTIES ARE
In the weight room, of course. So it's important to get down with all that weight room terminology. Cut, ripped, reps, lats, pecs, curls, dips, jacked, juiced – is this a weird lingo or what? Let's start with reps. Reps is simply short for—

"Ingrid?"

Ingrid looked up. Mary Jane, the chairside assistant, stood in the doorway that led back to the surgeries, the expression on her face a little exasperated, as though maybe she'd been calling Ingrid for some time. If so, Ingrid really hadn't heard. Reading – it didn't matter what – always did that to her.

"All set," said Mary Jane. Ingrid followed her. There were two chairside assistants: Mary Jane, who wore her gray hair in a bun and always had circles under her eyes, and a younger one, who changed every two months or so. Mary Jane motioned Ingrid to the chair and raised it just as Dr. Binkerman strode in, flexing his surgically gloved hands.

"And how's Ingrid today?" he said, looming into extreme close-up, his gaze locking on her teeth. Like Sherlock Holmes – *The Complete Sherlock Holmes* had been sitting on her bedside table for years – Ingrid was a habitual noticer of little things. Sherlock Holmes believed you could find out just about all you needed to know about people from little things; his method, as he told Dr. Watson more than once, was founded on the observation of trifles. Trifles were things like the single but surprisingly long white hair poking out of Dr. Binkerman's left nostril; the sleepy seed, lima bean colored, in the corner of his right eye; the pinprick-size blackhead on the end of his nose, a millimeter off-center. All these trifles added up to the glamorous Dr. Binkerman, hard-riding sheriff of the overbite range.

And what was the question? How's Ingrid today?

"She's fine," said Ingrid.

"Open, please," said Dr. Binkerman. He peered inside her mouth, felt around in back, where the screws were, with his rubbery fingers. "Been wearing the appliance?" he said.

"Uh-huh," said Ingrid.

"Every night?" Dr. Binkerman drew back, looking at her whole face for the first time, fingers out of her mouth now so she could speak clearly.

"Uh-huh," said Ingrid, although every night would be pushing it, if by "every night" Dr. Binkerman meant every single night, night after night after night ad nauseam. Ingrid didn't want to get to the nauseam stage, so she never wore the thing on sleepovers, for example, or when she fell asleep reading, or on Friday nights, when she gave herself a regular breather as a reward for getting through the school week; and there might have been other random misses from time to time. She was only human. Still, what business was it of his?

"Keep it up," said Dr. Binkerman.

Keep it up. He said that every time, and every time Ingrid replied, "I will." But this time, for no reason, she said, "For how long?" The words just popping out on their own, the way words sometimes did.

Mary Jane, sticking X rays up on the light box, paused for less than a second, just a tiny hitch in her movement. Dr. Binkerman blinked. "How long?" he said.

How long? Had Dr. Binkerman lost track of the whole point of this? "Till everything's all straight," she said. "Till I'm done."

Ingrid had noticed that people's lips often did things when they were thinking. Some people pursed them, some bit them, some sucked them in between their teeth. Dr. Binkerman was a biter. "Every case is different, as I mentioned way back at the initial consultation with your parents," he said. "You remember that conversation, Ingrid?"

Ingrid remembered: Mom hovering over morphing mouth schematics on the computer screen, Dad checking his watch. "Uh-huh," she said.

"Then you'll remember there are lots of variables," Dr. Binkerman said. He paused. "Like patient cooperation. But all in all, I'd say you were coming along right on schedule." He leaned forward again, pointy silver pliers in hand. "Are we due for an adjustment, Mary Jane?"

Mary Jane glanced at the chart. "Overdue."

Adjustment meant tightening. Tightening didn't hurt much while it was happening, but every turn of the screw made a squeaky sound that seemed to come from right inside Ingrid's head, and reminded her of the Shackleton IMAX movie she'd seen a few weeks before on a class trip – that scene where ice floes slowly crush the ship to death. Over Dr. Binkerman's shoulder, she saw that Mary Jane was watching. Ingrid read the straight answer to her how-much-longer question in Mary Jane's frowning eyes: *Till hell freezes over.*

"See the receptionist on your way out," said Dr. Binkerman.

Ingrid made her next appointment at the reception counter, then looked out the window to see if Mom or Dad was waiting in the parking lot. Mom drove a three-year-old green Mazda MPV van, an uncool car with uncool bumper stickers that said she supported National Public Radio and the Echo Falls Heritage Committee. Dad drove a silver Audi TT, a very cool car, no doubt about that, with no bumper stickers supporting anything, the only problem being that the TT was really a two-seater, with not much more than shelf space for Ingrid in the back. But shelf space covered in the softest leather Ingrid had ever touched, so it all balanced out, kind of.

Neither car was in the lot. Ingrid hadn't really expected them to be exactly right on time to the minute. Mom and Dad had busy lives. On the far side of the parking lot, a squirrel ran down a branch and leaped to the next tree. Three yellow leaves came loose and drifted to the ground. Ingrid watched how they landed, intact and undamaged, so softly you could hardly call it landing.

She sat back down, reopened *Seventeen*.

—repetitions. Meaning how many times you lift the weight. Reps are divided into sets. For example—

Ingrid tossed the magazine onto the next chair. She knew all this. They had practically a whole gym in their basement at home. Her brother, Ty – her parents had had only one acceptable name in them, and he'd come first – was into sports, and Dad, who was also into sports, especially Ty's, was building him up. Dad was into her sports too, or sport, since she'd rid herself of hockey – too cold – and softball – too slow – and was now down to soccer, the only one she'd ever liked in the first—

Soccer. Ingrid checked the clock on the waiting-room wall: 4:10. Practice was at 4:30. She'd completely forgotten soccer practice. Miss a practice, miss a game. That was Coach Ringer's rule number one. Was there anything more boring than sitting on the bench for a whole game? Other than math class, of course; that went without saying. And could you get around rule number one by skipping the punishment game? No, because rule number two was miss a game miss the next game. This had actually happened to Ingrid's friend Stacy Rubino, who'd gotten into a battle of wills with Coach Ringer that had spun into a death spiral of missed games and eventual demotion from the A travel team to the Bs. The Bs, who always inherited the uniforms worn by the As the year before. Say no more.

4:13. Ingrid glanced out the window: no green van, no silver TT. Her boots, shin pads, and sweats were in her backpack, slung over one shoulder and heavy with homework. She went outside to wait, in the hope of saving a minute or so. Why? Because being late for practice meant push-ups. Rule number three.

Ingrid stood in the parking lot. No Mom, no Dad. This would be a good time for a cell phone. Did Ingrid have her own cell phone? She did not. Did Ty have his own cell phone? Yes, he did. Were Mom and Dad's reasons for not giving her one yet anything more than complete b.s.? They were not.

A few more leaves drifted down. Probably 4:15 by now, maybe even later – Ingrid didn't know because her watch, Fossil, red face, red band, lay on *The Complete Sherlock Holmes* in her bedroom. Or maybe – uh-oh – in her desk at school. Red was Ingrid's favorite color, of all the colors the only one that said COLOR in big letters.

What was it now, 4:17, 4:18? Still time to get to the soccer fields. The drive only took a few minutes. You just turned right out of Dr. Binkerman's parking lot, went past Blockbuster and Benito's Pizzeria, the one with the thin-crust pizza she liked and—

A little spark went off in Ingrid's head, a lively, wake-up kind of spark she'd had before. It always meant one thing and one thing only: Inspiration had struck. Inspiration, a thought coming out of nowhere, like the apple falling on Newton's head, and this was a good one: Why not walk to soccer practice? Even though she'd never actually walked from Dr. Binkerman's to soccer practice before, she had to know the way, having been driven there a million times. So what was the big deal about walking? Why hadn't she thought of this before? In fact, why not run?

Ingrid ran – turning right out of the parking lot, zipping past Blockbuster and Benito's, and over a bridge. Bridge? Funny, she'd never noticed this bridge before – maybe you noticed a lot more when you were on foot, like the way the river flowed underneath, sliding along like one long jelly the color of Mom's good silverware when it needed a polish at Christmas, the only time it came out of the drawer.

One thing about Ingrid: She could run. She could run and she loved to run. "Look at her fly," Assistant Coach Trimble, who'd played for a UConn team that had gone all the way to the NCAA Division One Women's Championship game, would sometimes say. And Coach Ringer, who owned Towne Hardware, would reply, "Be nice if she kept her head in the game," or "When's she gonna learn a move or two out there?"

How about this for a move? Ingrid thought, swerving to kick a Coke can over a fire hydrant, catching up to it before it stopped rolling, kicking the can again, then again and again, while she thought *When the hell is Coach Ringer going to retire?* and *Does the fact that I hear them talking on the sidelines mean he's right and my head's not in the game?* and raced faster and faster down a street lined with shabby old gingerbread houses, their paint peeling and windows grimy with—

Shabby old gingerbread houses? Whoa. The Coke can clattered into the gutter and came to rest on a sewer grate. The only shabby gingerbread houses Ingrid knew in Echo Falls stood in the Flats, the oldest part of town, where the shoe factories and railroad yards had been long ago. The soccer fields were up the hill from the hospital, and that was nowhere near the Flats. Was it? Ingrid looked around. No hill, no hospital, just these gingerbread houses in a neighborhood not especially safe, come to think of it. The front door of the nearest one – just about the most decrepit of all, actually crooked to the naked eye, half the roof covered with a blue tarp – opened, and out came a woman with a shopping bag in her hand.

A strange woman: She was tall, and even taller in the gold spike heels she wore. What was the word? Lamé. Gold lamé spike heels, that was it. She also had on tights and a red-and-black-checked lumber jacket. Strips of silver foil were stuck in her hair, as though she was in the middle of a coloring treatment. Ingrid recognized the woman. She collected cans from trash barrels on Main Street and sometimes bought things at the tail end of tag sales in Ingrid's neighborhood, Riverbend. The kids called her Crazy Katie.

Wearing wraparound sunglasses even though it was starting to look like rain, she came down the front stairs, wobbling just a little. She ignored the cement path leading to the street, cutting across the bare-dirt yard, straight for Ingrid, who for some reason was rooted to the spot.

Crazy Katie walked right past Ingrid, missing her by inches and maybe not noticing her at all. She took a few steps down the sidewalk, then stopped suddenly and turned around.

"You lost?" she said. She had a deep, ragged voice, like a heavy smoker or someone who'd just finished screaming at the top of her lungs.

"Not really," Ingrid said.

Crazy Katie took off her wraparound sun-glasses and gazed down at Ingrid. She had pale irises, blue or green, but so light there was hardly any pigment at all. The whites of her eyes, on the other hand, had twisted red veins running all over them, so the effect of her gaze was painfully red.

"You look lost to me," she said. She took a step closer, gazed harder. "Like totally."

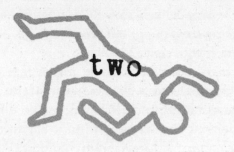

two

crazy katie was well within smelling range. She smelled like Grampy: cigarettes and booze.

"Little girlie, totally lost," she said. "Or else running away from home. Is that it? You running away from home?"

"No," said Ingrid, fighting the urge to back up a step.

Crazy Katie squinted down at her. "Bet you are," she said. "Bet your whole life's hit the fan and you're taking off. I'm a real good guesser." She stuck the sunglasses in her piled-up hair. "Or used to be," she said, her voice a lot quieter all of a sudden. She glanced around. Her gaze fell on the Coke can. She stepped into the gutter and scooped the can into her shopping bag automatically, like an assembly-line veteran; a shopping bag, Ingrid noticed, that came from Lord & Taylor. "You a Coke person or a Pepsi person?" said Crazy Katie.

Fresca was Ingrid's drink, but she said, "Pepsi."

"Me, too," said Crazy Katie. "Plus rye. What's your name, sister?"

Ingrid knew better than to give her name to strangers, especially strangers like Crazy Katie. On the other hand, she had to say something. But what?

"Forgotten your name?"

"No," said Ingrid. Who could forget *Ingrid*? Ingrid, a name that might as well have been Geek, Dork, or Loser, a name she absolutely hated, inspired by a long-ago movie star in Mom's all-time favorite movie, *Casablanca*, curse it forever. Why couldn't Mom have fallen in love with something starring Drew Barrymore? Drew Levin-Hill: cool, essence of. But no. When she was eight, Ingrid had finally thought up a nickname, but it hadn't caught on. Nicknames, she learned, were something others had to give you.

"Then what is it?" said Crazy Katie. "Your name."

Had to say something, real name out of the question, no fake names coming to mind except Miss Stapleton from *The Hound of the Baskervilles*. "Griddie," said Ingrid.

Crazy Katie's expression grew thoughtful, her forehead wrinkling, pushing ridges of dried pancake makeup out of the furrows. "Griddie," she said. "Cool. Mine's Katherine, but you can call me Kate." She held out her hand. Ingrid shook it.

Surprise. The only person who'd ever bought into her nickname turned out to be Crazy Katie. And a second, smaller surprise: how cold her hand was.

"Nice to meet you," said Ingrid. The handshaking was going on too long. The actual shaking part was over but Kate still hadn't let go.

"So what are you running away from, Griddie?"

"I'm not running away," said Ingrid, pulling her hand free. "I'm on my way to soccer."

"At the fields up by the hospital?"

"Yeah," said Ingrid, surprised that Kate would know a fact like that.

"How are you getting there?"

"Walking."

"Walking?" said Kate. "It's five miles from here."

"It is?"

"So. Lost after all."

"I wouldn't say lost."

"No?"

"How can you be lost in your own hometown?" Ingrid said.

"Let me count the ways," said Kate. With her free hand, she reached into the chest pocket of her lumber jacket, took out a cigarette and a lighter, and lit up, the lighter spurting a foot-long jet of flame. She took a deep drag. "Got any money on you, Griddie?" Smoke blew into Ingrid's face.

What kind of question was that? After most school days, the answer would have been no, but Mom hadn't had anything smaller than a ten for lunch money, so $8.50 was sitting pretty in the zipper pocket of Ingrid's backpack. Did Crazy Katie have robbery in mind? If so, could Ingrid outrun her? Ingrid glanced at those gold lamé stilettos and decided the answer was yes.

"'Cause if you do," said Kate, blowing more smoke, "I could call you a cab."

"A cab?"

"A taxicab."

Ingrid knew what a cab was, of course. She'd been in two, once when she and Mom had gone to New York to see *The Producers*, then on the vacation to Jamaica, where the Rasta driver had sung under his breath practically the whole way from the airport to the hotel, that Bob Marley song about burnin' and lootin'. But Echo Falls wasn't the kind of place where people took taxis. Had she ever even seen one in town?

"Otherwise," said Kate, "you're not going to make it."

"I've got eight fifty," Ingrid said.

"More than enough," said Kate. "Come inside." She went up the steps and opened the door.

Echo Falls was a pretty safe town. The local paper – which came out three days a week and no one took seriously (right off the top there was the name they hadn't been able to resist – *The Echo*) – printed the police blotter and Ingrid always went to it first thing. Crime in Echo Falls meant lots of driving under the influence, underage drinking (Stacy Rubino's brother, Sean, for example), and any-age drugging, some theft, some late-night mugging and second-home vandalism, bad checks passed at Stop & Shop, a little domestic violence, the occasional bar fight. No murder, no kidnapping, even in the Flats: a pretty safe town, but Ingrid knew better than to enter a stranger's house, and would never have done so in this case except for the tremendous crack of lightning that zigzagged across half the sky at that very moment, seeming to tear it wide open like a gutted water balloon, raining down an icy flood. Ingrid flew up the steps of the crooked gingerbread house and ducked inside, thunder booming around her.

Kate was already disappearing through a doorway at the end of a long dark corridor. The light was all fuzzy and grainy, the way it got sometimes in high-end movies. Ingrid waited in the entrance hall, the floor littered with unopened mail. She left the front door partly open, but the outside light hardly penetrated. To the right of the corridor, a staircase with warped wooden stairs led up into gloom. Ingrid smelled kitty litter. First she was the one actively detecting the smell; then it was coming to her, growing and growing, an inescapable stink. She looked around for cats and spotted none. From somewhere upstairs came a creaking sound, maybe a footstep.

Kate came back along the corridor, materializing out of the darkness. "All set," she said. "Be here any minute." She dropped her cigarette butt on the floor and ground it under her stiletto heel.

"Thanks," Ingrid said.

"No problemo," said Kate. "Want to wait in the parlor?"

"Outside'll be fine," Ingrid said, as thunder boomed again.

"Parlor's right here," said Kate, kicking open a door with the side of her foot.

The parlor: a small square room painted purple with gold trim, the paint peeling everywhere. A dusty chandelier dangled lopsidedly from the ceiling. The only furniture was a saggy and stained pink velvet sofa. Kate sat on it, patted the pillow beside her.

"I'm okay standing," said Ingrid.

"Suit yourself," said Kate. She felt around under one

of the cushions, fished out two cigarettes, one bent. She offered the straight one to Ingrid. "Smoke?" she said.

"Me?" said Ingrid.

Kate shrugged, stuck the straight cigarette back under the cushions, lit the bent one with another eruption of flame. "So what do you do, Griddie?" she asked from behind a cloud of smoke.

"What do I do?"

"With your life."

"I go to school," Ingrid said.

"That's it?"

"I play soccer." Which reminded her. She opened her backpack and took out her boots, bright-red Pumas with glittering red laces ordered special. Why not save time by putting them on now?

"But what's your passion?" said Kate.

Ingrid paused, the boot still in her hand. "My passion?"

"What you like to do the most."

That was easy. "Drama."

"You like acting?"

Ingrid nodded.

"Ever been in a play?"

"Lots," said Ingrid. "We did *Our Town* last spring. I was Emily in the birthday scene."

"Who is we?"

"The Prescott Players," said Ingrid.

Because of that fuzzy and grainy light, Ingrid couldn't be sure, but all of a sudden Kate seemed to go very white, and her mouth opened up, an empty black hole. Had smoke gone down the wrong way?

"Do you know the theater in Prescott Hall?" Ingrid asked. "That's where we perform."

Kate rose, her lips moving though no sound came out. She left the room – a little unsteady, maybe because of those stilettos.

"Is something wrong?" Ingrid said.

No reply. She heard Kate's footsteps on the stairs. Ingrid went into the hall, looked up the staircase, didn't see her. At that moment, a car honked outside. Through the partly opened door she saw a taxi waiting at the curb.

"Uh, thanks," Ingrid said, speaking back into the interior gloom. Then she moved toward the door, and as she did a huge cat, the biggest she'd ever seen, almost bobcat size, came gliding in from outside, tail hooked up high and a tiny blue bird in its mouth. Its hooked tail brushed her as it went by. Ingrid hurried out, slipping slightly on the unopened mail, and jumped into the cab.

"The soccer fields," she said.

"This is adjacent the hospital?" said the driver, toothpick wagging between his lips, face on the ugly border between beard and no beard.

"Yes, yes," said Ingrid, checking his ID posted by the meter: *Murad* and then a complicated last name.

"You are pressing for time?" he said.

"Yes."

He flipped the lever on the meter and made a quick U-turn, driving back the way Ingrid had come. The rain was falling hard as they passed Benito's Pizzeria, Blockbuster, and Dr. Binkerman's office, its parking lot now empty. A few minutes after that, they zipped by the hospital and stopped alongside the soccer fields. Empty soccer fields, not a soul in sight.

"What time is it?" Ingrid said.

The driver snapped open his cell phone. "Five on top of the button," he said.

Practice didn't end till five thirty. Where was everyone? Ingrid paid the driver – five dollars plus a fifty-cent tip, which was possibly not quite enough, but wouldn't a whole dollar have been too much? – and got out. The taxi drove off.

Ingrid walked over to a bench on the sidelines and sat down. Cold rain soaked her hair, her shoulders, her back. A thought came, a little late, like maybe she should have stayed in the taxi and had the driver take her home. What was the route from soccer to her house, 99 Maple Lane? Through the line of trees at the end of the field, Ingrid could see the red cross marking the helicopter pad on the hospital roof, and beyond that the spire of the Congregational church. From the church, you went by the village green and turned right at that corner with the Starbucks. Or was it the next corner, the one with the candy shop? Ingrid didn't know, but it was getting dark now. Time to go.

Ingrid rose just as a car came up the road. A minivan, actually, and green: a green MPV van. Ingrid started running.

Mom was already out of the car when Ingrid ran up.

"Ingrid," she said, rain dripping off the hood of her rain jacket. "Where have you been?" Those two vertical lines on Mom's forehead, the only flaws in her soft skin, were deeper than Ingrid had ever seen them, and her big dark eyes were open wide.

"Here," Ingrid said, moving around Mom to get in at the other side. Mom put out a hand to stop her.

"What do you mean, here?" she said. "I've been by three times and Dr. Binkerman's office had no idea you'd even left."

"I just got here," Ingrid said. "I decided to walk." Maybe leaving a message to that effect with Dr. Binkerman's receptionist would have been a good thing.

"You walked?" Mom said. "And you're just getting here now?"

"I got a little turned around," Ingrid said. All that other stuff – Crazy Katie, the purple parlor, the taxi – seemed too messy to bring up at the moment. "Where is everybody?"

"Soccer was canceled," Mom said.

"Canceled?"

"The rain, Ingrid. Mr. Ringer called hours ago. And I was at Dr. Binkerman's at four twenty-five."

"Oops," said Ingrid.

Mom gazed down at her. Not so much down anymore – almost eye to eye. "Nothing like this will ever happen again, will it, Ingrid?"

"Uh-uh."

"Do I need to explain why?"

"No."

Ingrid got in the car. Mom explained why all the way home.

three

ninety-nine Maple Lane was a

two-story Cape built in the 1950s with a master-
bedroom suite on the ground floor and three bedrooms
upstairs. The extra bedroom – now an office with desks
for Mom and Dad – and Ty's bedroom faced the street.
Ingrid's was at the back, looking out over the patio, the
garden, and the heavily wooded conservation land that
stretched all the way to the river: a quiet room, ideal for
reading. Ingrid lay in bed, her pinpoint light shining on
the open pages of *The Complete Sherlock Holmes*.

Sherlock Holmes was a cold man – although not as
cold as Dr. Watson made out – but you could learn a lot
from him. For example, right here in "The Red-headed
League," he tells Watson: "The more bizarre a thing is
the less mysterious it proves to be. It is your commonplace, featureless crimes which are really puzzling, just
as a commonplace face is the most difficult to identify."
Or, a few pages later, after Holmes has seen some clue
on the knees of the pawnbroker's assistant's trousers – a

complete mystery to both Watson and Ingrid – he makes a point of memorizing the order of the houses around Saxe-Coburg Square. "It is a hobby of mine to have an exact knowledge of London."

Ingrid stopped right there. Was it possible to imagine Holmes lost in London? No. London was his territory and he knew every inch. The obvious thought came next: Echo Falls was her territory, and she'd been lost in it that very day. There was nothing cute about that. It was just plain dumb. She decided to begin work on an exact mental picture of Echo Falls first thing in the morning.

Then she remembered that tomorrow was Friday, a school day. Uh-oh. Was there math homework? Oh, yeah, a bunch. Had she done it? Fat chance. And was there a reading packet, too, something about Shays' Rebellion? Who was Shays again? The red backpack, unopened, lay on the floor, probably in reach if she wriggled to the edge of the bed and made a good long stretch. Ingrid glanced at the clock. One forty-seven, practically dawn. Oh my God.

Ingrid switched off the pinpoint light and closed her eyes. They wanted to snap right back open, but she kept them shut. She had a vision of Crazy Katie taking a deep drag from the bent cigarette. Across the hall, Ty moaned in his sleep. Maybe he was having a bad dream. Ingrid felt on the shelf above her bed for Mister Happy, her teddy bear, old now and missing an eye, and tucked him in beside her. The rain started up again, pounding on the roof, flowing into the gutters and down the drainpipe outside Ingrid's window. She listened, isolating all the separate sounds of the rain. Soon her eyes stayed closed on their own.

She was in a little boat on a wild sea, but oh so snug, for some reason, and fast asleep.

"Ingrid!"

Fast, fast asleep, so delicious with the storm all around.

"Ingrid! It's ten after seven."

So snug, and even snugger if she rolled over and pulled the covers up like so. Mmmmm. Sleep in a full-force gale, the wind howling but Griddie so safe and—

"INGRID!"

Ingrid squeezed over against the wall, making herself practically invisible. "Five more minutes," she said, her voice thick, her lips almost glued together.

"You don't have five minutes, Ingrid."

"Four."

And then the intolerable. Snap – her covers were on the floor, whipped right off her, antisnug, definition of. Ingrid rolled over. Mom stood over the bed, dressed for work, arms crossed. Four was just a preliminary bargaining position; she would have settled for two or even one. One pitiful minute more of sleep.

"Were you up reading last night?" Mom said.

"No," said Ingrid, getting out of bed, her bare feet touching down on the icy floor.

"I see you didn't wear your appliance."

"Oops."

"What's the point of paying Dr. Binkerman all this money?"

"Search me."

"Watch your tone."

"But I really don't know."

"And this room is a shambles."

"I'll stay home and clean it," Ingrid offered, but Mom was already out the door.

Ingrid went down the hall to the bathroom. She knew that in parts of the world eight or nine people might share a single bathroom, maybe even more, maybe a whole village. She didn't feel that sorry for them: They didn't have to share with Ty.

Ty: who threw strike after strike on the baseball diamond but whose aim at the toilet was worse than a blind man's; who required four towels – or as many as were available – to dry himself and left them in a soggy pile; who'd started shaving, which meant using both sinks, his and hers, leaving blood-spotted meringues of foam in each; who, worst of all, was now a brand-new experimenter in the world of men's cologne. Ingrid stepped under the shower, hot and pounding, and gradually came to life.

Mom and Ty were gone by the time Ingrid went downstairs; the school day at Echo Falls High – home of the Red Raiders – started half an hour before the middle school, and Mom drove right by it. Ty got a ride every day, and in the foreseeable future would be turning sixteen, getting his license and driving himself to school in a Maserati or Rolls-Royce. Ingrid would be taking the bus till the end of time.

*   *   *

Dad was at the table, drinking coffee and reading *The Wall Street Journal*. Dad always smelled good, like a forest but very faint; whatever the trick was, Ty hadn't learned it yet. Dad was wearing one of those blue shirts with a white collar and white French cuffs, plus a black tie with orange tigers on it – Dad was a big supporter of Princeton football, although he'd gone to UConn. He was also the handsomest dad around.

"Hey, cutie," he said. "What's shakin'?"

"Not much. What's in the paper?"

Dad turned the pages. He was never in a big hurry in the morning. Dad was the financial adviser for the Ferrand Group, which was really just the Ferrand family, probably the richest in this whole part of the state – the middle school was named after them and so was a dorm at Princeton, where Ferrands had gone since forever and where Ty and Ingrid were headed too if it was the last thing Dad did – and Mr. Ferrand never got to work before nine. "Let's see," Dad said. "Unilever deal didn't go through, IBM sent another ten thousand jobs to India, plane crash in Benin, wherever the hell that is. The usual." He put down the paper and said, "When's your next game?"

"Dunno."

"Check the fridge."

Ingrid checked the schedule on the fridge. "Tomorrow at two."

"Home or away?"

"Home."

"Against whom?"

"Glastonbury."

"They're the ones with that big fullback? Redhead?"

"Maybe."

"Got to beat her to the ball, Ingrid."

Ingrid was hungry. That waffle on Dad's plate looked pretty good, but he ate the last bite before she could ask.

"Better get on the stick," Dad said.

Ingrid slung on her backpack.

"And work on that left foot of yours. Speed takes you only so far. Got to—"

"—master the fundamentals."

Dad laughed. He had a great laugh, rich and musical, and his eyes really did twinkle. "'Bye, cutie."

"'Bye, Dad."

He reached for the phone.

The bus stop was a block away, in front of Mia McGreevy's house. Mia: another cool name. Mia and her mother had come from New York the year before, after the divorce. The bus and Ingrid arrived at the same time, which was almost always the case.

"Hey, Mia."

"Hey," said Mia. She was tiny, with big pale eyes that always looked a little surprised. "Gum?"

"Yeah," said Ingrid, taking a lime-green piece of Bubblicious. She noticed Mia's mom watching from a window to make sure Mia got on the bus safely, maybe not yet realizing that Echo Falls wasn't the big bad city.

"You get that last algebra problem?" Mia said.

"Don't go there."

Mr. Sidney opened the doors. He had on his cap that

said BATTLE OF THE CORAL SEA.

"Mornin', petunias," he said.

"Hi, Mr. Sidney."

Girls were always petunia to Mr. Sidney. Guys were guy, as in "Take a seat, guy, and zip it." Ingrid and Mia filed past him and sat down at the back, as far from Brucie Berman as they could. Brucie sang "Am-er-i-can wo-ma-aa-aa-aan" as they walked by, ignoring him completely. They opened up their algebra notebooks and Ingrid started copying, fast as her pen would move.

Did it do her any good? No, all because of Ms. Groome, her Algebra Two teacher. There were four eighth-grade math sections at Ferrand Middle School – Algebra One for the geniuses, Algebra Two for good math students who didn't rise to the genius level, Pre-Algebra, which is where Ingrid would have been happily, if Mom hadn't called the school to complain, and Math One, formerly remedial math, for the criminal element. And what did Ms. Groome do to screw her up? Ms. Groome, who was making it her mission to single-handedly raise the SAT math scores of girls across the nation, whether they liked it or not, picked today to ignore the homework and spring a pop quiz instead.

Would she ever have a use for algebra in her life? Get real. Or any other form of math? Who are you kidding? Ingrid was going into the theater, as an actress or director, and what possible use would math be in the theater? Take this question right here, number one on the pop quiz: Factor the following quadratic polynomial: $4x^2 + 8x - 5$. Could Angelina Jolie do it? Or Elijah Wood? How about Shakespeare, for God's sake, if it came to that? Did they even have algebra when Shakespeare was around? She took another look at the stupid thing.

X. All these math people had a big – what was the word? Mom used it all the time – *fetish*. That was it. Fetish. Ingrid put her hand on her chin and started daydreaming about schoolboy Shakespeare forced to factor quadratic polynomials. Her gaze met Ms. Groome's.

Ingrid bowed her head over the test paper. $4x^2 + 8x - 5$. A fetish. They made a fetish about x, couldn't keep their hands off it. What was wrong with x just the way it was, kind of mysterious and interesting? X was way better than 39, say, or 1032, or even 999,999; way better than any so-called solutions. So-called solutions to nonproblems. How was $4x^2 + 8x - 5$ a problem? Like who did it bother? The whole thing pissed her off, big- time. She scrawled $(2x + 5)(2x - 1)$ in the answer column for no reason apparent to her, and went on to the next one.

Really annoyed now, Ingrid mowed through the numbers, squaring this, factoring that, equaling and not equaling, greatering and lessering, slicing and dicing, firing every math gun in her arsenal all the way down the page to the very last problem, the extra-credit one, which she knew was always a word problem, although she'd never before actually reached the end of a math quiz in order to try her luck. A little surprised, Ingrid glanced around to see if the test was still on, or whether Ms. Groome had called time and she just hadn't heard.

Still on: Three rows over, Mia was scratching out some calculation, the tip of her tongue showing between her lips, gloss a nice soft shade of pink – Mia had great taste – and Brucie Berman was picking his nose.

"Time," said Ms. Groome. "Pens down."

Ingrid downed her pen, leaving the extra-credit problem, some nonsense about trucks traveling in opposite directions, untouched.

Ingrid sat next to Stacy Rubino, her oldest friend, on the bus ride home. Mr. Rubino was an electrician who did the lighting for the Prescott Players, and Stacy always had the inside dope.

"Going to audition for the next play?" Stacy said.

"They haven't announced what it is yet," said Ingrid.

"*Alice in Wonderland*," said Stacy.

Alice: a plum role, plum of plums. "She's kind of an innocent," Ingrid said.

"A sap," said Stacy. "In the cartoon, anyway."

"I could play an innocent."

"Weren't you a pig in that musical last year?" Stacy said. "You can play anything."

"A pig?" said Brucie Berman, somewhere behind them.

The girls turned slowly to face him. Stacy was big and sturdy, could break Brucie in half no problem. Ingrid saw that Brucie had some joke all ready to go, something about pigs, but he swallowed it, his Adam's apple actually bobbing. The girls turned away. Brucie kept quiet the rest of ride, except for a little barnyard snort he made as he got off the bus.

No one was home at 99 Maple Lane: Mom and Dad still at work, Ty with the football team going through their pregame rituals. Ingrid picked up the Friday edition of *The Echo* from the driveway and went inside. Week over. Ah. She took a deep breath, felt a lovely relaxation spread through her. How did hot chocolate sound? Perfect. She dropped *The Echo* on the kitchen table, made herself hot chocolate with milk, not water, nice and creamy. How about a little treat to go with it? Ingrid stood on a chair so she could reach the cupboard and found a bag of oatmeal cookies. Oats were good for you. She took two.

Ingrid sat at the table, dipped one of the cookies in her mug of hot chocolate, glanced at *The Echo*. Boring things appeared on the front page, like coverage of the garden club and Senior Center bingo, and it got more boring inside, except for the sports, where Ty was mentioned almost every week during football and baseball seasons, and even Ingrid had gotten in once or twice.

But not today. Today the front page had a big photograph of a woman. Ingrid almost didn't recognize her at first, probably because her hair was cut short and neat and her skin seemed smooth and young. It was Crazy Katie. The headline read: LOCAL RESIDENT FOUND MURDERED. The subhead: ASSAILANT UNKNOWN.

four

Longtime Echo Falls resident Katherine Eve Kovac was murdered Thursday, according to Echo Falls police chief Gilbert L. Strade. The body of Ms. Kovac was found by a neighbor shortly after 8 P.M. The neighbor, whose name had not been released by the police at press time, went to Ms. Kovac's house at 341 Packer Street to complain about the activities of Ms. Kovac's cat. Allegedly finding the front door open, the neighbor went inside and found the body. The neighbor immediately called 911. Sergeant Ronald Pina arrived shortly thereafter and found signs of a struggle and evidence of strangulation. According to Chief Strade...

The kitchen door opened, and Ingrid looked up in alarm, as though she'd been caught at something. It was Mom.

"Hi, Ingrid," she said. "That sure looks good."

Ingrid slid her hand over the paper. Her heart was beating fast and light, like a tom-tom. "What does?"

"Your snack."

"Oh," Ingrid said. "Want some?"

"Just a bite," said Mom. She broke off a tiny bit of oatmeal cookie – Mom watched her weight constantly, gave up something like bread or pasta almost every month – dipped it in the hot chocolate, and popped it in her mouth.

"Mmmm." She kicked off her heels and slipped into her sheepskin slippers, always her first move coming home from work. "How was your day?"

"Okay."

"Anything interesting happen?"

"Not really."

"Not even in English or history?"

"We didn't have English today," Ingrid said.

"What about history?"

Ingrid couldn't remember anything specific, but she knew history was on the schedule Fridays. "We had history."

"What are you taking right now?"

"Shays' Rebellion."

"God," said Mom. "I've completely forgotten what that was about."

Ingrid, unable to enlighten her, said nothing. Mom was opening her mouth to say something else – probably some follow-up question – when the phone rang.

"Carol Levin," Mom said. She listened for a moment and said, "That's under agreement, but I've got something very similar on Overland Drive. In fact, there's an open house scheduled this—"

Ingrid stopped listening. Her gaze was pulled right back to the paper, as though *The Echo* had developed some powerful force field. A suffocating feeling tightened in her chest. She read the whole article, way too fast to absorb much but powerless to slow herself down. Two sentences popped out at her, one in the middle: "Ms. Kovac had lived alone in the house at 341 Packer Street for many years." And the very last one: "Anyone who saw or spoke to the victim within the last few days or anyone with other helpful information is asked to call the Echo Falls police."

Ingrid felt strange, cold all over her body but lightheaded, as though she were burning up with fever. She glanced at her mother. Mom was talking about the new septic regulations, a spiel Ingrid had heard so often by now, she practically knew it by heart. She turned back to the picture of Crazy Katie. It was a good-quality photograph, especially for *The Echo*. The eyes seemed to be looking right at you, like they were sizing you up.

Ingrid read that last sentence again. Call the Echo Falls police? And say what? *Please don't tell my parents, but I was hanging out with Crazy Katie after school.* And how would that even help? What possible useful information could she have? Absolutely none, zip, zero, nada.

Except.

Except for that footstep overhead in a house where Crazy Katie had lived alone for many years. Meaning: Who was up there?

"Ingrid? Did you not hear me?"

Ingrid looked up. Mom was off the phone.

"What?" Ingrid said.

"Are you all right?" Mom said, those vertical lines on her forehead deepening. "You look pale."

Mom had feelers for how she was feeling. "I'm fine," Ingrid said.

"Then better bundle up."

"Bundle up?"

"Friday night," Mom said. "Football. Sure you're all right?"

The Red Raiders Boosters Club, of which Mom was secretary and Dad, who'd played for the Red Raiders – star quarterback and team captain – was past president, threw a tailgate party, nonalcoholic of course, at every home game. Ingrid's job was grilling burgers, which meant making sure they didn't burn and saying things like: "Yes," when asked by high school kids if she was Ty's sister, and "Did they have football back then?" when told by old people that Dad had been a big football star in his day. Old people didn't seem to laugh often, but when they did, they loved it, kind of surprising themselves by how much, Ingrid thought. That didn't include Grampy, who didn't really fit the category and never came to football games. "Had it up to here," he said. He said that about a lot of things.

The parking lot filled up and Ingrid got busy, burgers arranged in a careful system on the grill at first, and soon not. Beyond the near goalpost, she could see the teams stretching, the Red Raiders in red, the visitors in white with green trim. She spotted Ty, number 19, the only freshman on the varsity, off by himself, bouncing up and down. Ty could run. Running ran in the family. Ingrid was starting to think about that when smoke rose up from the grill, reminding her at once of Crazy Katie lighting up. Was everything going to remind her of Crazy Katie from now on?

Stacy came over. "What's a flea-flicker?"

"No idea," Ingrid said. "Why?"

"The other team's going to try a flea-flicker on the very first play," Stacy said. "I heard their coaches talking about it."

"Want a burger?" Ingrid said.

"No money on me."

"Here," said Ingrid, forking a slightly too-blackened patty into a bun and handing it to her. "Compliments of the Boosters."

"Boosters rule," said Stacy, squirting on some ketchup and taking a big bite. "Think we should tell anybody? Ty maybe?"

"About what?"

"The flea-flicker."

Flea-flicker. What could it be? "Watch the burgers," Ingrid said.

She hurried across the parking lot, around the end zone, and up the sideline. The Red Raiders were in their formations now, the offense practicing plays against the defense, like they always did at the end of warm-up. Ty, a defensive back, was only a few yards from her. He looked huge in his pads and uniform, almost like another person; except for his face, small behind the bars of the mask.

"Ty," she called, in kind of a stage whisper.

No reaction.

"Ty." A little louder.

But nothing.

Then came some shouted gibberish, "Thirty-six, red left, hut, hut," and everybody crashed together, grunting and bellowing. Number 43 knocked Ty to the ground. Ty sprang back up with a sort of roar, like he was all charged up from getting pummeled. Ingrid had seen a show on the Discovery Channel about territorial skirmishes between troops of chimpanzees. This was just like that.

"Ty," she called, full volume now.

Ty and number 43 were face-to-face, banging their heads together, completely oblivious to her. Ingrid stepped across the sideline. Both players whirled around immediately.

"What the hell?" said Ty.

"It's important," Ingrid said.

"Get off the field," Ty said. His eyes were maniacal.

"But—"

He yelled something obscene at her.

"You're a stupid jerk," Ingrid said.

"Power goat left, on two, hut, hut, HUT."

Crash. Ty got knocked down again. Ingrid left him there, went back to the grill, took over from Stacy.

"How did that go?" Stacy said.

"Hard to say," Ingrid said. "They seem to be under a spell right now."

Stacy laughed. "Wanna come over for the night?" she said.

That sounded good. Stacy's father was a genius when it came to electricity, and the Rubinos had a kick-ass entertainment center in their basement – forty-two-inch plasma screen, booming surround sound, two big corduroy couches with fleece blankets, popcorn machine, tons of videos including *Ferris Bueller's Day Off*, all of the *Fawlty Towers* series, *Rushmore* and *Billy Madison*. Ingrid had spent many weekend nights at Stacy's. The two of them went all the way back to before preschool, had started playing together when they could barely walk. Ingrid could tell Stacy anything; and tonight she had something to tell. She was about to say yes when Stacy's thick eyebrows shot straight up, the way they did when she had an idea or got excited by something.

"Hey," Stacy said. "Did you hear about Crazy Katie?"

Ingrid came very close to saying, "Oh my God, wait till you hear this." It was the perfect moment to tell Stacy her secret. But for some reason, Ingrid did not. Instead she looked away and said, "Somebody said something about it." Kind of mumbled it, actually, and felt her face turning red.

"Get this," said Stacy. "Her name wasn't really Crazy Katie."

"Of course not," said Ingrid, hearing her tone sharpen suddenly, as though she had some reason to be mad at Stacy.

"What's with you?" said Stacy.

"Nothing." Ingrid remembered: *You can call me Kate.* At that moment, she realized she'd liked Crazy Katie.

"I meant she had a last name," Stacy was saying. "I know Crazy's not a real name."

"Sorry," Ingrid said.

"It was Katherine something," said Stacy. She saw Joey Strade going by. "Hey, Joey."

Joey stopped and turned. "Yeah?"

"C'mere," said Stacy.

Joey came over. "What was Crazy Katie's real name?" Stacy said.

Joey was in their grade, a big pudgy kid with a cowlick that stood up at the back of his head like a blunt Indian feather. He was also – key fact popping up suddenly in Ingrid's mind – the son of Gilbert L. Strade, chief of police.

"Katherine Kovac," Joey said.

"So what's the Crazy thing all about?" Stacy said.

"She was weird," Joey said. His gaze met Ingrid's. "She had mental problems." Ingrid felt a little stab of guilt, as though she were hurting Kate in some way. But how could you hurt a dead person?

"Why would anyone want to kill her?" said Stacy.

He shrugged. Ingrid noticed that Joey, whom she'd never paid much attention to, seemed to have this new direct way of looking at you. And maybe he wasn't as pudgy as he used to be.

"Any suspects?" Stacy said.

Joey shrugged again.

"Did she have any relatives?" Stacy said.

"I don't know," said Joey. "Why are you asking me?"

"Duh," said Stacy.

* * *

A flea-flicker turned out to be a play where the quarter-back hands off to the running back and just when everybody on the defense thinks it's going to be a running play and comes hurrying up, the running back flips the ball back to the quarterback, who throws it to a wide-open receiver way downfield. Ingrid watched it unfold like a dream on the white-and-green team's very first play, eighty yards for a touchdown.

"Was that a flea-flicker, Dad?"

Dad's eyes shifted toward her in surprise, then returned to the field. He was leaning forward on their bench halfway up the stands, totally tense. "The silver lining with flea-flickers is they can only work it once a game."

But on the very next series the white-and-greens did it again. Sixty-three-yard touchdown.

"At least Ty was the closest one," Ingrid said.

A big vein throbbed in Dad's forehead. "He's the one getting beat most of all," Dad said, lowering his voice.

"I'm sure it's not just—" Mom began.

"—like a drum," Dad said.

The coach took Ty out. He didn't come back, just sat on the bench the whole game, slouching more and more. Final score: white-and-green 43, Red Raiders 6.

The ride home in the van was grim, Ty's face blotchy, Dad's knuckles on the steering wheel white, Mom's lips colorless. Ingrid shouldn't have been there at all, should have been with the Rubinos, on the way to their entertainment center, but Dad had said no.

"Ingrid's got a game tomorrow. At least there won't

be the excuse that she didn't get a good night's sleep."

"It is just a game," Mom said after a while.

"It's a commitment," said Dad.

The phone was ringing when they got home. Ingrid picked it up.

"Ingrid?"

"Yes?"

"It's Joey."

Ingrid was silent.

"Joey Strade."

"Hi."

"Hi."

Then came a little pause. Boys had called her before, but only to find out homework assignments. She and Joey didn't have any classes together.

"How's it going?" Joey said.

"Okay."

"Tough game," Joey said.

"Yeah."

"We got smoked."

"Yeah."

"What'd your brother say?"

"Nothing."

Another pause.

"See how big their number sixty-five was?"

She'd missed that.

"Six four, two eighty," Joey said. "And he's only a sophomore."

"So he'll be like what, seven hundred pounds by the time he gets out of college?" Ingrid said.

Joey laughed.

More pausing. Was this her first real call from a boy?

"Do you like video games?" Joey said.

"Some of them."

"Like what?"

She named a couple.

"Me, too," said Joey. "I just got the new Fortress Xylon."

"Is it good?"

"Haven't tried it yet," Joey said. "I was thinking of this weekend. Trying it, I mean."

Another pause. It went on and on.

"Guess I better go," Joey said.

"Me too."

"See you."

"'Bye."

As far as a good night's sleep went, Ingrid would have been better off at Stacy's on one of their most chocoholic, DVD-crazed nights. First came the memory of Crazy Katie and her raggedy voice, asking what Ingrid's passion was. Then came Joey, who wasn't as pudgy as he used to be and had a direct way of looking at you. What color were his eyes? Ingrid hadn't noticed, and that wasn't like her at all. Joey. She added him up: not so pudgy, direct look, blunt Indian-feather cowlick, liked video games, laughed at her jokes. Anything else? Oh, yeah: son of the police chief.

A nervous feeling – suffocation plus weight-in-pit-of-stomach – stayed with her all night. What was the lesson of the flea-flicker fiasco? That maybe people didn't react so kindly to sharers of supposedly helpful information, that maybe keeping your big mouth shut was the way to go. Toward dawn, when the first faint rays of skim-milky-blue light came through her curtains, Ingrid, rolling over for the billionth time, realized the name for this new feeling. It was dread.

Ingrid pulled Mister Happy a little closer. He hadn't been much of a help all night. That was a first.

five

saturday mornings were never about feeling tired. Even during soccer season, Ingrid could sleep in until ten at least, the A team never playing before noon. But this Saturday morning, after the night of the billion tosses and turns, she could barely get up. Outside her window, leaves were blowing around and the tops of the trees in the town woods were waving back and forth like giants whipping themselves into a frenzy. It looked cold out there, and any other Saturday morning she might have lingered in bed, watching the spectacle and feeling cozy.

But not today.

Ingrid went into the bathroom, always tidy and nice smelling on Saturday mornings since Mrs. Velez cleaned on Fridays and Ty slept until noon or even later. There she was in the mirror. Oh my God. Dark circles, hair ridiculous, and what was that, right under where her cheekbone would have been, if she had cheekbones? A zit. And not just a regular zit, but a zit with a blackhead in the middle – a one-in-a-million dermatological freak show, maybe the basis for some researcher's prize-winning paper. Ingrid went down to the kitchen.

"You ask him," Dad was saying. He was at the table, buttering an English muffin. "Why is it up to me?"

Uh-oh: Mom and Dad, not getting along. Not getting along came with all sorts of telltale signs, such as that narrow-eyed look of Mom's and that lumpy muscle that twitched on the side of Dad's face. Ingrid tried to remember: Hadn't they been getting along lately, at the Booster Club tailgate last night, for example? But maybe not getting along was unacceptable Booster Club behavior and they'd just been pretending.

Mom was at the counter, spooning coffee into the filter basket. "But you won't have any problem spending the money," she said.

Every word a total mystery. Then they noticed her.

All smiles. "Hi, cutie," Dad said. "Bet you had a good sleep."

"How much?" Ingrid said.

Dad laughed.

"Did you wear your appliance?" Mom said.

Was there any point in telling the truth about a stupid little thing like the appliance when you were simultaneously withholding information in a murder case? *No*, she thought. "Yes," she said.

"Good," said Mom.

Pure logic. But to her surprise, Ingrid felt bad just the same. And again that feeling of dread awoke inside her, suffocation in chest, heavy weight in stomach. What kind of a world was it where if a good person did one tiny bit of wrong, everything fell apart, while bad people smoothed their way through heaps of wrong? Was that like math, some complicated equation between good and evil? Hold it right there, girl. Math sucks and you suck at math: Be real.

Ingrid opened the fridge. On a normal Saturday morning she'd be starving, in the mood for Mom to rustle her up eggs, bacon, toast, but today she found herself just staring at what was in there.

"Ingrid?"

She felt Mom's feelers out.

"Yeah?"

"Look at me."

Ingrid turned.

"Are you all right?"

"I'm fine."

"You're sure? Because you look a little—"

"She just told you she was fine," Dad said.

Mom faced him, eyes narrowing like cocked weapons. The top of Dad's robe had opened a little, exposing some of his rusty-blond chest hair. He tugged it closed.

"I was talking to my daughter," Mom said, one of those over-the-top things Mom sometimes said for no reason Ingrid could make out. Dad picked up his plate and went into the dining room.

Was this the moment to spill the whole Crazy Katie thing? Maybe not perfect, but that heavy weight inside wouldn't go away. Ingrid opened her mouth. Nothing came out. It was so quiet, she could hear the drip drip of the coffee in the pot. An irrelevant thought came out of nowhere: Maybe it was time to get a new dog.

Flanders, who had disappeared three years before, would lie under the kitchen table at awkward times like this. Offering him a treat had been a good way to break the silence. Under the table now lay a single dustball, missed by Mrs. Velez.

Ingrid ate plain yogurt and a banana for breakfast, finishing neither, and the silence continued, unbroken.

Club soccer, maybe to show they had nothing to do with school soccer, like they were above it, didn't wear the red of all the Echo Falls school teams, sporting instead a shade of green Ingrid loathed. Lima-bean green, dried-snot green – the worst. Which was why she treasured her bright-red Puma boots with the glittery red laces almost bright enough to hurt your eyes, ordered special, red boots that Coach Ringer had frowned on at first, but Assistant Coach Trimble must have stepped in because now half the team was wearing them, swearing they were the fastest shoes on earth. Ingrid loved those red Pumas – red Pumas, size seven. But right now, she couldn't find them.

She tried all the usual places. The mudroom – footballs, baseballs, bats, gloves, soccer balls, jackets, including Ty's brand-new varsity jacket with Ty on one arm, 19 on the other, and RED RAIDER FOOTBALL on the back. The front hall – antique hat stand with no hats; oil painting of the actual falls in Echo Falls, painted by a semiknown nineteenth-century painter and inherited from Grammy when she died, a few years before Ingrid was born; a deep-blue marble floor, devoid of shoes. Then her bedroom, the landing between the garage and the kitchen entrance, the laundry room, where her uniform was washed and folded on the dryer. No red Pumas.

"Anybody seen my boots?"

No answer.

A complete mystery.

"Time to get in gear," Dad said.

"I can't find my boots."

Dad came into the laundry room. He thought. When Dad thought, his eyes shifted to one side and up a little, like he was looking in a rearview mirror. "When was practice?"

"Thursday."

"Didn't it get canceled?"

Ingrid felt her own eyes shifting too. "Yeah."

"So maybe they're still in your backpack."

Back to the mudroom, backpack hanging on a wall hook. Ingrid looked through, found crumpled assignments and lots of wholesome snacks Mom had put in during the week, all uneaten, given Ingrid's preference for chips and candy bars in the cafeteria, but no red Pumas.

"There must be old ones around somewhere," Dad said, losing patience.

Ingrid had old ones, a size too small and black. She squeezed her feet into them.

"Feeling fast today?" Dad said as they got in the TT and it slowly filled with his forest smell.

"Yeah," Ingrid said, although she couldn't remember feeling slower.

"Keep working the ball in the corners."

"Yeah."

"And use that left-footed little fake on the red-haired girl. She overcommits."

"Yeah."

"Are you listening?"

"Yeah."

"What did I say?"

"Left-footed fake." A tricky little jitterbug thing she'd never executed properly, not even in practice.

"Good girl."

Coach Ringer, the last of the original founders of the Mid-State League – going back to when bears roamed free in Echo Falls – was a short round guy with a droopy mustache and a drippy nose on cold windy days, like this one. He always wore a black-and-gold hooded sweatshirt that said TOWNE HARDWARE on the back, SCREWS FOR YOUSE SINCE 1937, the dumbest slogan Ingrid had ever seen. Assistant Coach Trimble was tall and lean, wore running tights and a UConn soccer jacket, looked like she could do something amazing, like outrun a deer or kick the ball right through you.

Coach Ringer liked to gather the team around him in a tight circle for a pregame pep talk, of which there were two kinds, a long rambling one if they'd been losing and a short confusing one if they were on a roll, like they were now, winners of three in a row.

"Hey," said Coach Ringer. "Listen up."

They all stopped talking, or at least talking loudly.

"Today," said Coach Ringer, "I want you to remember one" – he searched for the right word; when Coach Ringer searched for the right word, his jaw came jutting out like he was going take a swing at somebody – "thing," he went on, finding the word. "Remember one thing and one thing only, and this is it, so listen up. That means everybody. The thing to remember is this. Listen up. We're gonna make them play the way *we* want them to play." That was it? Oh, no – was he going to say it twice? For a moment, Ingrid thought maybe not. But then, raising his voice this time and spacing out the words: "We're gonna make them play the way *we* want them to play. Got it?"

The girls all nodded, ponytails sticking out sideways in the wind. Ingrid said, "I vote they play with their shoelaces tied together."

A pause, followed by muffled laughter. Coach Ringer turned red. "Twenty-two," he said, calling her by her number, "on the bench."

Ingrid sat on the bench, steaming. She felt Dad's eyes on her from the stands across the field.

Coach Ringer concluded his pep talk the way he always did. "Anything you wanna add, Coach Trimble?" In the kind of tone that invited a no.

Coach Trimble had been assisting with the As for two years now, and many parents couldn't wait for Coach Ringer to retire to Florida. She said what she always said: "Play hard and play to win."

It sounded like one of those meaningless sports clichés. But at that moment, sitting angrily on the bench at soccer field number one up the road from the hospital, the wind blowing and the temperature falling, winter just around the corner, Ingrid realized she'd never actually heard it except from Coach Trimble, so it couldn't be a cliché. She glanced up, met Coach Trimble's gaze. Coach Trimble didn't have friendly eyes. Not that they were unfriendly, either, just impossible to see behind, at least for Ingrid. And all of a sudden, Ingrid got what Coach Trimble was trying to tell her: Playing hard wasn't the same as playing to win. Playing to win was something else entirely, a whole new way of seeing the game. A revelation: Ingrid's mind started buzzing.

"Ingrid," said Coach Trimble.

"Yes?" said Ingrid.

"Earrings."

Ingrid felt her earlobes: her little gold studs, still in place. She'd been playing soccer since the age of four, knew that for safety reasons no jewelry was allowed on the field, knew the ref would boot you out of the game if you were wearing any, and for the first time in all those years had screwed it up. Why now? Ingrid unfastened the earrings, spotted Dad in the stands. He was watching her, arms folded across his chest. Ingrid gave the earrings to Coach Trimble for safekeeping.

Her punishment lasted for five minutes, which was how long it took for them to go down one zero.

"Head in the game, twenty-two?" said Coach Ringer, hands behind his back, unlit cigarette twitching between his fingers.

Ingrid nodded.

"Get in there."

Ingrid got in there. And then, despite the sleepless night and too-tight boots and forgetting about the earrings, Ingrid ran out there and played the best soccer game of her life, by far. Everything was different somehow. The field was smaller, for one thing. And the ball, which had always had plans of its own, almost as though it were a member of a third team, was suddenly, if not a friend, at least predictable. Even the big red-haired sweeper, with her booming kicks and aggressive elbows, was starting to be predictable. Take that spin move of hers: The game wasn't ten minutes old before Ingrid saw it coming and, instead of following her, took two simple steps the other way, stole the ball, and went in on the goalie all alone. Lower left corner – GOAAAAAAAL! Ingrid always heard that Hispanic announcer in her head when she scored a goal, which was not often. But she scored another one before the half – GOAAAAAAAAL! – and assisted on a second. And in the second half, a third – GOAAAAAAAAL! – using that left-footed jitterbug fake to perfection. Hat trick. Echo Falls parents must have been cheering on the sidelines, but Ingrid didn't hear, didn't even sense Dad's presence, another first. She was locked in.

Ingrid stayed locked in until almost the end of the game. With a minute or two left, score Echo Falls 5, Glastonbury 2, the red-haired girl came dribbling up out of the corner and Ingrid moved in on her. It happened to be the corner of the field closest to the road, and right behind the red-haired girl, Ingrid couldn't help but see a taxi driving up. And behind the taxi: a police car. They slowed down. The taxi driver's window slid open, and Ingrid saw his unshaven face, toothpick dangling from his lips: Murad, with the complicated last name. He pointed at something. The field in general? Her in particular? Were they going to stop and get out? No. They seemed to be speeding up, seemed to be—

Ingrid opened her eyes. Coach Ringer, Assistant Coach Trimble, and the ref were crouched in a circle around her.

"Ingrid?" said Coach Trimble. "Are you all right?"

"What happened?" Ingrid said.

"You got hit by the ball," Coach Trimble said.

"Right in the coconut," said Coach Ringer.

Ingrid had no memory of it. She shifted her head – that hurt – and saw all the players kneeling, proper procedure when a player was down; the red-haired girl knelt close by, looking worried. Dad stood on the sidelines, ready to charge out and embarrass her at any moment.

"I'm fine," Ingrid said.

Coach Ringer held up three fingers. "How many?"

"Three fingers and a ring with big yellow jewels." She sat up. That hurt too, but not bad. What did she remember? Taxicab and police car. She looked around, maybe a bit wildly: gone.

"Easy now," said the ref.

Red veins crisscrossed the whites of the ref's eyes, as though she hadn't slept well either. One of those sparks went off in Ingrid's mind, a spark of inspiration, half memories fusing with probability. But this moment of inspiration was different from all the others because there was no excitement to go along with it.

She had left her red Pumas at Crazy Katie's.

six

An IM from Powerup77 (Stacy): heard u were gr8 today

Gridster22 (Ingrid): uh thanks

Powerup77: whassup?

Gridster22: nada

Powerup77: nada--that another name for joey?

Gridster22: huh?

Powerup77: heard he called u

NYgrrrl979 (Mia): hi--moi is here--joey strade called the i-girl?

Gridster22: for godsake

Powerup77: yup he did

NYgrrrl979: he's cute

Powerup77: joey?

Gridster22: howja know he called?

Powerup77: secrets safe w/me.

NYgrrrl979: hey--you guys hear bout crazy k?

Gridster22: brb

But Ingrid didn't come right back. She put up her away message and lay down on her bed. Her head hurt, but that was nothing compared to the thought of those red Pumas left behind at Crazy Katie's house. Ingrid had gone to a soccer camp at Loomis in August, taking the boots with her, of course. A fun camp – she'd roomed with Stacy and they'd met girls from all over the Northeast, some of them awesome players. A fun camp, but with strict rules about name tags; name tags on every piece of clothing and even on the shoes, the camp issuing little metal disks with holes in them, for slipping right on the laces. INGRID LEVIN-HILL, 99 MAPLE LANE, ECHO FALLS, CT. After camp Ingrid had kept the tags on – a cool souvenir. She might as well have spray-painted on Crazy Katie's front door: FOR MORE INFO CONTACT GRIDSTER22@AOL.COM.

She had to think. Who was the best thinker she'd ever come across? Sherlock Holmes, by far, the only drawback being he wasn't real. Ingrid took *The Complete Sherlock Holmes* off her bedside table and leafed through. When Holmes was doing his deepest thinking, he fell into a sort of trance, played the violin, or snorted cocaine. The violin route was out: Ingrid was hopeless at music, couldn't carry the simplest tune. As for cocaine, Holmes hadn't had the benefit of the DARE program to set him straight.

Ingrid closed her eyes, slowed down her breathing, tried to fall into a trance. After more than enough of that, she got up and started pacing around, more her style anyway. In "A Scandal in Bohemia" Holmes says, "It is a capital mistake to theorise before one has data." What data did she have? Start with Murad the taxi driver, leading a police cruiser up to the soccer fields. That had to mean the police now knew that on the day of the murder, a girl had gone by taxi to the fields from outside Crazy Katie's. Did they also know that Kate had called the driver? Possible, but not a fact, not real data. But it was a fact that the police didn't know the identity of the girl, because if they did they'd have scooped her up already. Therefore they either hadn't found the red Pumas or had found them but not examined them carefully, hadn't checked those identity disks from camp. That left two possibilities. One: The boots were at the police station, sitting in a drawer until someone – like Joey's dad – put two and two together. Two: They were still inside Kate's house, waiting to be discovered.

Ingrid stopped pacing. The problem with deep thinking was it could lead to unpleasant conclusions. Like this one, for example. If the shoes were still at Kate's house, Ingrid had to get them back, and soon. How soon? Don't put off until tomorrow what can be done today. Who said that? Benjamin Franklin?

It wasn't going to be easy. Could she even find Kate's house? Down in the Flats, but where? Ingrid hadn't even had time to start her project of learning the whole layout of Echo Falls. This was all happening very fast.

Ingrid started pacing again, faster now. Outside, beyond the backyard, a huge bird, maybe a hawk, rose over the town woods and spiraled up, shrinking and shrinking in the blue sky. *Boom.* It hit her: *The Echo* had printed Crazy Katie's address.

Ingrid sat at her computer and went to *The Echo*'s site, a homey little site featuring a photo of the falls in winter, a big clump of ice about to shoot off the edge. LOCAL RESIDENT FOUND MURDERED. Ingrid scrolled through the article, found the address: 341 Packer Street. She went to MapQuest.com, clicked on Directions, typed *99 Maple Lane* and the rest of her address in the From box and *341 Packer Street* in the To box. The directions popped up: Start out going north on Maple Lane. Distance 0.1 miles. Turn left onto Avondale Rd. Follow...

"Ingrid."

Mom, right outside the door. Ingrid clicked on the Close button and MapQuest vanished.

"Yeah?" she said.

The door opened. Mom was dressed in weekend

clothes – jeans, corduroy barn jacket, Burberry scarf. "All set?" she asked.

"For what?"

"Grampy's."

"Grampy's?"

"Don't tell me you forgot. What's getting into you these days, Ingrid? We're supposed to be there at five and it's already twenty of."

Grampy's. Something about bringing him an old photo of the farmhouse that Mom had had framed. "Do I have to?" Ingrid said.

"Don't start. Grampy likes seeing you."

Any – Ingrid didn't want to use the word break-in – any visit to 341 Packer Street would have to happen at night, and night was still hours away. She might as well go to Grampy's. Ingrid went down to the mudroom, put on her red North Face jacket. The door to the basement was open and she heard Ty grunting down there, and Dad saying – almost shouting, really – "One more, come on, one more, push, push, push, that's it." She found herself remembering a scene in some movie about the Romans with the galley slaves rowing into battle, chained to their benches.

Ingrid had two grandfathers: Mom's dad, a retired accountant who lived in Florida with his girlfriend, and Grampy, who lived alone on the old family farm where Dad had grown up, the last farm left inside the town limits of Echo Falls. No actual farming went on there anymore, because Grampy had had it up to here with the cows, horses, chickens, and harvesting the corn, and how he supported himself wasn't exactly clear, since he'd refused all offers to sell off any of the land.

Mom handed Ingrid the photo as they got in the car. "What do you think?"

Ingrid examined the photo, a black-and-white that showed the farmhouse on a spring day – she could tell from the blossoms on the apple tree – and a spring day long past, on account of the old gangster-movie-type car parked in front. "The house was smaller back then," Ingrid said.

"I meant the frame," said Mom.

"Nice," Ingrid said, although she didn't like it.

"You don't like it."

"I do."

They drove in silence for a while. Ingrid paid attention to the route, trying to form a mental map. Mom drove up Maple Lane, past Avondale, turned right on Spring, which – hey – changed its name to River. She knew River, one of the main streets in Echo Falls. It cut around the town woods and then ran beside the bike path by the riverbank. There were Rollerbladers on the bike path today. One was a boy in a T-shirt, no jacket, even though it was pretty cold, a boy who looked like Joey Strade. Ingrid gave him a quick sidelong glance as they went by. Joey, for sure.

Mom crossed the river, turned onto Route 392. It grew hilly, the houses farther apart and run-down. A beer can rolled across the road and got squashed with a little *thmmp* sound.

"Mom?"

"Yes?"

"Do we have a lawyer?"

Mom's eyes shifted. "That's a funny question. Why do you ask?"

"No reason." But Ingrid was starting to wonder if breaking into Crazy Katie's house was really something she could do. The dread feeling came back, stronger than ever. Maybe a lawyer could somehow fix things behind the scenes and no one would ever have to know anything.

"Is something wrong?" Mom's voice rose, real anxious, just like that. She got so jumpy sometimes.

"No," Ingrid said. Maybe if Mom's tone had been different, she might have said something else.

"Is one of your friends in trouble?"

"No."

The first of Grampy's fence posts appeared on the right, the fields all brown and bare.

"You can always tell me anything, Ingrid," said Mom, trying to be calm but sounding even more worried. "I hope you know that."

"There's nothing to tell," Ingrid said. "I was just curious." If only Mom weren't so tense.

After a little pause, Mom nodded. "Whatever legal work we have, wills and such, we give to Mrs. Dirksen."

"You and Dad have wills?"

"Of course."

"But you're young," Ingrid said. "Comparatively."

Mom laughed. "It's irresponsible not to."

Ingrid gazed at Mom's profile, tensing back up after the laugh. It was a bright day, and Mom's crow's feet showed clearly, plus a new little crescent line in her cheek. Mom was responsible, no doubt about that. They turned into Grampy's long, rutted driveway.

"What's Mrs. Dirksen like?" Ingrid said.

"Very nice."

Very nice and a woman, maybe the warm and nurturing type. Why not? Like any moviegoer, Ingrid knew the police caution by heart. She had the right to a lawyer.

Grampy was out back, chopping wood, wearing a T-shirt and dirty canvas pants. He wasn't tall but had broad shoulders and cords of muscle that still stood out on his arms even though he was seventy-eight. Split logs were flying everywhere.

"Hi," said Mom. "Aren't you cold like that?"

Grampy looked up in midswing. "Nope," he said, and brought the ax down hard, splitting a log neatly in two and burying the blade in the chopping block. He left it there, the ax handle quivering.

"I've brought that picture," Mom said.

Grampy wiped his nose on the back of his forearm. "Hey, kid," he said to Ingrid.

"Hi, Grampy."

"Let's get some of this wood inside," he said. "Then we can palaver."

They each carried an armful through the back door and into the kitchen. Grampy had a great kitchen, with wide-plank pine floors full of knots and a huge fireplace where whole pigs had been roasted at Christmastime long ago. Grampy arranged some of the logs in a pyramid on the grate, tossed in a match, and poof – fire. Just like that, no paper, no kindling. Dad always used an artificial log to get the fire started.

Mom showed Grampy the picture. Grampy put on his glasses, gave it a quick look. "Nineteen thirty-seven Buick," he said. "Absolute piece of crap." He went to the sink, turned on the tap, drank from it.

"Would you like some tea?" Mom asked. "We can talk about where to hang it."

"Hang it wherever you want," Grampy said.

Mom put the kettle on. "How about beside the armoire in the living room?" she said.

"Living room, dining room, bathroom, wherever," said Grampy.

Mom picked up the picture and took it to the living room. Grampy turned to Ingrid.

"Want to roast up some marshmallows?" he said.

"Yeah."

"In the cupboard," Grampy said, pointing at it with his chin.

Ingrid opened the cupboard, found a jumbo bag of peanuts in the shell, a can of Planters salted peanuts, a jar of peanut butter, and peanut brittle, but nothing else.

"Goddamn," said Grampy.

"Want to come see?" Mom called from the living room.

"It's not goin' anywhere," Grampy said.

Mom returned, poured the tea.

"We're out of marshmallows," Grampy said.

"Seven-eleven should have them," Mom said.

"It doesn't matter," Ingrid said.

"I have a hankering for roasted marshmallows," Grampy said.

Mom put on her jacket. "I'll be right back."

Mom left. Grampy opened another cupboard, the one under sink, and took out a bottle of brandy. He sat at the table, poured some in his tea. Steam rose from the mugs, and logs crackled in the fireplace.

"What do you think of the police in Echo Falls?" Ingrid said.

"Can't trust a cop," said Grampy. "That's a given."

He poured in a little more brandy.

"Do you know Mrs. Dirksen, the lawyer?"

"Or a lawyer," said Grampy. "Lawyers'll screw you six ways from Sunday. Had it up to here with lawyers. Cops and lawyers both – trouble, pure and simple. What else do you want to know?"

Tell Grampy everything? Seemed like a crazy idea, but maybe not. Their eyes met. Ingrid was searching for where to begin when Grampy's eyes darkened, like he was suddenly angry.

"And throw in doctors while you're at it," he said. "Plus accountants. Never got good advice from an accountant, not once. Know what happens when you rely on some bozo?"

"What, Grampy?"

"Whatever's good for them," said Grampy. "Know who to rely on?"

"Who?"

"Yourself. No one's gonna look out for you like you. Stands to reason." He gulped back the rest of the tea, rose. "Speaking of which," he said.

"There's no time," said Ingrid.

"Got to be quick, that's all," said Grampy. He took a box of ammo from a drawer, opened the broom closet, and pulled out the .22 rifle and the .357 automatic. They went outside, hurried past the woodpile and around the barn. For one brief moment Ingrid wondered whether he'd cooked up the whole marshmallow scheme just to get rid of Mom. Could she tell from the expression on his face? No. It was businesslike, but not quite – what was that little upturn at the corners of his lips?

On the other side of the barn stood the corral from when Grampy had kept horses. The sun, low and red, gleamed on a row of Coke bottles lining the top of the far rail, maybe a hundred yards away.

"Here you go," said Grampy, handing Ingrid the .22.

Ingrid took her stance the way he'd taught her, feet apart, nicely balanced. She laid the butt against her shoulder, released the safety, got the farthest Coke bottle to the left in the middle of the sight. Then she took a breath and let it out slowly, relaxing inside until she saw nothing but the very center of that Coke bottle and squeezed the trigger the way Grampy said to, like she wanted just a little bit of toothpaste but all at once. Then came the bang and kick. The Coke bottles stood undamaged.

Grampy looked surprised. "Must not be focusing," he said. "Pretend it's the enemy."

"I don't have enemies," Ingrid said. "And even if I did, I couldn't shoot them."

"A deadly enemy," Grampy said, perhaps not hearing her. "When there's no choice, him or you." He got a faraway look in his eyes. "Past the point of fear."

"What does that mean?"

Grampy blinked. His eyes returned to normal. "Sometimes fear helps," he said. "Like fear of flunking a test, so you study. But when bad's going to happen for sure, fear only hurts."

Ingrid raised the .22, again got the farthest Coke bottle to the left in the sight. She tried to pretend the Coke bottle was a deadly enemy but failed because she couldn't picture a face. Then it hit her that Crazy Katie had had a deadly enemy with a face, no question. She breathed in and out slowly, went still. The Coke bottle seemed to grow in the sight, bigger and rounder. Him or you. She gave the trigger that toothpaste squeeze.

Blam. The Coke bottle shattered in a million pieces. The sun caught them in midair and made a rainbow.

"R-I-P," said Grampy.

Ingrid took aim at the next bottle. Squeeze. Shatter. Another little rainbow bloomed over the end of the corral. Was anything more fun than this? She was getting the third bottle in the sight when Grampy said, "Damn."

Ingrid looked up, followed his gaze. Out on Route 392, the green MPV was already coming back. Mom was so quick about everything, quick and efficient. She was also antigun, to the max, would go into orbit if she ever found out about their little hobby.

"Your turn, Grampy," Ingrid said.

He raised the handgun. *Blam blam blam:* All the

Coke bottles exploded off the rail, making a whole series of rainbows that shimmered for a moment and fell apart. Grampy was a great shot. He'd fought on some island in the Pacific and refused to ride in the Mazda or any other Japanese car.

They were having a second mug of tea – Grampy's heavily laced with brandy – when Mom came in with the marshmallows.

"What a peaceful scene," Mom said. "Like from a Norman Rockwell painting."

Grampy took another sip.

"Thanks for the marshmallows," Ingrid said. "Who wants some?" No takers. Not surprising on Mom's part, the way she watched her weight, but hadn't Grampy said something about a hankering for marshmallows? Ingrid stuck one on a fork and went to the fire. Flames licked around the marshmallow, slowly browning it. Ingrid got a little mesmerized; fires did that to her.

Over at the table, Mom had sat down opposite Grampy.

"I hope you like the picture. Mark found it at the library fundraiser."

Ingrid, gazing into the fire, heard the slurp of Grampy taking another drink.

"He's on the board now," Mom said.

Slurp.

Mom lowered her voice. "Mark and I have an idea we'd like you to think about."

A long pause. The skin of the marshmallow caught

fire, blackening just the way Ingrid liked it.

"It involve selling off my land?" said Grampy.

"Only a very small section," Mom said. "From the old tractor shed down to the back road. The Ferrand Group—"

"Where is he?" Grampy said.

"Tim Ferrand?"

Something crashed. Ingrid turned to look. Grampy's mug lay in pieces on the floor. "I'm not talking about any damn Ferrand vultures," Grampy said. "I'm talking about Mark." Grampy started shaking; he didn't look so strong all of a sudden. Ingrid's marshmallow slipped off the fork and fell into the fire. "Why'd he send you out to do the dirty work? What kind of man does that?"

"It's not dirty work," Mom said. "And besides, I'm the one in real estate. If you'll just listen, Pop" – she called him Pop? – "I'm sure you'll see how different this is from any other—"

"It's not for sale," Grampy said. "Not from the shed to the back road, not an acre, not one square inch." He got up, found another mug. "You go on back and tell him."

Mom and Ingrid got into the car.

"What was that all about?" Ingrid asked.

"Nothing," Mom said. She turned too fast out of Grampy's driveway and the tires squealed. That wasn't like Mom at all. They rode the rest of the way without a word.

Night had fallen, a dark, moonless night. Mom's

headlights cut two weak yellow beams in the blackness. Ingrid forgot about the land behind the tractor shed and the Ferrand Group. Dark and moonless: She understood the meaning of that right away. This night was made-to-order for doing what she had to do. Her mind was made up: Grampy and Benjamin Franklin stood behind her.

seven

downstairs Mom's and Dad's voices rose and fell in irregular patterns, like waves on the monitor of a sick patient. Ingrid got busy at the computer. MapQuest said that the distance from 99 Maple Lane to 341 Packer Street was 4.2 miles with lots of lefts and rights: a long and complicated journey at night. As Ingrid studied the map, she saw something she'd never realized before: Her neighborhood, Riverbend, and the Flats weren't really that far apart as the bee flies, or the crow, or whatever the expression was. All you had to do was cut through the town woods. The distance looked like half as much as going by road, maybe even less.

Ingrid knew there were paths in the woods. She'd done lots of exploring back when Flanders was alive, knew how to get to the kettle pond and the big rock with RED RAIDERS RULE spray-painted on the side. Three or four paths came together at the big rock. She'd just have to find one leading off to the left, like so, and in what couldn't be more than four or five minutes, she'd be popping out somewhere on Packer Street. From there she could simply read the house numbers. All she needed was a flashlight.

Ingrid searched around, found her camp flashlight in the closet, under her sleeping bag. She switched it on: nice and bright.

What else? Dark clothes. Ingrid chose jeans, brown hiking boots, a black fleece jacket, and a matching pompom hat that said STOWE on the front. She checked the time: 11:37. Mom's and Dad's voices had faded away. Ingrid stepped out of her room, listened. She heard the kettle whistling. That would be Mom, waiting up for Ty, who had a midnight curfew. Ingrid got in bed, lights off, clothes on, and waited.

A car pulled up outside at 12:05. A door banged shut and the car peeled away, which meant some older kid and not a parent was driving. A minute later, Mom said something that ended on a rising note, and Ty said something not much longer than a grunt. That would be Mom asking about his evening and Ty saying as little as possible. Then came his footsteps on the stairs, lots of flowing and splattering liquid sounds from the bathroom, footsteps again. To her surprise, they kept going, past Ty's bedroom. There was a soft knock on her half-open door.

"Ingrid?" Ty said. "You awake?"

"Yeah."

"Hear you had a good game today," he said. "Nice job."

"Thanks," Ingrid said. Wow. Had that ever happened before, or anything even close? No.

"Night."

"Night."

Ty went into his room and closed the door.

Ingrid waited for him to fall asleep, waited for the house to go completely quiet. And while she waited, she had a thought: What about asking Ty to go with her? She'd never shared any secrets with him before, but she'd never had any to share, nothing important. He was her big brother, after all. What was the point in having a big brother if not for times like this?

Ingrid clipped the flashlight onto a belt loop, went down the hall, stood outside Ty's door. She heard him talking in a low voice. He was on the phone. And what was that smell? She took a quiet sniff. Not quite the same smell as Grampy's brandy, but not that different. Ty had been drinking. The big-brother plan wasn't going to work.

Down to the basement, across the TV room, maneuvering around all the unseen weights, to the walkout sliding door at the back of the house. It wasn't locked. Ingrid took that for a sign. She slid it open without making the slightest sound and stepped into the night.

A surprisingly cold night, with the wind whipping across the patio, cutting through Ingrid's fleece jacket. Behind her, a TV screen light shone in Mom and Dad's room, sending a trembling blue oblong into the darkness. Ingrid skirted its edge, then hurried across the yard and into the trees.

Her eyes adjusted to the darkness. It came in different shades: the sky the lightest, a kind of charcoal; the tree trunks and branches, mostly bare, a little darker; the ground darker still; and the path black. Night was nothing to fear. The world stayed exactly as it was during the day – only the lighting changed, like when Mr. Rubino worked the board for the Prescott Players. Ingrid followed the trail into the woods, a path that seemed to shine like polished black coal. She didn't even need the flashlight.

How about counting steps? Might be a good idea, giving her some idea of the distance. Ingrid started counting, had reached 679 when something rose in front of her, the same shade of darkness as the trees, but much bigger, big and looming. The rock? Ingrid switched on the flashlight. Yes, the rock, almost the size of a small hill, with RED RAIDERS RULE spray-painted on the side, plus peace signs, hearts with arrows through them, and a few anatomical scribbles. The rock already. This was going great. Griddie – night tracker extraordinaire.

Beyond the rock lay the Punch Bowl, a kettle pond formed by a long-ago glacier. Ingrid felt the rising dampness, cold on her face. Flanders had loved diving into the Punch Bowl for sticks she threw. Once Flanders got started, he just wouldn't stop and he had this annoying way of poking you in the leg with the stick as a signal for more. He'd been a hyper dog, with a crazy tail-biting thing when he really went over the top, and he hadn't liked being patted either. But she missed him, especially right now.

Ingrid studied the paths that came together by the big rock. There were four: the path she'd been on, another going right, around the Punch Bowl, a third leading straight ahead, and a fourth bearing left. Bingo. Ingrid cut the light and set off on the path bearing left.

The path took her up a long rise. The trees seemed to grow closer together, and maybe because of that the different shades of darkness began to blend and the path lost its polish, making it harder to see. But she didn't want to switch on the flashlight; better not to see than to be seen.

Ingrid kept going, a little slower now, the only sounds her own breathing and the occasional crunch of a twig or acorn beneath her feet. She'd lost count. From above came a strange beat, heavy, regular, getting louder. Ingrid felt a whoosh of air above her head, and an instant later a branch creaked, very near. Oh my God. Flashlight. She jabbed the beam toward the sound. An owl, huge and white, with pointy devil ears, sat on a branch that overhung the path, less than ten feet away. Its eyes, the color of liquid gold, gazed right into the beam, maybe blinded. Ingrid had never seen an owl before, not in the wild. A funny thought. How could this be the wild? She was practically in her own backyard.

Somewhere far away a dog howled, very faint, but the owl seemed to hear. Its head turned slowly, reaching an impossible angle; then the owl spread its wings – so wide – and in two heavy flaps rose off the branch, out of the beam, and into the night. Ingrid switched off the flashlight, kept going. Was the owl another good sign? Had to be: She felt a sense of kinship with it, both of them up to something in the night woods.

The path leveled out, bent around an enormous tree

trunk, rose again, and then began sloping down. A light blinked in the distance, then another, then a lot. Two or three minutes after that, Ingrid stepped out of the woods and into an alley behind a tall, narrow house. A window opened on the top story. Ingrid heard music. A lit cigarette came spinning out. The window closed. Ingrid stepped on the butt, squished it out.

She walked around the house, came out on the street, not far from the corner. It was quiet: no one around, cars parked on both sides, gingerbread houses, all run-down. None of the streetlights were working, so Ingrid had to go close to the corner to read the sign: Packer Street. She turned back to the narrow house, read the number by the porch light: 339. Ingrid recognized the darkened house next door but checked the number anyway, just to be sure: 341. She followed a narrow walkway around to the alley and stared up at the back of Crazy Katie's house, where not a glimmer of light showed.

How to get in? That was a question she hadn't considered, maybe should have at the start, when instead she was goofing about Benjamin Franklin.

There were four windows at the back of Crazy Katie's house: a basement window, barred over; one on the first floor; and two more above, out of reach. There was also a door, which she tried first. Locked, no surprise. She stepped over to the first-floor window, put her hands on the glass, pushed up. It didn't budge. Was there anything lying in the alley she could stick in between the sill and the bottom of the window? Nothing she could see in the dark, and she couldn't risk using the flash: Music leaked into the alley from 339, the thumping bass rappers liked. It might have been coming right out of the ground.

Ingrid knelt by the basement window, examined the grate. It was made of thick crisscrossed metal bars with arrowhead-shaped ends, the whole thing attached to the wooden siding of the house. Ingrid put her hand on one of the bars, gave a hopeless little tug. The grate came right off, screws or bolts or whatever they were ripping out of the rotten wood. She almost tipped over backward.

Ingrid examined the window. It wasn't the kind that went up and down, more the kind attached at the top that might swing up and in if given a push. Ingrid gave it a push. It swung up and in, then got stuck, leaving an opening about a foot wide. She gazed in, saw nothing.

Ingrid got facedown on the ground, wriggled back into the opening feetfirst; not a very big opening, but all she needed. Halfway in, she felt around with her feet. No floor. She lowered herself a little more, a little more, still not finding it. She ended up hanging there in the basement, fully stretched and clinging to the windowsill, her feet dangling in midair.

Choice one: She could try to pull herself up, start over. That meant doing an actual pull-up. Ingrid had done pull-ups before, two in a row at soccer camp, for example, but she hadn't been wearing boots and all these clothes. She tried an experimental little pull-up, rose an inch or so. She'd been much stronger in the summer.

Okay. Choice two: She could just let go. Alice, down the rabbit hole.

eight

how long a fall? That was hard to judge, but long enough for a cry to spring from Ingrid's lips despite the importance of absolute silence at a time like this. And then, crash, with a capital C, and all the other letters capitalized too. *CRASH.* A paralyzing landing and she crumpled up, the wind knocked out of her. Maybe paralyzed for real. Then came cacophony, more concentrated noise than she'd ever heard in her life: a wild multichannel soundtrack for a movie – banging trash cans, hubcaps rocketing across a resonating floor, whole glass factories shattering; a wicked symphony that went on and on. When it was over, the silence that followed was even worse. Except for one final sound: the high window banging shut.

Ingrid got her breath back. She tried to wriggle her fingers. They wriggled. Could she move? Yes. She rolled over, got to her knees. Flashlight: still on her belt loop. Was it working? Yes. Ingrid panned the beam across the room, a furnace room full of shadows, cobwebs, newspaper stacks, junk. The trash cans she'd landed on had spilled garbage all over the place. The hubcaps were close to real hubcaps – trash-can lids; and the glass factories were smashed glass cabinets full of ceramic knickknacks, now mostly in pieces. Dust motes by the billion floated in the flashlight beam.

Ingrid rose, picked up her pom-pom hat, brushed something horrible and sticky from her hair. Other girls – smarter ones – were home in bed now, happily—

She froze. A voice spoke in the alley. She switched off the flash.

"Wha' the hell was tha'?" a man said.

"Wha'?" said another man.

"You din hear nothin'?"

"Wha'?"

Then came a tiny splashing sound, maybe two parallel splashing sounds. After that Ingrid heard a quick *zip zip* of zippering up.

"Dju see a light?"

"Wha'?"

"Light on in Katie's cellar."

"Nope."

"Nope?" Pause. "Don' matter anyhow. Here's to Katie."

"Katie."

Ingrid heard what might have been bottles clinking together.

"Hey! Wha's with the grate?"

"Grate?"

"Window grate. Lookit."

"Stick it back on."

Grunt. "Like so?"

"Close enough."

Drunken footsteps moved off.

She wanted to get out of there, get back to her own bed. But the window was closed now and well out of reach, the grate back on. She had no choice but to go up the crude wooden stairs she'd spotted on the far side of the room.

Ingrid mounted the stairs, all of them creaky and coated with dust. At the top she came to a partly open door. A calendar from the Norwich National Bank hung on it. The month was June, the year 1987. Ingrid calmed down. No one in the house, nothing to be alarmed about. Night was the same as day except for lighting. And those boots: She had to have them. Get a grip.

Ingrid pushed the door open, found herself in the kitchen. She beamed the light around: back door leading to the alley, heaps of dishes in the sink, a half-full glass of water on the counter, fridge in the corner, humming away. Ingrid opened it. There was food inside – chocolate milk, Smucker's blueberry jam, three pink-glazed doughnuts. So weird: Kate dead, but her life kept on going a little while longer. She'd probably been looking forward to those doughnuts.

Ingrid walked down the long corridor to the purple-and-gold parlor. What had happened here? She'd taken out the red Pumas with the idea of putting them on to save time. Then the taxi had beeped and she'd hurried out. So the boots would have been right here. Ingrid shone the light around. No boots, nothing on the floor at all. She tried the sagging pink couch, on top and under, found cigarette butts and empty brandy bottles just like Grampy's, but no red boots.

Where else? Maybe nowhere, maybe time to go. She'd made an honest effort, if breaking into a house in the middle of the night could be called honest. Then she remembered assistant Coach Trimble: Playing hard, an honest effort, wasn't the same as playing to win. Ingrid went into the hall, gazed at the stairs leading up into darkness, up where she'd heard a footstep although Crazy Katie lived alone, up where she really didn't want to go.

Ingrid climbed the stairs. At the top was a room barred off with a strip of yellow police tape. She stood next to it, shone her light into the room beyond, a bedroom, although that wasn't the first thing she noticed. The first thing she noticed was the sprawled outline of a human body, chalked on the floor. The second thing she noticed was the pile of shoes beside the closet door. The gold lamé stilettos were there. So were the red Pumas.

POLICE LINE, it said on the tape. DO NOT CROSS. Ingrid knew that was important, all about protecting evidence. She also knew that she wasn't Kate's killer, and therefore the red Pumas couldn't really be called evidence, were just on the wrong side of the tape by accident. What harm could possibly result if she simply ducked under the yellow tape, like so, walked carefully around the chalked outline, and picked up the red Pumas – yes! – while touching absolutely nothing else? No possible harm whatsoever. Ingrid held the Pumas tight. Griddie: playing to win.

She turned to go, already planning her exit strategy –

touching nothing, using that back door to the alley, home before you knew it – when her beam lit on a stack of playbills on the bedside table. And not just any playbills, but playbills from the Prescott Players, old ones, yellowed and beat up with age. Funny, the way she'd been telling Kate about the Prescott Players and up here in her bedroom were these playbills. The top one featured a production of *Dial M for Murder*, a play Ingrid had never heard of, and showed a photo of a young blond actress with frightened eyes facing a silhouetted man. Was there something familiar about that actress? Ingrid bent closer. Yes. Kate, even younger and prettier than in *The Echo* photograph. The very moment Ingrid made that connection, a windowpane shattered somewhere downstairs.

She cut the light at once, stood very still, listening. Had she imagined it? Or had the sound come from the alley, not from inside the house? Ingrid listened with all her might, heard nothing but her own heartbeat, pounding in her ears. The imagination could be very powerful, plus those two drunks might be walking back, dropping bottles in the alley, so chances were—

A footstep on the stairs. Ingrid heard it, clear, distinct, real.

Those little creatures, rabbits and such, that freeze at the sight of a rearing snake and wait meekly to die: for a moment she knew what they felt, understood preferring death to terror. Then she remembered what Grampy said about the point where fear stopped helping and started hurting. She dove under Crazy Katie's bed.

Another footstep, soft but closer. Then a few more, followed by silence. Ingrid pictured someone standing by the police tape. She even thought she sensed the force of a straining human mind. A narrow beam of light flashed on, arced across the floor, then up and out of her sight. She heard a soft grunt: a man ducking under the tape. Ingrid knew it was a man from the sound of the grunt.

The footsteps drew closer. The feet themselves came into view, lit by the soft edges of the narrow beam: dirty, man-size tennis sneakers with those three Adidas stripes, spattered with dark-green paint.

The feet were still. Ingrid heard the man breathing. Could he hear her? She held her breath. The feet shifted a little. Something shuffled. A playbill fluttered to the floor, inches from Ingrid's face – the *Dial M for Murder* playbill. The man made a sound in his throat, harsh and metallic. Then came another grunt and a gloved hand appeared, long and narrow, feeling under the bed. The fanning fingers came so close to Ingrid's face that she could feel the breeze, smell the combination of glove leather and absorbed sweat. The hand encountered the playbill, settled, picked it up.

The Adidas feet moved away. A small circle of light jerked across the opposite wall in the direction of the door and vanished. The man grunted once more – that would be him ducking under the yellow tape. His steps faded away, down, down. Ingrid, her ear already to the floor, listened hard, thought she heard a door close down below – that would be the kitchen door leading to the alley. She let out her breath, what was left of it, which wasn't much.

It was cold in Kate's house, but Ingrid was sweating. She was also shaking a bit, lying there under the bed. The house was silent now. Did that mean it was safe to come out? Ingrid didn't know. She stayed right where she was for a long time. Nothing changed. The silence went on and on.

Ingrid crawled out from under the bed, making no noise at all. She tied the red Pumas together, slung them around her neck. With her hand over the flashlight lens, she had a quick look around the room. Under the reddish light that escaped between her fingers she saw the stack of playbills still standing on the bedside table. *Dial M for Murder* was no longer on top. Ingrid leafed through: In fact, the *Dial M for Murder* playbill was gone.

Ingrid stepped around the chalked outline, crouched under the yellow tape, started downstairs, hand still covering the lens. Almost at the bottom, she heard a car pulling up. Then came a sound she was familiar with from *Cops*, Stacy's favorite show: the crackle of a police radio. Ingrid hurtled down the last few steps, swung around the stair post into the long corridor. A powerful searchlight from outside was shining through the parlor window.

Ingrid raced down the corridor, into the kitchen, to the back door, broken glass crunching under her feet. She yanked the door open. At the same moment, she heard the front door opening at the far end of the corridor. A man called out: "Hey!"

Ingrid sprang out the door, ran across the alley and into the woods, faster than she'd ever run in her life. A searchlight beam cut through the night, just missing her.

The man called out: "Stop! Police!"

But Ingrid didn't stop, couldn't stop. The searchlight beam angled through the trees, momentarily revealing a path ahead. Ingrid took it. The right path? The right direction? She didn't know. She just kept running. And she could run.

"Stop! Police!"

The searchlight went out. From behind came the sound of heavy charging footsteps, ripping through underbrush, coming closer and closer. How was he doing that if he wasn't even using his searchlight? Ingrid realized her flashlight was still on, bobbing along like a lure. She snapped it off.

A tremendous crash not far behind her, followed by a cry of pain. A brief silence, except for her own panting breath, and then a police radio crackled through the woods. Ingrid kept going, slower now without the flashlight, but she left the crackling sound behind. No one came after her, no one who made noise or aimed a light. Soon her eyes adjusted to the darkness, and the path began to shine again like polished coal. She ran.

Ingrid could run. Running ran in the family. She ran until she could run no more, which must have been a long time. Shouldn't she have reached the big rock by now? Ingrid peered into the darkness, saw no sign of that looming shadow. She listened, heard nothing but a dog howling, somewhere up ahead.

Ingrid kept going, walking now and starting to feel a

chill, her sweat cooling. Where was the big rock? The path suddenly split in two, two polished black tracks, forming a Y. Ingrid didn't remember any Y. Left or right? Right seemed best for no reason she could explain. Why hadn't she taken up the hobby of learning Echo Falls years ago?

Play to win, she told herself.

This path to the right had lots of twists and turns, twists and turns she didn't remember. The sound of the howling dog grew louder and louder, very near, then stopped abruptly. Ingrid stopped too. She took the risk of switching on her flashlight. There on the path, not ten yards away, stood a big dog, its eyes yellow and opaque.

"Good dog," she said.

The dog growled.

Okay. This was probably the wrong path anyway. Her best bet would be returning to the Y intersection, trying the left-hand path. Ingrid started back. She heard the dog taking off after her.

Ingrid whipped around, aimed the flash in the dog's face. The dog froze, one forepaw poised in the air, like one of those well-trained pointers. But this was not a well-trained pointer. Close up, this dog, collarless, turned out to be kind of fat and dumb-looking, with floppy ears and droopy eyes. Ingrid held out her hand. The dog wagged its tail and came forward. She patted its head. It pressed its head against her hand. Simple as that. They were pals.

"Where's out?" Ingrid said.

The dog ran in a little circle, stopped by the nearest

tree, and lifted his leg.

"You're a big help," Ingrid said.

She backtracked to the Y intersection, took the left fork this time, the dog trotting along beside her. The left fork led down a long hill and then came to a three-way split, one path going left, one right, one straight ahead. Where was the rock? The previous left fork must have been a mistake. If so, shouldn't she take the right-hand path now, as a correction? Ingrid took the right-hand path, the logical choice, the choice Sherlock Holmes would have made. She tried to think of any similar situations Holmes had been in and remembered none.

The right-hand path went up a rise, got narrow and almost disappeared, then came out at an opening in the woods. Ingrid found herself on the top of a hill. Down below flowed the river, silvery black. The river? Didn't that mean she'd gone in the exact wrong direction? The river was on the other side of the woods from her house, miles and miles away, so far she'd never even considered walking to it. And the falls: She could hear them, not too distant, making a sound like people going *shhhh*. That would mean ... yes: Topping a hill on the opposite bank stood Prescott Hall, the old mansion that housed the Prescott Players, all its tall leaded windows dark. Curiouser and curiouser. Prescott Hall was nowhere near 99 Maple Lane. Griddie, deep down the rabbit hole.

The sky wasn't quite so nightlike by the time Ingrid finally found the big rock. She was so cold, so tired by then that she hadn't noticed the coming of day, and was even slow to recognize the significance of the fact that she could read RED RAIDERS RULE without a flashlight, the only way she could read it now in any case, the battery having gone dead.

"Good boy," she said, although the dog had done nothing to help, leading her down false trails every time she'd decided to trust his animal instincts. Ingrid took the right-hand path by the rock, this right-hand path the correct one for sure, and headed for home.

Day was breaking beyond any doubt when Ingrid stepped out of the woods and into her own backyard, a gray dawn with thick clouds covering the whole sky. Ninety-nine Maple Lane was quiet. Ingrid crossed the yard, slid open the door to the basement.

"Go home, boy," she said, very quietly.

The dog wagged his tail but didn't go anywhere.

"Go."

Ingrid went inside, closed the door. She hurried into the basement bathroom, looked at herself in the mirror.

Oh my God. Filthy, scratched, blue lipped; and what was that in her hair? A clump of rice in congealed plum sauce? How had that happened?

Ingrid cleaned herself up, not well but quickly, and went into the laundry room. Her yellow pajamas with the red strawberries were folded on the drier. She threw all her clothes into the washer, except for the shoes she'd been wearing and the red Pumas, which she left on the floor, and put on the pajamas. As for the red Pumas – she didn't love them anymore.

Now to get upstairs and into bed. Ingrid went up, into the mudroom, almost there. Then she heard someone coming down the hall from the master bedroom. Could she reach the stairs to the second floor? Not in time.

Ingrid slipped into the kitchen instead, sat at the table in the breakfast nook, took a banana from the fruit bowl. Mom came in, wearing her quilted blue housecoat, eyes puffy, hair all over the place. One small part of Ingrid, maybe getting smaller, was telling her to fly across the kitchen, fling her arms around her mother and say, "Oh, Mom."

"Ingrid!" Nothing in Mom's tone was saying "hug me". "You're up early."

"Uh-huh," said Ingrid noncommittally, peeling the banana. And anyway, wasn't it all over now?

Mom gave her a long, suspicious look.

"Did you wear the appliance?" she said.

twenty minutes later, Mom had gone out for Sunday bagels and lox and Ingrid was in her own blessed bed, Mister Happy tucked in beside her. Seconds after that she was asleep. Stormy seas rose all around her, but she was snug in her sturdy boat – dry, warm, safe.

"Hey."

Ingrid opened her eyes, the lids almost glued together with eye crust. Ty was at her door.

"Phone," he said, and tossed it to her.

She missed. The phone bounced on the bed, hit the wall. She grabbed it.

"Hello?"

"Ingrid? Jill Monteiro." Ingrid sat up; Jill Monteiro was director of the Prescott Players. "I hope I didn't wake you."

"Oh, no," said Ingrid. "Not me."

"We'll be auditioning for *Alice in Wonderland*

Tuesday at five," Jill said. "Hope you can make it. There're all kinds of good parts."

"Like Alice?" Ingrid said, unable to stop herself.

Jill laughed. She had a great laugh, surprisingly deep and wicked; she'd used it once in a real Hollywood movie called *Tongue and Groove*, all about home-renovating hijinks with Will Smith and Eugene Levy. Straight to video, but JILL MONTEIRO was on the box, tiny but there.

Alice: a plum role. Ingrid had a copy of the book on her shelf. She took it into the bathroom, poured a huge hot bubble bath, got in, and started leafing through the pages. The trick was going to be keeping Alice from sounding like a geek. Ingrid practiced saying "he's perfectly idiotic," "the stupidest tea party I ever was at in all my life," "mustard isn't a bird," and "you're nothing but a pack of cards," trying to inject at least a bit of cool. Acting was all about cool; she'd learned that at the movies.

When Ingrid went downstairs, she found everyone in the TV room, Dad and Ty watching football, Mom going through some listing sheets.

"I found your boots," Mom said.

"Oh."

"Don't you want to know where?"

"Okay."

"In the laundry room."

"Oh."

"Try to keep track of your things, Ingrid. I put the boots over there by the—" Mom paused, looked out the slider. "There's a strange dog in the yard," she said.

They all looked. A strange dog – with floppy ears and droopy eyes, coat a kind of tweedy brown – but not strange to Ingrid. He stood right outside the slider, peering in, tail wagging as if he'd spotted someone, although the only thing in his line of sight was the StairMaster.

Dad and Ty turned back to the TV.

"Did you see that hit?" Dad said.

Mom got up, went to the slider.

"Go on, go home," Mom said. The dog wagged his tail, still looking off in the wrong direction. "He's not wearing a collar. Anyone seen this dog before?"

No one answered, Dad and Ty probably too into the game to have even heard, Ingrid because, well, because where would she start?

Mom took her cell phone out of her pocket, called the shelter, described the dog. That was Mom, organized, quick, on task. No such dogs reported missing in Echo Falls, and the shelter didn't do pickups on weekends.

"He's kind of cute," Mom said. Ingrid saw where this might be going, tried to head it off.

"He's the dumbest dog on the planet," she said.

Mom looked surprised. "What makes you say that?"

Uh-oh. Those feelers of Mom's: almost impossible to out-think them. "Just look at him," she said. It was true. He was the kind of dog that in a cartoon would harrumph a lot and play second fiddle.

"I think he's cute," Mom said. She opened the slider.

The dog came right in as if totally familiar with the

place, trotted past Mom, and stood in front of Ingrid, mouth open and tongue hanging out.

"He likes you," Mom said. "Give him a pat."

Ingrid gave him a pat. He did that head-pressing thing, shoving his head against her hand.

"Mark," said Mom. "Look how the dog likes Ingrid."

Dad didn't hear: Football put males in a trance, maybe a handy fact to keep in mind.

"You know what I'm thinking, Ingrid?" Mom said.

Ingrid knew, but she said, "What?"

"If no one claims him, maybe we should at least give him a temp—"

Mom's phone rang. She listened for a moment, hung up. "We'll talk about it later. I've got to go show Blueberry Crescent."

"What's the price on that?" Dad said, eyes on the screen.

"They're asking three thirty," Mom said.

Mom left. A few minutes after that, Dad got up and said, "Maybe I'll go into the office for a while."

"What about the game?" Ty said.

"It's getting out of hand," Dad said.

"Seventeen-ten's not out of hand," Ty said.

"I'll tell that to Tim Ferrand when my report's not ready," Dad said. He left too.

Ingrid sat on the couch near Ty. The dog followed, stood at her feet; didn't sit, just stood there. On the screen a player in green and gold knocked down a pass and did a funny hip-hop dance.

"You should try that," Ingrid said.

"Are you nuts? I'd be off the team."

"I meant after you made a great play."

"When's that going to happen?"

Ty had never asked her a question like that, like he was leaning on her or something. "You're just a freshman," Ingrid said. "The only one on the varsity."

"Not for long," Ty said.

"That can't be true," Ingrid said. "You're so fast."

Ty snorted.

"How were you supposed to know about that stupid flea-flicker?" Ingrid said; unless he'd listened to her, but too late to bring that up.

And maybe she should have kept her mouth shut completely, because Ty turned on her, his face going bright red. "What the hell do you know?"

That annoyed her, especially after all she'd done to try to warn him, annoyed her enough to change her mind about keeping her mouth shut. "I'd know enough not to fall for it twice," Ingrid said.

What happened next was so fast, Ingrid didn't understand at first, didn't even feel the pain. Ty sprang across the couch and hit her. Maybe he was aiming for her arm or shoulder; his fist did graze her shoulder, but where it landed was on her right eye. Ingrid fell sideways, hand going up to her eye, hardly aware of Ty bolting out of the room, kicking something, yelling, "I hate football."

Now she felt the pain. Not enough pain to make her cry, but she was crying anyway. Nothing like this had ever happened. Ty's speech could be rough sometimes, and when they were much younger he'd gone through a stage of shutting her in the broom closet when Mom and Dad were out, but he'd never actually hit her, and she'd have thought they'd outgrown the possibility by now.

Ingrid felt the dog pressing his head against her leg. She stopped crying, gave him a pat. He pressed harder.

"You're pretty strong for a fat guy," she said, brushing tears away on the back of her sleeve.

He wagged his tail, a scraggly thing with burrs in it. A TV commentator said, "That's what they call lowering the boom." Ingrid got up and switched him off. She heard water running in the pipes: Ty taking a shower, or washing his face. She didn't want to be in the house. Confiding in Ty: She'd actually considered that?

"Come on, boy," Ingrid said. She got her jacket from upstairs and opened the slider.

He came out and shook himself the way dogs do when they're wet, which he wasn't, of course. "Know any tricks?" she said.

He pressed his head against her leg.

"That's not a trick."

Ingrid picked up a twig. At the mere sight of a picked-up twig, Flanders would have been springing up and down and barking his head off. This dog didn't seem to notice. He was looking at nothing in particular.

"Here's a stick," Ingrid said, waving it before his eyes. She flicked it backhand about ten feet away, right in front of him. "Go get it. Get the stick."

His mouth opened and his tongue appeared. He gazed off into the middle distance. That was it.

"Come on," Ingrid said. She walked over to the twig,

picked it up. He stood beside her, watching. Watching her do the retrieving, you could almost think, like he was the one doing the training. You could almost think that, but not if you looked at his dumb face, which reminded her of Nigel Bruce, who'd played Dr. Watson to Basil Rathbone's Holmes. Ingrid had all the videos.

"Smell the stick," Ingrid said, holding it close to his nose. He averted it slightly, a strangely delicate movement, like an aristocrat who'd been offered a pastrami sandwich.

"Go get it," Ingrid said, throwing it again. She pointed.

This time the dog ambled off in the general direction of the twig. He came quite close, actually stepping over it, before making a sharp turn and heading into the woods.

"Hey!"

He kept going, past the oak with the split trunk where she and Ty had built a tree house, now in disrepair, around a bend and out of sight.

"Hey. Come back here."

Ingrid ran after him, not her fastest, no way she could run her fastest, still sore all over from the night in the woods. And the woods were the last place she wanted to be right now.

"Dog!" She didn't even know his name. "Come here."

Ingrid tore along the path, back in the damn woods. Up ahead she caught sight of him squatting, the lower half of him all urgent and straining, his head in the clouds.

"Stay."

But he didn't stay. As soon as he was done, he took off again, trotting in his clumsy way, like that beer-belly guy who jogged past their house every Sunday.

"Come back, you moron."

But he didn't. The stupid jerk got all the way to the big rock before Ingrid caught up with him. He'd come to a stop, was just standing still, almost alert-looking, sniffing the air.

"Move an inch and you're dead," Ingrid said.

The dog turned his head backward in her direction, one of those weird angles dogs can do.

"I mean it," Ingrid said.

A man stepped out from behind the rock. He was very big, with broad shoulders and a barrel chest. The dog saw him and wagged his scruffy tail.

"Just who are you planning to kill?" the man said.

Ingrid backed up.

"I wasn't—" she began.

And then someone else stepped out from behind the rock, someone in an Echo Falls Pop Warner jacket, someone she knew.

"Ingrid?" said Joey Strade.

"Hi," Ingrid said.

"Hey," said Joey. He rocked back and forth a little.

"Manners," said the big man.

"This your dog?" Joey said.

"Kind of," said Ingrid.

"Manners means introduce me to your friend," said the big man.

"Oh yeah," said Joey. "Ingrid, my dad."

"Nice to meet you, Ingrid," said Chief Strade, holding out his hand.

Ingrid shook it, the biggest hand she'd ever seen in her life.

Joey gave the dog a pat. The dog did his head-pressing thing with Joey. "What's his name?" said Joey.

Why were all questions suddenly so hard? "Nigel," Ingrid said.

"Nigel?"

"Yeah. He tried to get away, sort of."

"You should put his tag on," said Chief Strade. "In case he does it again."

"It's in the laundry," Ingrid said. Chief Strade gave her a close look. "The collar, I mean," said Ingrid. "Very dirty. Dogs, et cetera." *Shut up, for God's sake.*

"Got a little shiner there," said Chief Strade.

"Huh?"

"Over your right eye."

Ingrid's hand went to it involuntarily. That hurt. "I fell," she said. "Chasing this stupid ... chasing Nigel."

Chief Strade was still giving her that close look. He had a big nose, big chin, big ears, but his eyes were small, half hidden by the kind of heavy brow ridges Neanderthals had. "You live near here, Ingrid?" he said.

"Yeah," said Ingrid, waving vaguely.

"Whereabouts?" said Chief Strade.

Before she had to answer, a crackling sound came from his jacket pocket. Chief Strade took out his police radio and said, "Strade," moving away a little.

Ingrid's eyes met Joey's. They both looked away.

"Nice dog," Joey said.

"Uh-huh," said Ingrid.

"Nigel?"

"Right."

"How'd you come up with that?"

"Something wrong with it?"

"No," said Joey. "It ... um ..."

Over by the rock, Chief Strade was saying, "Separate cells."

"Like, fits him," Joey said. "The way he looks."

"Uh-huh," said Ingrid, watching Chief Strade. "What are you guys doing here?"

"My dad's actually working," Joey said. "I'm just tagging along. Something weird happened last night."

"Oh?"

"Remember the woman who got killed?"

"Katherine Kovac," Ingrid said.

Joey gave her a quick look, a little like his dad's, but Joey was much better-looking, didn't have that Neanderthal thing going on. "Yeah," he said. "Some guy broke into her house down in the Flats. I guess he made a lot of noise, because there were like two or three calls to the station. Sergeant Pina chased the guy into the woods. My dad was hoping maybe he dropped something."

"Did he?" said Ingrid, trying to sound casual. Sergeant Pina umpired Little League and Babe Ruth baseball, also girls' softball from time to time, including back when Ingrid still played. He was a good umpire, made an effort to keep all the kids relaxed, was great at learning their names and remembering them. Hers, for example.

"Not that we found," Joey said. "But my dad thinks whoever did the break-in was probably the killer."

"Why would the killer do that?"

"Lots of reasons." Joey said.

"Like?"

"I don't know," Joey said. Chief Strade was coming back. "Why would the killer do the break-in last night?" Joey said. "Ingrid wants to know."

"Does she?" said the chief. "Good question. We're about to find out."

"What do you mean?" Joey said.

"We got them," said the chief.

"Them?" asked Ingrid before she could stop herself. What them?

The chief gave her another look, but quicker this time; he was in a hurry.

"Couple of lowlifes who live on the same street," he said. "They left a bottle in the alley out back with prints all over it. We think they used it to smash the window on the back door. Their prints are inside, too. As for the night of the murder, their stories don't add up, not one little bit."

"So what's going to happen?" Joey said.

"Booking them on murder one," said the chief, "soon's we get to the station."

"Murder one," said Joey; his body made a little motion, almost a shiver, in his Pop Warner jacket.

Chief Strade turned to her. "Better get some ice on that eye."

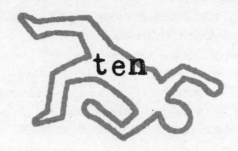

ten

ingrid went back in through the slider and up to the kitchen, Nigel following. Ty was doing homework at the table. Homework. Did she have any this weekend? She kind of thought so.

Ty looked up. His gaze went right to her eye. He looked worried – was he thinking bye-bye to that Rolls-Royce or Maserati due on his sixteenth birthday? Nigel spotted a bagel half under the table – sesame – darted across the floor, and scarfed it up.

"His name is Nigel," Ingrid said.

"Nigel? How do you know?"

"Because I named him."

"Nigel? That's the dumbest—"

Mom came in through the door that led to the garage, carrying two pizzas from Benito's.

"Ingrid! What happened to your eye?"

Ingrid looked at Ty. She let a nice long pause go by, building suspense like a Hollywood pro. "I fell," she said at last.

"You fell?"

"Playing with Nigel. I'm fine. Don't worry."

"Who's Nigel?" Mom said.

"The dog, Mom," Ingrid said, still watching Ty. "That's the name we gave him, Ty and me."

"Nigel?" Mom said.

"It was Ty's idea, but I like it too."

Mom turned to Ty, surprised. "'Nigel' was your idea?"

Ty's face went through a bunch of expressions, all comical from where Ingrid sat. "Yeah," he said.

"Ty was really psyched about it," she said. "Weren't you, Ty?"

"Yeah."

"Tell Mom where you got the idea."

He was kind of squirming now. This must have been how it felt to be a grand inquisitor in the Spanish Inquisition: pretty damn good.

"Where I got the idea," Ty said. He gazed down at Nigel licking sesame seeds off the tiles. "He … looks like a Nigel. Like, it fits him."

Mom bent down, getting a good close-up of Nigel. "You know something, Ty? You're absolutely right. It's perfect."

Her gaze shifted to Ty, seemed to be seeing him in a new light, as though she'd spotted some previously hidden talent.

Mom opened the pizza boxes – a large pepperoni, olive, and garlic, and a medium arugula and goat cheese. "Someone call Dad," she said.

"He's not back yet," Ty said.

"From where?" said Mom.

"He had to go to the office," Ty said.

Mom lost track of what she was doing for a moment, as though hearing some distant sound, then finished serving out the pizza.

There were still two slices of the pepperoni when Dad came back, taking off his leather coat and saying, "Hi, everybody. That looks good." He sat down opposite Ingrid. She waited for that piney smell to waft her way, but it didn't.

"You had to go to the office?" Mom said.

Dad nodded. "Ten-o'clock meeting tomorrow. Tim's gotten interested in electroplating technology for some reason. There isn't one company in the whole sector I'd put a dime into but—"

Ingrid stopped listening. Murder one. The killers, those two drunks in the alley, were in jail, their finger-prints all over Kate's place, their stories not adding up. And she had the red Pumas. So it was over, right? There was nothing to tell anybody ever.

Except: The man who'd broken into Kate's house, ducked under the police tape, and stood over the bed had been so quiet, whereas the drunks were noisy. Plus she hadn't smelled any alcohol. But weren't those just two tiny impressions she could have easily gotten wrong? And what did they add up to anyway compared to Chief Strade's expertise? A feeling of relief should have been washing over her at this very moment. But it wasn't. Ingrid would have given a lot to know if one of those men in jail owned Adidas sneakers spattered with green paint.

"Ingrid? I asked you a question."

Ingrid looked up. Dad was talking to her.

"What happened to your eye?"

"I fell. Out playing with Nigel."

"Nigel?"

Ingrid pointed under the table. Dad looked down.

"Nigel," he said. "Cool name."

"Ty came up with it," Mom said.

Dad beamed at Ty. Ty gave him an aw-shucks look so fake that the dumbest parents in the world would have seen through it; but not Mom and Dad.

"So we're keeping him?" Dad said.

"Unless someone puts in a claim," said Mom.

Dad tossed Nigel a piece of pepperoni. Almost casually, Nigel opened his mouth and caught it, like a smooth shortstop making a routine play.

That night Nigel followed Ingrid up to her bedroom, tried to climb on the bed. "On the floor," Ingrid said, pointing. Nigel circled and circled, finally settled on a spot. Ingrid lay down, pulling Mister Happy in beside her. It had to be the two drunks. And she had the boots back safe and sound, as though she'd never been in Kate's house at all, the whole episode deleted. The seas rose around her. She slept. The little boat was not so snug anymore, but she slept.

When she woke up in the morning – "Ingrid! Don't make me call you again!" – Nigel was on the bed and Mister Happy, somewhat gnawed, was on the floor.

"Bad dog." But he was too warm and fat and cuddly

to get mad at. "Don't hog the pillow."

"INGRID!"

"Mornin', petunia," said Mr. Sidney as Ingrid got on the bus.

"Morning, Mr. Sidney."

Mr. Sidney checked the rearview mirror, his eyes barely showing under the bill of his BATTLE OF THE CORAL SEA hat, and said, "Guy in the back – zip it."

Ingrid sat beside Mia.

"Hey," Mia said. "You're wearing eye shadow."

Ingrid had made up both eyes. A good solution – they now looked much the same – even though she was a little sketchy with makeup, having tried it only once or twice, and never out in the world. Ingrid batted her eyelids.

"Cool," Mia said.

"Cool in da pool," said Brucie Berman, somewhere behind them.

"Zip it, guy," said Mr. Sidney.

Ingrid noticed that Mia's own eyes didn't look very happy. After their divorce, despite the fact that Mia's dad had stayed in New York and never came to Echo Falls, he and her mom still managed to fight several times a week, usually on the phone but sometimes by e-mail. Mia knew that part because her mom wasn't good on the computer and sometimes copied Mia by mistake, nasty messages popping up in her inbox. Ingrid was trying to find the right thing to say when the bus pulled into Ferrand Middle School.

* * *

Ms. Groome handed back the math quiz. In red at the top: an *A. A? A!* Ingrid had never got an A in math in her life. She flipped through – check mark after check mark, right to the end, where she'd left the extra credit problem undone. Wow. A breakthrough. She noticed that under the A, Ms. Groome had written "Please see me after class."

Griddie the math whiz trailed after the other kids when the lunch bell rang, stopped by Ms. Groome's desk for her pat on the back. "Hi, Ms. Groome," she said. "You wanted to see me?"

Ms. Groome looked up. It was her first year in Echo Falls, but before that she'd taught in Hartford for a long time. Ms. Groome put down her red pencil.

"You got all the questions right," she said.

"Not the extra credit," Ingrid said, in the interest of modesty.

"Up till now," said Ms. Groome, "you've been carrying a C plus."

No denying that: It was what made the A feel so good.

"So," said Ms. Groome, "this is unexpected."

Exactly. They were on the same page. Surprises were nice. If you got A after A after A, the whole thing would get old pretty fast.

"Therefore," said Ms. Groome, "I want you to tell me honestly whether this is your own work."

A weird thing happened at that moment: Ingrid's body understood what Ms. Groome was saying before her mind did. Her face went a bright hot red and she had trouble getting her breath. "Are you saying I cheated?"

"I'm not saying anything," Ms. Groome said. "I'm asking."

"I didn't cheat," Ingrid said. Her face got hotter and hotter, probably making her look guilty when she wasn't the least bit guilty.

"Mia is a very good math student," Ms. Groome said. "On last Monday's homework she got only one wrong, number thirty-seven. You got only one wrong as well, which rarely happens, even when you complete the assignment. The exact same problem, thirty-seven, the exact same error."

Ingrid remembered copying Mia's work on the bus Friday morning; had she done it Monday too? Possible. Was it cheating? Kind of. But not the same as cheating on a quiz. "I didn't cheat on the quiz," Ingrid said.

Ms. Groome gazed at her. Silence went on and on until Ingrid had to say something. "I don't sit anywhere near Mia."

"True," said Ms. Groome. "And no one who sits around you got better than a B." She rose, took Ingrid's quiz over to the board. "If you didn't cheat, is there any reason you couldn't solve these problems again?"

"No," said Ingrid. There was no other answer.

"Then why don't we take number one?" Ms. Groome wrote on the board: "Factor the following quadratic polynomial: $4x^2 + 8x - 5$," and handed Ingrid a piece of chalk.

Ingrid stared at the problem. Four x squared plus eight x minus five. Vaguely familiar, but no answer jumped out at her. Worse, her mind refused to help. For some reason it started tossing up all kinds of irrelevant stuff, like Angelina Jolie, Elijah Wood, Shakespeare, Arabs. Algebra was an Arabic word. *Al* meant *the* in Arabic and *gebra* probably meant *gibberish*. Ingrid touched the chalk to the board, hoping something might happen. It didn't.

"Well?" said Ms. Groome.

Ingrid turned to her. Ms. Groome had a broad, still face, almost like a piece of statuary, that could look you in the eye forever. Ingrid knew how important it was to look her right back but couldn't quite do it.

"I didn't cheat on the quiz," she said, suddenly sure that her face wore the same mulish look she sometimes saw on Ty's, not attractive, not innocent. Plus the eye makeup, which Ms. Groome seemed to be noticing at that very moment, no doubt thinking *The kind of thirteen-year-old girl who wears eye makeup to school is the kind who cheats.*

"I can't prove you did," said Ms. Groome. "Not without an honest admission." She waited. Ingrid said nothing.

Ms. Groome laid Ingrid's test on the nearest desk, wrote on it with her red pencil, handed it to Ingrid. The A was now an F.

"If you choose to appeal this grade," said Ms. Groome, "speak to the principal."

Ingrid sat next to Stacy on the bus ride home. She was telling her all about Ms. Groome when a police cruiser sped by, the word CHIEF in gold letters on the door.

"He's a real jerk," Stacy said.

"Who?"

"The chief. Joey's dad."

Ingrid's heart started going, that quick tom-tom beat. "What makes you say that?"

"The DUI thing."

Stacy's brother, Sean, had been picked up for driving under the influence a few months before. "But how was that the chief's fault?" Ingrid said. "Wasn't Sean drunk?"

"Point oh nine on the Breathalyzer," said Stacy. "Know what the limit is? Point oh eight. The chief could have cut him a break."

"Why didn't he?"

"Because he's a hard-ass," said Stacy. Stacy glanced at her. "Like Ms. Groome."

Was Chief Strade a hard-ass? Meeting him in the woods, Ingrid hadn't gotten that feeling. But it wasn't going to matter – as long as the right guys were in jail.

eleven

there were no more Prescotts in Echo Falls, hadn't been for thirty years, but Prescott Hall still stood on a hill across the river from the main part of town. That side of the river had been rural until very recently: Grampy's farm could be seen from the long gallery, if it hadn't been closed off. Most of Prescott Hall was closed off – whole floors and wings, plus most of the back including the kitchen, pantry, and morning room, and all of the cellar, where the renovation was scheduled to begin, under the direction of the Echo Falls Heritage Society, of which Carol Levin-Hill was vice president in charge of acquisitions. The Heritage Society now owned Prescott Hall and had a ten-year plan to fix up the whole thing; Tim Ferrand was in charge of fundraising and had already given one hundred thousand dollars of his own money.

Ingrid often heard her mother talking about all this on the phone, but it didn't interest her very much. What interested her was the fact that some long-ago Prescott had married a wannabe stage actress and converted the ballroom into a beautiful theater that sat 300 people. Mahogany seats, red carpeting, polished oak stage, lovely red curtains decorated with gold-embroidered masks of comedy and tragedy: all this the home of the Prescott Players, Jill Monteiro, director.

Ingrid had never met anyone like Jill Monteiro. Jill was an artist, not wannabe but real. Besides her role in *Tongue and Groove*, she'd done two off-Broadway plays, guested as a nervous flight attendant on *Friends*, and created a one-woman show based on the life of Jackie Onassis that she'd performed at colleges all over New England.

"Hi, everybody," she said, standing at the front of the stage, a slim little figure dressed in black, with curly black hair and big dark eyes. "What a great turnout, and I'm glad to see some newcomers."

Ingrid, sitting in an aisle seat ten or twelve rows back, glanced around. She saw lots of the same people who auditioned for every production, like Mr. Santos of Santos's Texaco, who did a great wiseguy accent (even when he wasn't in a wiseguy role) and Mrs. Breen, the teller at Central State Savings and Loan, who couldn't learn her lines but could cry on cue, real tears just pouring down her chubby face (an effect that had made her performance as Mrs. Claus in the Christmas pageant really stand out); but there were also some she didn't know; and oh my God – who was that just coming in at the back? Not ... but it was.

Chloe Ferrand.

Chloe Ferrand, daughter of Tim, Ingrid's dad's boss,

was the most beautiful thirteen-year-old girl in town, maybe the most beautiful girl in town period. And certainly the only one to be recognized as officially beautiful by the outside world: She was already represented by a real modeling agency in New York and had appeared in the Plow and Hearth catalog twice, once in sheepskin slippers and once lounging by a stack of Georgia fatwood kindling. Ingrid and Chloe had played together when they were little, but Chloe had left the public-school system at the end of sixth grade and now attended Cheshire Country Day. C.C.D. had its own theater program, for God's sake. So what was Chloe doing here? Only one reason Ingrid could think of: Alice. Chloe wanted the role.

"… have to take other parts," Jill was saying. "And there won't be enough parts to go around, but everyone who wants will get some job in the production. Any questions?"

Mr. Stubbs of Stubbs Engineering stuck up his hand. "How are we going to do the parts where Alice gets smaller and bigger?"

"We'll get to that, Gene," Jill said. "Did everybody sign in on the clipboard? Scripts are down front, with Post-its marking the audition scene for each role. Wait in the green room for your call."

Ingrid loved the green room. Some Prescott had gone all out. The walls were rich and creamy, with fluted green marble columns painted on them, the floor was a checkerboard of green and cream tiles, and the furniture was all green leather.

Ingrid sat on a footstool in the corner, examined the

script. "*Alice's Adventures in Wonderland,* by Lewis Carroll. Adapted for the stage by Jill Monteiro." She turned to the page marked with the Alice Post-it: an excerpt from the mad tea party scene. There were only two speaking roles, Alice and the Mad Hatter.

HATTER: Have you guessed the riddle
yet?
ALICE: I give up. What's the answer?
HATTER: I haven't the slightest...

"Hello, Ingrid."
Ingrid looked up: Chloe.
"Hi," Ingrid said.
"How's everything?" Chloe said.
"Good."
"Cool," Chloe said. "How's what's-her-name?"
"Stacy."
"Yeah."
"Good."
Chloe nodded. A wisp of golden-blond hair fell over one eye; she tossed it back into place, a little movement that seemed to attract all the light in the room. "Interested in any role in particular?" she asked.
"Alice," said Ingrid.
"What a coincidence," said Chloe. "You'd be great."
"Thanks."
"But maybe even better as the White Rabbit."
"The White Rabbit?"
Chloe nodded encouragingly. She had the brightest smile in creation, would probably be doing Crest com-

mercials any day now. She also seemed to have a tan, although it wasn't a month for tans, even for the Chloes of the world. Not summer, not Christmas, not spring break.

"You've got a tan," Ingrid said – couldn't stop herself.

"Barbados," Chloe said. "Just for the weekend. How long have you had braces?"

"Ingrid Levin-Hill," called someone from the green-room door. "You're next."

Already? She hadn't even read the scene once. Ingrid rose, a little unsteady.

"Break a leg," said Chloe.

There were two stools onstage. Ingrid sat on one. Mr. Santos sat on the other, the script in his huge hand, oil stains under the fingernails.

"Anytime," said Jill Monteiro, from somewhere in the darkened seats.

"Me?" said Mr. Santos.

"From the top," said Jill.

Mr. Santos frowned at the script. "I'm at the top," he said. He shook himself, as though discarding the character of Mr. Santos and allowing the inner Mad Hatter to emerge, then cleared his throat, forcefully enough to cause bleeding, Ingrid thought, and spoke through gritted teeth: "Okay, paisan, time's up on that freakin' riddle."

Out in the darkness, something dropped on the floor. Ingrid opened her mouth, closed it, began again: "I give up." Her instinct was to be breezy in the tea-party scene, but following Mr. Santos's lead, she tried nervous instead, flashing him an anxious glance. "What's the answer?"

Mr. Santos laughed suddenly, startling her – a loud, cruel, triumphant laugh, but more Daffy Duck than Joe Pesci. For such a big guy, Mr. Santos had a surprisingly high voice. "How the hell would I—" he began, before a cell phone rang in the pocket of his overalls. "Geez." He fished it out and said, "Santos," listened for a moment, then rose and peered past the footlights, shading his eyes. "Hey. Screwup down at the station. Be back as soon as I can, okay?"

Jill's voice came out of the darkness. "No hurry," she said.

"Thanks," said Mr. Santos. He turned to Ingrid and in a stage whisper said, "That scared look you did – wow. Just like Diane Keaton in *Godfather Two*."

Mr. Santos left. Jill called out, "Send another Mad Hatter." Then to Ingrid: "This will probably be a little more conventional." And to herself, so quietly Ingrid almost didn't hear: "Please God."

A man walked onto the stage, script in hand. Ingrid had never seen him before. He was tall, with short-cropped gray hair, high cheekbones, and only one or two wrinkles, but deep.

"Your name, please?" said Jill.

He gazed into the orchestra seats. "My name is Vincent Dunn," he said.

"Thanks for coming out," Jill said. "This is Ingrid."

He turned to her. "Hello, Ingrid." He had a soft voice, kind of a monotone.

"Hi," said Ingrid.

He sat on the vacant stool.

"Whenever you're ready, Mr. Dunn."

"Vincent, please," he said in his quiet voice. He glanced down at the script. His face seemed to change, although Ingrid was at a loss to say exactly how, but it became a little unstable. And when he spoke, his voice had changed too, no longer a monotone but not musical either: It was too discordant for that.

"Have you guessed the riddle yet?" he said; there was a slight pause before *riddle*, and the word itself seemed to squirm around aggressively, like a living thing. Maybe it was the aggression part that reminded Ingrid of her talk with Ms. Groome, and the way Ms. Groome had trapped her with questions.

"I give up," Ingrid said; and heard defiance in her tone, defiance she wished she'd mustered with Ms. Groome. She hadn't cheated on that quiz. "What's the answer?" Ingrid said, making it a demand.

"I haven't the slightest idea," said Vincent Dunn, slowing down the rhythm slightly on *idea* to suggest just the opposite of what he was saying, that he knew the answer damn well.

The script now directed *(wearily)* for the next line of dialogue, but Ingrid found herself narrowing her eyes and sharpening her tone. "Why waste time asking riddles that have no answers?"

"Aha!" said Vincent Dunn, reading from the script: "Another riddle!" He smiled like he was enjoying himself.

"Not all questions are riddles," said Ingrid, giving him the schoolmarm effect, straight from Ms. Groome.

Now for the first time, Vincent Dunn raised his eyes from the page and looked at her. A long time seemed to pass. "Your hair wants cutting," he said.

"You should learn not to make personal remarks," Ingrid said, maybe getting too prissy; she wanted a do-over on that one. "It's very rude."

He gazed at her for a moment, as though offended, then changed completely, growing brisk and hostlike: "I want a clean cup," he said. "Let's all move one place down." All at once, utterly insane.

Ingrid tried some exasperation, Scarlett O'Hara style. "This is the stupidest tea party I ever was at in all my life!"

Vincent Dunn went still, then delivered the last line on the Post-it page in a quiet, reasonable tone that was somehow still insane: "Who's making personal remarks now?"

A moment of silence. Jill Monteiro came down the aisle and into view beyond the glare of the footlights.

"Interesting," she said. "A little … darker than I'd imagined, but interesting. Have you done much theater, Mr. Dunn?"

"Vincent, please," he said, back in the soft mono-tone, his face again inexpressive. "A little bit. Years ago."

"Where was this?" said Jill.

"Various places. Nothing worth mentioning."

"Are you new in town?"

He nodded, then looked down at his feet. He wore brown leather lace ups like Dad's, but scuffed and with-out those tiny holes in the toecap. Could middle-aged men be shy? Vincent Dunn seemed to be. "I thought maybe this might be a way of meeting a few people," he said.

"It's a great way of meeting people," Jill said. "And I'm delighted you came out. In fact, Vincent, with Mr. Santos called away, would you mind staying out here while we run through the other Alices?"

"Not at all," said Vincent Dunn.

"And one other thing," she said. "I was thinking – depending on the abilities of whoever got the role – of having the character sing the little song that's in the book. The words aren't coming to me offhand but it goes to the tune of 'Twinkle Twinkle Little Star.' Can you sing, Vincent?"

"A little," he said. He licked his lips and sang.

> "Twinkle twinkle little star,
> How I wonder what you are.
> Up above the world so high,
> Like a diamond in the sky.
> Twinkle twinkle little star,
> How I wonder what you are."

It was beautiful. He hit every note and had a much bigger voice than Ingrid would have guessed; but more than that, he gave you the feeling of great big universe and little lonely guy.

"Wow," said Jill. Ingrid knew Jill was much too professional to give anything away at auditions, but she did now.

He looked at his feet.

Ingrid got off her stool. "Thanks, Mr. Dunn."

"Vincent," he said to her. "Please."

"And thank you, Ingrid," Jill said. "I'll let you know by tomorrow." She called to someone in the wings: "Send in Chloe Ferrand."

Ingrid went into the entrance hall, a huge octagonal room hung with artists' renderings and blueprints of the reconstruction plans, and looked out the window. No silver TT, no green MPV. She sighed. After a minute or two she began sidling back toward the theater. She opened one of the doors, stood behind the last row of seats.

Up onstage, Chloe, glowing in the footlights, was saying: "Why waste time asking riddles that have no answers?" Her voice ran up and down the scale like a flute. She shook that blond wisp out of her eye, all girlish innocence and wide-eyed freshness, at the same time impossibly good-looking, oozing stage presence.

Vincent Dunn said, "Aha. Another riddle." He smiled again as though enjoying himself, maybe this time even more. Even more. Did that mean Chloe was doing better? One thing was certain: Ingrid hadn't looked like Chloe up there, not close. A thousand Dr. Binkermans couldn't take her to that level. After a minute or two she knew she'd blown it, her reading way off the mark.

Ingrid went home in a gloomy mood. Wide-eyed freshness was obviously the way to go. What had she been thinking?

The Echo lay on the kitchen table.

Big headline: TWO ARRESTS IN FLATS MURDER. No surprise there, but seeing it in print gave her a jolt anyway.

The Echo had pictures of the men, two scuzzy-looking guys named Albert Morales and Lon Stingley. They shared a basement apartment on Packer Street, were currently unemployed, and had long criminal records – drug possession, public drunkenness, vagrancy, car theft, shoplifting. Ingrid went over that part twice. What was missing? No crimes of violence, no breaking and entering. She gazed at their faces, faces with too much hair, too many scars, not enough smarts. The bigger the crime, Holmes said, the more obvious the motive. That was one of his basic rules. So what was the motive here? Ingrid had heard these men, drunk, yes, but sounding mournful about Kate's death, as though they'd liked her. Did that mean they hadn't done it? Did it mean one of them couldn't have broken in and stood over the bed? Why repair the grate first? Why repair it at all? And what was the point of that break-in? Ingrid had no answers. Why couldn't this have been an airtight case?

Full-length photos might have helped, especially if they'd showed Albert Morales or Lon Stingley in dirty Adidas sneakers spattered with green paint. But these were just their faces. She stared at the photos until they turned into meaningless dots.

twelve

wednesday after school. Ingrid home alone. She sat at the kitchen table, math homework in front of her, rain whipping by outside at a sharp angle. She counted the problems – six factoring, eight solving for x. X, that obsession of Ms. Groome and all her buddies in the math police.

Ingrid gazed at the page in the textbook, saw a maze, a thicket, a minefield, endless. Suppose she could do each problem in two minutes; the whole thing would take six plus eight makes fourteen times two – twenty-eight minutes. Practically a whole half hour, a serious amount of time, torn right out of her life, lost without a trace, wasted forever. A sin.

"Can you believe this, Nigel?"

Nigel, sleeping on the floor, one paw awkwardly over his face as though warding off the light, had no response.

But what about if she went a little faster, one and a half minutes per problem? That would be … let's see, fourteen times a minute and a half, minute and a half being tricky ... twenty-one minutes. Still too big a chunk of time. One a minute would make fourteen minutes, but even that, so close to a quarter of an hour, was too much. Math homework was worth ten minutes, not a second more. That meant doing better than one problem a minute.

How much better? How quickly did she have to do each problem to get the whole stupid thing over with in ten minutes? Was there a way to figure it out? Time – ten minutes. Problems – fourteen. What else was there? Just the amount of time per problem, which was what she wanted to know. Call that G, for Griddie.

She wrote G on a corner of the textbook page, remembering too late the rule about not writing in textbooks. G was the time for one problem. For all of them, it would be ... fourteen times G. She wrote 14 in front of the G. Total time: 14G. But total time was also ten minutes. Hey. $14G = 10$. So G ... turned out to be one of those messy divisions that wouldn't come out even, forty-two point something. Call it forty-three. Forty-three seconds. Hey! That was the answer. Wow. Forty-three seconds per problem, painlessly quick, if you wanted to be done in ten minutes. But impossible, at least for her. She sucked at math.

The phone rang. Ingrid grabbed it, thinking *Jill Monteiro*, her heart racing even though she knew she'd blown the audition. But it wasn't Jill.

"Ingrid? Hi."

"Hi Joey."

"Hi."

"Hi."

"What's happening?" Joey said.

"Homework," said Ingrid.

"Me too. Math."

"Me too."

"Um," said Joey. "Who have you got?"

"For math?"

"Uh-huh."

"Ms. Groome."

"You're in Algebra Two?"

"Yeah."

"I'm in Pre-Algebra. Mr. Prindle."

"What's he like?"

"Gay."

"Gay gay?"

"No," said Joey. "Just gay."

There was a silence.

"How's Nigel?" Joey said. "Your dog."

"He's sleeping right now," Ingrid said. "He sleeps a lot."

Another silence. "Do you think dogs dream?" he said.

"Yeah."

"About what?"

Ingrid glanced at Nigel. If he was dreaming, there was no sign. "I don't know," Ingrid said.

"You think there's a way to find out?" Joey said.

"What dogs dream about?"

"Uh-huh."

"You mean like an experiment or something?"

"Yeah."

An interesting idea, the kind she wouldn't have had in a million years. "You could do something for the science fair," she said.

"I've already got a project."

"What is it?"

"I'm building a catapult."

"A catapult?"

"Like in *Lord of the Rings* where the orcs lobbed the bodies into Minas Tirith."

"Cool."

"Not full-scale," said Joey. "I could lob maybe mice."

"That wouldn't be as scary," Ingrid said.

Silence.

"You could see it, if you want," Joey said.

"The catapult?"

"Uh-huh. After school. I'm on bus two." She'd need a note to change buses. "My dad could drive you home."

"That sounds—" Beep. "Joey? Hang on a second. I've got another call. Hello?"

"Hello. Tim Ferrand. Is Mark there?"

"Hi, Mr. Ferrand."

A little pause. "Ingrid?"

"Hi. He's not here."

"Do you know where I can reach him?"

"Probably at the office."

Mr. Ferrand's voice, kind of impatient to begin with, got a little sharper. "I'm at the office."

"Oh."

Click.

Ingrid hit flash to get back to Joey.

"Joey?"

"Hi."

Beep.

"Hang on." She hit flash again. "Hello?"

"Hey." Stacy. "You watching TV?"

"No."

"Turn on channel nine. Quick."

Ingrid switched on the under-cupboard TV, found channel nine. A reporter was standing in front of 341 Packer Street, and the writing at the bottom of the screen read ECHO FALLS MURDER. "... suspects lived two doors down," the reporter was saying. The camera panned down the street, zoomed in on 337. There was a FOR SALE sign outside – Riverbend Properties, the company Mom worked for. "Morales and Stingley were arrested by Echo Falls police on Sunday," the reporter said. Footage came on of police marching Morales and Stingley into the station.

"Are they nasty-looking or what?" said Stacy.

But Ingrid wasn't looking at their faces. She was bent close to the screen, peering at their shoes. Morales wore beige work boots; Stingley, who walked with a pronounced limp, dragging his right leg, had on black hightops. That didn't prove anything: Somewhere in the basement apartment at 337 Packer Street there might be a pair of paint-spattered Adidas sneakers. But one thing Ingrid knew: Whoever had broken into 341 and stood over the bed hadn't walked with a limp. Did that mean Stingley, at least, was innocent for sure? That feeling of dread stirred inside her.

The news shifted to another story – people lined up at a convenience store for lottery tickets.

"Stace? I'll call you back."

She hit flash.

"Joey?"

No one there. The door opened and Mom came in with a bag from Ta Tung Palace. "Who's Joey?" she said.

"Joey?"

"Didn't you just say Joey?"

Ty came in behind Mom, dumped his backpack on the floor.

"Not there, Ty, please," said Mom. She looked tired. "How many times do I have to ask you?"

"You're so uptight," Ty said, grabbing the backpack, rounding the corner, tossing it into the mudroom, where it knocked something over. He looked tired too.

Mom turned to Ingrid, her eyes a little confused. Ingrid could tell she couldn't remember what they'd been talking about. Just as well.

They sat down to dinner: spring rolls, dun dun noodles, orange chicken, Szechuan shrimp with onions. Nigel woke up. Ingrid got out the chopsticks – Chinese food always tasted better with chopsticks.

"Where's Dad?" Ty said.

"Working late," said Mom. "Anything interesting happen today?"

Ty shrugged.

"Ingrid?" Mom said.

Ingrid, chopsticking up a slippery shrimp no problem, like she hailed from Haiphong, said, "Not that I can think of."

"What's happening in English?"

"We're reading poems."

"Such as?"

English was Ingrid's favorite subject, by far, but today's class seemed long ago. She realized she was tired too, the whole family tired at once. "There was one about daffodils."

Mom's eyes brightened. "'I wandered lonely as a cloud,'" she said, "'That floats on high o'er vales and hills, When all at once I saw a crowd, A host, of golden daffodils.'"

"Hey," Ingrid said.

Ty paused in midchew. "How do you know that?" he said; midchew of an orange chicken ball, Ingrid saw.

"I just do."

"But how?" Ingrid said.

Mom looked a little embarrassed. "Don't laugh," she said. "But as a kid, I wanted to be a poet. My poetry was terrible, so I decided to memorize great poems in the hope it would rub off."

"Like how many?" Ty said.

"How many poems?" said Mom. "Oh, I don't know, lots. I got good at it – I guess that was my talent, memorizing poetry."

"Say some more," Ingrid said.

"Of 'Daffodils'?"

"Something else."

Mom thought. Then she said:

> *"That sunny dome! those caves of ice!*
> *And all who heard should see them there,*

And all should cry, Beware! Beware!
His flashing eyes, his floating hair!
Weave a circle around him thrice,
And close your eyes with holy dread,
For he on honeydew hath fed,
And drunk the milk of Paradise."

"What the hell's all that about?" said Ty.

"Something scary," said Ingrid. "What is it about, Mom?"

Mom didn't answer the question. Instead, she smiled a wise sort of smile, and in a quieter voice, recited:

"I say that we are wound
With mercy round and round
As if with air."

"Hey," Ingrid said.

Mom didn't look so tired anymore.

The door opened, and Dad came in with a bouquet of mixed flowers in his hand. He handed them to Mom.

"They're beautiful," Mom said. "What's the occasion?"

"No occasion," said Dad. He sat at the table. "I'm starving," he said, and started eating out of a carton.

"Let me get you a plate," Mom said. She got him a plate; opened a bottle of wine, too, which normally happened only on weekends. Dad took a big drink.

"Long day?" Mom said.

"No complaints," Dad said. "That Blueberry Crescent sale go through?"

130

"Not yet," said Mom. "They're haggling over whether the freezer stays or goes."

"What's your cut?"

"One and a half percent of three twenty."

"Forty-eight hundred," Dad said. He was amazing with numbers. And Mom had all this poetry in her. Together they had it made.

"Let's go somewhere," Ingrid said.

"What do you mean?" said Mom.

"With the forty-eight hundred. Chloe Ferrand went to Barbados for the weekend."

"When were you talking to her?" Dad said.

"At the audition." Ingrid glanced at the clock. Maybe Jill wasn't even going to call, would be e-mailing the bad news instead. Yeah, that was it.

Dad dipped a spring roll in plum sauce; Chinese food was great, and plum sauce most of all. "The Ferrands and us aren't in the same league," he said.

Ingrid knew that, of course, but it was depressing to hear it coming from Dad. "He called, by the way," she said.

"Who?"

"Mr. Ferrand."

"When was this?"

"A while ago."

"Why didn't you tell me?"

Uh-oh. Some kind of mood change – why, she had no idea. "I just did," Ingrid said, maybe a little rudely, but it came out so fast.

"Thanks," said Dad, rude right back. He took out his cell phone and went into the dining room. "Tim?"

he said, and closed the door.

Ingrid cleared the table. Mom loaded the dishwasher. Ty went into the little pantry and started eating something that made crunchy sounds, probably potato chips. Dad returned, shaking his head.

"He's in some kind of a mood," Dad said.

"Why?" asked Mom, pushing the energy-saver button on the dishwasher.

"No idea," Dad said.

Strange, thought Ingrid, Dad's moods and Mr. Ferrand's. She made a big decision: No way she was going to work for anyone but herself.

The phone rang. Ty stepped out of the pantry, answered it.

"For you," he said, handing the phone to Ingrid.

Yes, potato chips: Their oil was now all over the receiver, and therefore on her hand and in her hair, just washed this very—

"Ingrid?"

Jill Monteiro. Ingrid went still.

"Or," said Jill, "should I say Alice?"

thirteen

happiness, essence of.

Ingrid fell asleep happy – except for the little glitch of not having called Joey back – and woke up happy.

Alice!

In Wonderland!

Unstoppably happy. Did it matter that cold rain was still slanting down and it looked really miserable outside? No. Or that Ty's toilet-aiming skills had been at their all-time worst this morning? No. Or that he'd used up all her favorite shampoo, sold only at salons, forcing her to wash her hair with a bar of Ivory? No.

Ingrid went downstairs, skipping the last few, skidded around the corner and into the kitchen. Mom and Ty were already gone; Dad sat at the table, drinking coffee and reading *The Wall Street Journal*.

"Someone's feeling pretty good," he said.

"Who wouldn't, Dad? I got the part." She almost couldn't stop herself from saying it again. *I got the part.*

He smiled at her. "Have some breakfast."

Ingrid glanced at the clock. "No time."

"That's all right," Dad said. "I'll drive you."

"Yeah?"

"Got to go in early anyway."

Ingrid fried up an egg, toasted an English muffin, spread it with lots of butter and raspberry jam, sat down.

"What's in the paper?" she said.

"Interest rates are going up."

"Is that good?"

"Not for business."

"Then why are they doing it?"

Dad looked over the top of the paper. "Not much choice," he said. "It's like surfers on a wave – they can change the direction they're going a little bit, but they can't change the wave at all."

"So the economy's like out of control?" Ingrid said.

"Depends who's doing the surfing," Dad said, and turned the page.

Ingrid took a big bite of her English muffin, toasted to perfection, the butter partly melted, the jam still cold from the fridge – that first bite, just heavenly. "How did the Ferrands get so rich?" she asked.

"They got in early on some nickel mines in Canada, back in the thirties. Angus Ferrand, Tim's grandfather, I'm talking about."

"But he must have had money to start with."

"Not much. But he married a Prescott."

"From Prescott Hall?"

"Right."

"And who did they marry?" Ingrid said.

Dad laughed. "I don't know. Their money goes way

back to the Civil War. They had a foundry right below the falls where the Little League complex is now. Made shovels and shipped them down the river."

"The Prescotts got rich by making shovels?" Ingrid said.

"For burying the dead," Dad said.

"Hey." There was so much killing, you could get rich making the shovels to bury the dead? "Why don't they teach us this in school?" Ingrid said.

Dad shrugged, spooned more sugar into his coffee. He liked lots.

"What happened to the Prescotts?" Ingrid said.

"They kind of dwindled away," Dad said. "I think one still lived up in the Hall when I was a kid. He took off for Alaska or someplace."

"Did you ever see the Prescott Players back then?" Ingrid said.

"Going to a play?" said Dad. "Does that sound like Grampy to you?"

Ingrid laughed.

Dad got a look in his eye. Every once in a while, especially if encouraged at all, he told a really stupid joke. One was on its way.

"What do you call a guy who jumps off a bridge in Paris?"

Ingrid waited.

"In Seine," Dad said.

"Please," said Ingrid.

Dad drove her to school. She sat up front in the TT, which didn't happen often. The sound system was awesome.

Ingrid punched in Roxy 101.

"Turn it down," Dad said.

Ingrid turned it down. The rain fell harder. Little branches lay on the pavement. Dad checked the outside temperature and said, "Two degrees lower and you'd have a snow day."

"Damn," Ingrid said. She had a complicated thought, all about the existence of numbers everywhere – interest rates, thermometer degrees, even Civil War dead – affecting her life whether she understood how or not. "I'm starting to do a little better in math," she said.

"Good to hear," said Dad. Ingrid smiled. "Won't get into Princeton without practically an eight hundred on the math SAT."

Ingrid stopped smiling. "Does it have to be Princeton?"

"Or any other top school. But Princeton's very special."

"How?"

"How is Princeton special?" Dad said. "You'd be set for life. Look at Tim Ferrand."

"But you said the Ferrands got rich by marrying the Prescotts."

Dad's voice rose. "That's only part of the story," he said. "Why do you argue when I give you good advice?" He punched the off button on the radio.

"It's a long way off, Dad. I'm in eighth grade."

"Last grade that doesn't count," Dad said. "And that's not even true, not in math. You've got to come out of this year on the calculus track."

"What's that?"

"Algebra, geometry, precal, calculus."

"Or what?"

"Princeton won't even look at you."

Rain pelted down. The drops got long and silvery, as though icing over. "Princeton's orange and black, right?" she said.

"Their colors?" said Dad. "Yeah."

"Who's red?" said Ingrid. If Princeton didn't want her – and that was already crystal clear – she didn't want them.

"Red?" Dad said.

"Of the ... top schools."

"Stanford. Cornell. Harvard is crimson, which is pretty close."

"Not really," Ingrid said. What was crimson? Just a mealymouthed color that didn't have the guts to be red.

They rode the rest of the way in silence. The future looked grim. There wasn't even a Prescott left to marry.

Math, first period. Ms. Groome usually began the class by collecting homework, walking up and down the rows. Ingrid, her mind on those surfers making insignificant little movements on a mighty wave, might have missed something Ms. Groome said.

"Ingrid? Is there something wrong with your hearing?"

Ingrid looked up. Ms. Groome was looming over her.

"Your homework, please," Ms. Groome said.

At that moment, way, way too late, Ingrid realized that she hadn't actually done her homework. Instead, she'd spent her time making calculations about how long homework would take if she were speedy; calculations in ink, written in the margins of her textbook, this same textbook that now lay on her desk, open to that very same page; a page Ms. Groome was staring at.

"I ... uh," Ingrid said. "Forgot."

Ms. Groome's glasses were smeared with fingerprints that made a kind of glare, hiding her eyes from view. "You forgot to do your homework?"

Ingrid nodded. She could have said she was sorry, but then Ms. Groome would have had an opening for saying sorry doesn't cut it or something along those lines, and what was the point of going through all that?

"And did you also forget the rules about defacing textbooks?" said Ms. Groome.

Ingrid nodded again. This time she did come close to saying sorry.

There was a long silence. The silence ended when Brucie Berman sneezed, so loudly it had to be on purpose. Someone giggled. Ms. Groome picked up Ingrid's textbook. "Unacceptable," she said, and returned to her desk, shutting Ingrid's textbook in the top drawer.

Ms. Groome taught a lesson all about distance, rate, and time problems, trucks and trains passing each other, going in different directions, arriving in places like Cleveland, Des Moines, or Kalamazoo, but when? Ingrid, concentrating hard, resolving to do better on account of the calculus track and her newfound realization that math was all around, ended up understanding the lesson perfectly. Later, in the hall, the guidance counselor handed her a note. She'd been reassigned to Pre-Algebra, Mr. Prindle's class, starting tomorrow.

*   *   *

Ingrid saw Joey in the dismissal lineup. He was wearing his Pop Warner jacket, and that out-of-control blunt Indian feather thing was sticking straight up from the back of his head.

"I didn't call you back last night," she said.

"Uh-huh."

"Things got busy."

"Yeah."

"And now guess what?"

"What?"

"I'm in your math class."

"How did that happen?"

"Ms. Groome."

"That sucks," said Joey.

"Yeah."

"Um. Want to come over and see the catapult?"

"I didn't bring a note for the bus."

"Oh."

"But maybe ..." Ingrid took out her math notebook, useless now, tore out a page, and wrote "My daughter Ingrid will be taking bus two today. Sincerely, Carol Levin-Hill."

"I don't know," Joey said, reading it upside down.

"Don't know what?" said Ingrid.

"If ..." said Joey.

Ingrid handed the note to the bus monitor and got on bus two. Unlike a lot of kids, she'd never forged a note from home before, but today was different. Just like Grampy, she'd had it up to here.

*   *   *

Joey lived in the Lower Falls neighborhood. The houses were smaller and closer together than in Riverbend, with lots of pickups in the driveways. Joey took out a key, opened the side door. Ingrid went in.

"This is the kitchen," Joey said.

Ingrid could see that. It was very tidy, with a sailing-ship calendar on the wall and two places set at the table. "Want something to eat?" Joey said.

"I'm all right."

Joey opened a cupboard, took out a bag of potato chips. He offered them to her. She shook her head. He ate a few, then a few more, offered the bag again. This time Ingrid took a handful.

"Okay," Joey said. "I'll show you the thing."

They went into the living room.

"You've got a woodstove," Ingrid said. Coals glowed through the glass window.

"Heats the whole house," Joey said. "Pretty much."

Paintings hung on the walls, all of sailing ships. A chessboard sat on a table between two chairs, the pieces in some kind of midgame formation.

"Who plays chess?" Ingrid said.

"Me and my dad," said Joey. "Do you?"

"No."

Joey opened a door. "It's down here," he said. He flicked on a light. They went down to the basement.

"You've got a workshop," Ingrid said.

"Yeah."

An amazing workshop, with a long bench, different power saws, a vise, tons of tools, lots of stuff Ingrid didn't even know the names of. On the end of the bench stood the catapult, about three feet high, made of some yellowish wood that seemed to glow under the workbench lamp.

Ingrid went over, touched it.

"No modern materials or techniques," Joey said. "I got the plans from a book about the Hundred Years' War."

Ingrid had never heard of the Hundred Years' War.

"They weren't fighting the whole time," Joey said.

"Does it work?" said Ingrid.

"I told you," Joey said. "Tack down the leather string."

"Here?"

"Yeah."

"Now crank the wheel."

Ingrid turned the wooden wheel, a little thing, beautifully made.

"You can do it harder than that."

Ingrid cranked harder. The arm of the catapult began to bend. She felt its strength.

"Now put this in the bowl."

He handed her a golf ball. She stuck it in the bowl at the end of the catapult arm.

"Unhook the string."

Ingrid reached for it.

"Get your head out of the way first."

She got her head out of the way, unhooked the string. The catapult arm snapped forward with a tiny whoosh of air, flinging the golf ball across the room in a blur. It thumped against a punching bag that Ingrid hadn't noticed and bounced on the floor.

She turned to him. They looked at each other for a moment. "If there's time before the fair," Joey said, "I'll build a little castle to knock down."

Ingrid nodded. For some reason, it sounded like one of the best ideas she'd ever heard.

There wasn't much space between them, the way they were standing, close to the catapult. Joey leaned across that space, face first, a very awkward movement, leading with his mouth. Ingrid, like a figure in a dream, turned up her own face. Their lips came together. Ingrid's eyes closed. She felt his arms going around her. She put hers around him. Ingrid had done plenty of hugging – Mom, Dad, Stacy, Mia, other friends, Grampy once or twice, Aunt This and Uncle That – but nothing compared to this. She opened her eyes to see what he was doing. He was watching her. She'd never been so close to someone's eyes before. At that moment a door opened upstairs and Joey backed away, fast, like from an electric shock.

"My dad," he whispered. And then, out of nowhere, "Divorced."

A voice called from upstairs. "Joe?"

"Down here," Joey said.

Heavy footsteps started down the stairs.

"Ingrid's here to see the catapult," Joey said.

Chief Strade came into view, wearing his uniform. "Is she?" he said.

"You remember Ingrid," Joey said.

"From the woods," said Chief Strade. "Nice to see you."

"Hello, Mr. Strade," Ingrid said. "It's one heck of a

catapult." Possibly the dumbest remark of her life.

"Not bad," said the chief. "I'll just get supper started. You're invited."

"Thanks, I—"

"Fire up the grill, Joe."

"It's raining, Dad."

"Stopped twenty minutes ago," said the chief. "You didn't notice?"

fourteen

they ate at the kitchen table, under the sailing-ship calendar. It was different from dinner at Ingrid's. First, it was called supper. Second, it was happening earlier. Third, they were eating steak, banished from the Levin-Hills' table because of mad cow. Ingrid loved steak, especially medium rare and juicy, just like this.

"Been saving these," said the chief, loosening his tie, a navy-blue tie that matched his uniform shirt. "How's yours?"

"Great," Ingrid said.

"Pass down that A1, Joe, where she can get it."

"That's all right," Ingrid said.

"No A1?" said the chief. "How about ketchup?"

"I like it just like this," Ingrid said.

"Me, too," said the chief. "Joe puts sauce on everything."

"That's not true," Joey said, although his steak was swimming in A1 and there was a pool of ketchup on the side.

The chief rolled up his sleeves – his forearms were huge, the links of his steel watchband stretched to the max – and poured himself a beer. Ingrid and Joey had milk – whole milk, which she'd hardly ever even tasted. So good, like a meal all by itself. There was a lot to be said for eating at Joey's.

"How's school?" asked the chief.

"Good," said Ingrid.

"Ingrid's one of the brainy kids," said Joey. She felt something press against her foot.

"That's clear," said the chief.

Joey's foot. "I'm not," said Ingrid. How could a foot pressing against another foot feel this good?

"What's your favorite subject?" the chief asked.

"English." Joey pressed a little harder; it actually sort of began to hurt.

"Least favorite?" the chief said. "Send those rolls around, Joe. And the butter, for Pete's sake. What's wrong with you?"

Joey withdrew his foot fast.

"Math," said Ingrid.

"Ingrid's—" Joey began, and then stopped himself. She knew what he'd been about to say, knew he'd realized he'd be opening a can of worms.

But too late. "Ingrid's what?" said Chief Strade.

"Uh," said Joey.

"I'm going to be in Joey's math class," Ingrid said. "Starting tomorrow."

"Pre-Algebra?" said the chief.

"Yeah."

"Where were you before?"

"Algebra Two."

"Her teacher was a jerk," Joey said, a streamlet of A1 leaking from the corner of his mouth. Ingrid felt the crazy temptation – totally whacked – to mop it up with her napkin.

"How so?" said the chief.

"It doesn't matter," Ingrid said.

"Just being a jerk," said Joey.

"Who's the teacher?" the chief said.

"Ms. Groome," Joey said.

His father nodded, chewing slowly. Joey's eyes narrowed.

"You know her?" he said.

"Is she new?" the chief said. "From Hartford?"

"You know her?" Joey said again.

"I think she's going out with Ron Pina," said the chief.

"You mean like dating?" Joey said. "But Ron's a cool guy."

"Who's Ron Pina?" Ingrid said.

"Sergeant Pina," Joey said. "He works with my dad."

Ingrid, putting more butter on her roll, froze: Sergeant Pina.

"How's he doing, anyway?" said Joey.

"Be on crutches for six weeks," the chief said.

"What about that hunting trip to Wyoming?"

"Had to cancel, and they're fighting him over the deposit," the chief said. "Pass those potatoes down where Ingrid can reach them, Joe."

Joey passed the potatoes. "Sergeant Pina was the one

146

who chased the guy into the woods," he said. "He ran into a tree."

"Oh," Ingrid said. A baked potato she was transferring from the bowl to her plate somehow got loose and fell to the floor. "Sorry," she said, reaching down to pick it up, lying right next to one of the chief's enormous feet. The laces of his black shoes were untied, black shoes that gleamed even in the dim light under the table; she could smell the polish and see where – what were those things called? bunions? – deformed the leather.

"That's all right," the chief said. "Take another."

Joey put another potato on her plate. "Ingrid's into Sherlock Holmes," he said.

She glanced at him. How did he know that? He must have been talking to her friends. Ingrid wasn't sure whether she liked that or not.

All the heavy features on the chief's face seemed to lighten up. Was he really a hard-ass, like Stacy thought? "'There is nothing more deceptive than an obvious fact,'" he said.

"'The Boscombe Valley Mystery'" said Ingrid. One of her favorites.

The chief grinned. His teeth were huge, too, all different shapes. "I'm a big fan," he said. He clinked his glass against Ingrid's. "Wonder what he'd think of the case."

"The Crazy Katie case?" Ingrid asked.

The chief's grin went away. "That's what people called her," he said, "but there was never any evidence of actual insanity and no criminal record whatsoever.

She did have her share of problems."

"Mental problems, right, Dad?" said Joey.

"Don't know if you'd call them mental problems," said the chief. "She got eccentric over the years, but at one time she must have been pretty normal. They say she was engaged to the most eligible bachelor in Echo Falls."

"Who was that?" Ingrid asked.

"Philip Prescott," said the chief.

"Of Prescott Hall?"

"Yup. The last of the Prescotts."

"The one who took off for Alaska?"

The chief gave her a quick look. "How'd you know that?"

"Ingrid's Alice," Joey said. "In the Wonderland play."

The chief glanced at him in a way that said *Is this my son?*

"My dad told me," Ingrid said.

The chief nodded, helped himself to another steak from the serving platter, cut it into bite-size chunks. "That's the story," he said. "Long before my time, of course. This must have been thirty years ago or so. I was a kid back then, younger than you two."

"Here in Echo Falls?" Ingrid said.

"Oh, no. Thirty years ago I'd have been in Germany. Army brat."

"He lived in Omar, too," said Joey.

"Oman," said the chief.

"Amen," said Ingrid; it just popped out, completely ludicrous.

But the chief seemed to find it very funny. His eyebrows, thick and almost meeting in the middle, shot up and he laughed and laughed. "That's a good one," he said. "Have another steak."

"I couldn't."

"This one's barely two bites." He plopped one on her plate. "They say her problems started up after he disappeared."

"He just took off for Alaska?" Ingrid said. "Out of the blue?"

"He wrote a farewell letter to *The Echo*," the chief said. "We found it among her effects, saved all these years."

"What did it say?"

The chief reached for his briefcase, standing by the fridge. He opened it on the table and handed her a yellowed newspaper clipping.

My friends, Ingrid read.

"Read it out loud," said Joey.

"'My friends, this may come as a surprise, but after our wonderful production of *Dial M for Murder*, I feel a sudden and very deep need to refresh myself. My plans take me far away, to Alaska or even beyond. I want honest physical work, space, a chance to work things out in my head. Please don't think badly of me. Sincerely, Philip Prescott.'"

"That's so weird," Joey said.

"What do you think, Ingrid?" said the chief.

Ingrid thought. She hardly ever got sick, so hardly ever stayed home from school; but when she did, she watched those afternoon shows on TV, soap operas, so unreal. Philip Prescott's parting letter reminded her of those shows. "Yeah," she said. "It's weird."

"He never came back?" said Joey.

"Nope," said the chief. "Never heard from again."

"What happened to all his money?" Joey asked.

"I wondered about that," said the chief. "So I called old Mr. Samuels over at *The Echo*. If there's an Echo Falls historian, it's Mr. Samuels. Seems there wasn't much Prescott money left by then. They hadn't really worked for a generation or two. What was left behind got used up in taxes and maintenance over the years."

Ingrid handed him the clipping. As he put it back in the briefcase, she noticed some color photographs in there. The corner of the top one showed Kate's body on the floor, her arm flung out, almost as if reaching toward a pile of shoes in the corner. On top of the pile lay the red Pumas.

The chief pushed himself up from the table. "Wash up, Joe," he said. "I'll take Ingrid home."

A question popped up in Ingrid's mind. "What's *Dial M for Murder* about?" she said.

"No idea," said the chief. He smiled at her. "Let me guess – you want to be an actress too."

Or a director. But those were secret ambitions, so Ingrid said, "I don't know what I want to be yet."

"Give a thought to criminology," said the chief.

Out in the driveway, Ingrid started to get into the police cruiser. "Off duty," said the chief, gesturing to a pickup parked on the street. He drove her home in that.

"Want some music? Joe likes music in the car."

"Mr. Strade?" she said.

"Yeah."

"These men – Albert Morales and Lon Stingley – why did they kill her?"

"The motive?" said the chief. "We don't know that."

"Isn't it a pretty big crime not to know the motive?"

He glanced at her. "What do you mean?"

"'The bigger the crime the more obvious, as a rule, is the motive,'" Ingrid said.

The pickup slowed down slightly, as though the chief's foot had come off the pedal. "'The Blue Carbuncle?'" he said.

"'A Case of Identity'," said Ingrid.

He glanced at her again. "Right," he said.

They turned onto River Road; Ingrid put a name to the street at once: She was learning Echo Falls. It was dark now, the river sliding by black and shiny, like licorice. Once there would have been barges out there, loaded up with shovels for the gravediggers.

"Just between you, me, and the lamppost," said the chief, "very few cases end up being one hundred percent tidy."

"What's untidy about this one?" Ingrid said.

The chief laughed. "Poor little Joe," he said.

"What do you mean?"

"Nothing," said the chief. "I'll tell you what's untidy about this case. First, Morales and Stingley left prints in the house but only in the kitchen, and she was killed upstairs. We've got witnesses who say they sometimes socialized with her, so the prints could date from some other time. Second, they really don't seem to know anything about the break-in that happened the next day."

"Why is that important?"

"Because there's evidence of tampering at the crime scene. Who would take a risk like that other than a guilty party?"

"Tampering?" said Ingrid.

"Meaning that the crime scene was changed." Before Ingrid could say she knew what tampering meant, he went on, "Plus there's the problem of Stingley's physical condition."

"He limps. I saw it on TV."

"Says he stepped on a land mine in the Gulf War, although the fact is he never served in the military and was born with a clubfoot. But it's hard to imagine just about anybody not being able to get away from him."

"Then what makes you think he did it?"

"Morales ratted him out. We hadn't been questioning him more than twenty minutes before he described the whole thing, how the victim and Stingley ... uh, went upstairs together, then he heard noises but got there too late."

"Maybe he's just protecting himself," Ingrid said. "Maybe he did it."

"That's exactly what Stingley said the second we told him Morales's story," said the chief, turning onto Maple Lane.

"This tampering," Ingrid said. "What kind of changes were you talking about?"

They pulled up in front of 99, all lights shining inside. "Nice house," said the chief. He turned to her.

"You know the way Holmes always talks about the observation of trifles?"

"Yes."

"After the break-in, I took a pretty close look at the crime scene. That's basic. And something bothered me. Couldn't put my finger on it. But procedure says to take photographs before the body is removed, so back at the office I had a look at them. Sure enough, something was missing."

"What was that?" Ingrid said.

"A pair of red shoes. Can't make out what kind, maybe those bowling ones. But we're working on it."

"You ... you think it's important?" Ingrid said.

"Got to be. Who else would do that but a guilty party, like I said?"

"Guilty of what?" said Ingrid.

"Maybe they had an accomplice," the chief said. "It's even possible that they were set up and the real killer is still loose." He glanced out the window. "Starting to rain. Better get inside."

Ingrid went into the house. Her legs felt wobbly. Mom was waiting on the other side of the door.

"I had a very disturbing call from the guidance counselor today," she said.

Dad called from the living room: "Is that her?"

fifteen

dad had explained the whole calculus track thing to Mom. If Ingrid dropped down to Pre-Algebra now, the calculus track was out and all hope of Princeton or any other top college or university was dashed forever, at the age of thirteen. Mom went into the school the next morning, met with Ms. Groome and the guidance counselor, and made a deal. Ingrid's math homework would be monitored for the rest of the year, meaning Mom or Dad had to sign a slip saying they had seen the completed assignment and that Ingrid had done the work herself. As a bonus, Mom threw in the fact, unknown to Ingrid until that moment, that she'd been grounded for a month. The reward was getting to stay in Algebra Two with Ms. Groome.

"Grounded?" Ingrid said in the hall outside the guidance office, the deal done, just her and Mom.

"They weren't going to go for it otherwise," Mom said. "I could sense it."

"What am I?" Ingrid said. "A real-estate deal?"

"Ingrid. Don't be silly."

Ingrid stormed away.

She sat in history class, smoldering. They were learning about Tom Paine. Ingrid was barely listening, just enough to form the impression that he'd done some smoldering too. A real-estate deal. Toss in the freezer, the pool table, the curtains in the den, the patio furniture, the hunting prints, the portable safe. Ingrid had heard it all. She knew real estate backward, could ace the licensing exam right now. Sometimes she wondered how Mom could stand it, all that infighting over commissions, co-brokes, advertising, show fees, up time. No more. Mom had just thrown her to the wolves, was clearly suited to that harsh world, maybe even destined to— *Bzzz.*

One of those little sparks of inspiration went off in Ingrid's head: The keys to every listing hung on a Masonite board across from Mom's desk at Riverbend Properties. "Every listing" had to include 337 Packer Street, the house where Albert Morales and Lon Stingley had their basement apartment. Was a pair of paint-spattered Adidas sneakers lying around some-where in there? She had to know. This was all about shoes, especially now that Chief Strade thought the owner of those red ones might have been in on the mur-der. *Oh, by the way, Chief, they're mine.* How was that going to work?

Powerup77: Grounded?

Gridster22: yup

NYgrrrl979: me too

Powerup77: you too?

Gridster22: what for?

NYgrrrl979: told my mom to fo

Gridster22: why?

NYgrrrl979: Im tired of being in the middle – now she's suing him again

Powerup77: life sucks

NYgrrrl979: aint that the trut

Gridster22: :)

Powerup77: whaddaya mean :)

Gridster22: just felt like it eat drink and be merry, you know? :) :) :)

Powerup77: you're whacked

Gridster22: the whole town is whacked – philip prescott broke crazy k's heart and ran off to alaska :) :) :)

Powerup77: huh?

Gridster22: never to be heard from again :) :) :)

NYgrrrl979: you getting this from joey's dad?

Powerup77: joey joey joey

Gridster22: she saved his letter all these years
:) :) :)

Powerup77: STOP INGRID

Gridster22: : (

Powerup77: prescott was a jerk

Gridster22: maybe still is

NYgrrrl979: google him

A great idea. Mia was smart. They Googled Philip Prescott.

One relevant hit – linked to prescottrevival.org, the site Mom had designed for the Heritage Committee. Philip Prescott was barely mentioned, but there was lots of stuff about the renovation; Ingrid had scanned in some of the visuals herself.

"Ty? I'm going into the office for a while. Better let Nigel out."

Gridster22: cul8r

Stacy typed in *whats w/her?* but Ingrid, already rushing downstairs, didn't see it come up on the screen. Mom was putting on her coat.

"Going somewhere?" Ingrid said.

"The office," said Mom. "Just for half an hour."

"Maybe I'll tag along."

Mom raised an eyebrow.

"Going a little stir crazy in here, Mom."

"But it's only day one," said Mom.

"STIR CRAZY," Ingrid said.

"Okay," said Mom. "I don't see why not."

Ten minutes later, the key to 337 Packer Street was in Ingrid's pocket.

Being grounded didn't mean missing organized activities. Mom dropped Ingrid off at Prescott Hall for the first *Alice* rehearsal. She went into the huge octagonal entrance hall. A tall man with short-cropped gray hair was standing in profile to her, examining the reconstruction plans. It took her a moment to place him: Vincent Dunn. She hadn't realized quite how tall he was. He put on half-glasses and bent closer to one of those artists' renderings.

"Hi, Mr. Dunn," she said.

But he didn't hear. Ingrid could almost feel how hard he was concentrating on the picture. She went closer to see what was so interesting. Her shoe squeaked on the marble floor.

Vincent Dunn jumped, almost right off the floor, as though she'd given him an electric shock. He whirled toward her, eyes wide. She jumped too.

"Sorry, Mr. Dunn," she said. "I didn't mean to scare you."

"You didn't scare me," he said, his voice a bit snappish. It softened as he went on. "Surprised would be more like it." He gazed down at her without recognition.

"I'm Ingrid, Mr. Dunn. We auditioned together."

"Ah," he said. "You got the role?" Now he did look surprised. But just for a moment. Then he said, "Congratulations," and held out his hand. Ingrid shook it, a very long, delicate hand like the hands of saints in paintings by that Spanish painter El Greco.

"Thanks, Mr. Dunn," Ingrid said.

"You did a wonderful job, of course, very acute," he said. "And call me Vincent."

"Vincent," she said.

"Ingrid," he said, making a little bow; she'd never been on the receiving end of a bow before. "How appropriate for an actress." He looked doubtful for a moment. "You've heard of Ingrid Bergman?"

"I'm kind of named after her," Ingrid said.

"Your parents are movie buffs?" said Vincent.

"I wouldn't say that," Ingrid said. "But my mom's favorite movie is *Casablanca*."

Vincent seemed to think that over. His eyes, dark and liquid, got a faraway look. "Have you seen *Gaslight*?" he said.

"Is that a movie?" said Ingrid.

"Schlock, like *Casablanca*," said Vincent. "But she was much better in it."

Ingrid too thought that *Casablanca* was schlock.

They were going to get along just fine. She turned to the artist's rendering on the wall. "What were you looking at?" she said.

He glanced at it without much interest. "Nothing, really."

"This is a real big project. My mom's on the committee, and I helped with the website."

"There's a website?"

"Prescottrevival dot org."

Something about that struck Vincent as funny. He laughed, a short, sharp laugh, much louder than his speaking voice.

"What's so funny?" Ingrid asked.

"Oh, you know. Internet, Web, dot, backslash, all that."

Ingrid didn't quite follow. She looked a little closer at the artist's rendering, one she'd scanned onto the site herself. Vincent was right: It wasn't very interesting, just showed everything all dug up during the construction phase.

"They're redoing the whole foundation," Ingrid said.

Vincent opened his mouth to say something, but before he could, the inner door opened. A tall man came out, although not as tall as Vincent, more Dad's height; a tall man she hadn't seen in a year or two. He wore a trench coat of soft black leather and had a perfect haircut.

"Hi, Mr. Ferrand," Ingrid said, wondering *What's he doing here? I got the part.*

He glanced down at her, at first like Vincent without recognition; then it came to him. "Ingrid," he said; the sight of her didn't seem to please him. "I suppose congratulations are due."

"Thanks a million, Mr. Ferrand," which was maybe pushing it, since his cheeks went a little pink.

"I just dropped Chloe off," he said. "She's accepted the March Hare role. Chloe's always been a team player."

"That's good news," said Vincent, coming forward. "Vincent Dunn," he said. "Mad Hatter. I thought her audition was splendid."

"Tim Ferrand," said Mr. Ferrand, shaking hands. "Maybe you'll rise to director one day."

Vincent smiled. He had perfectly shaped teeth, but yellow. "I have no ambitions on that score," he said.

Mr. Ferrand nodded. He glanced at the drawings and blueprints on the walls with distaste. Ingrid knew what he was thinking: *I'm paying for a big chunk of this and what does my daughter get? The March Hare.*

They sat in a semicircle on stage, Jill in the middle, her black curly hair shining, her whole body radiating enthusiasm. "Let's all introduce ourselves, real names first, characters second," she said. "And feel free to throw in a word or two about what you'd like to accomplish with this play. Let's start with you, Mr. Santos."

"Harvey Santos," said Mr. Santos. "Accomplish? I dunno. Maybe get some good reviews, open up new avenues, you know what I'm saying? Take that heavyset guy in *Analyze This* and *Analyze That* – why couldn't I put on a few pounds, play him?"

A brief silence fell after that, the only sound Ingrid could hear a mean little voice in her own head: *No additional pounds necessary.*

"And your role here in *Alice*?" said Jill.

"Caterpillar," said Mr. Santos.

"Meredith O'Malley." Meredith O'Malley wore a miniskirt and a little top, resembled Marilyn Monroe, the way Marilyn Monroe might have looked if she'd lived to middle age and let herself go. "I play the Dormouse. What I'm so hoping for with this play –" beginning to slide into a British accent, always a danger with Meredith – "is that we all dig down deep to expose the rough edges of our characters, the raw emotions, good along with the bad."

She put a finger to her collagen lips in thought. That gave Ingrid a chance to remember where she'd heard most of that speech, and recently – on *Inside the Actors Studio*, where that intense bearded guy let Hollywood stars shoot off their mouths for hours; always so disappointing, compared to what they could do in the movies.

"I want," said Meredith, "to expose the character beneath the character." Finger quotes – plump and red-nailed – around that second *character*.

Character beneath the character? You're a rodent, for God's sake.

"Chloe Ferrand." Chloe had her hair up, that spectacular golden-blond hair of course, and looked a lot older than thirteen. "The March Hare." Everyone waited for her to say more – she had one of those faces that could make you wait, no denying that – but she did not.

"Vincent Dunn," said Vincent. "The Mad Hatter." He licked his lips, lips almost colorless but a tongue surprisingly red. "As for my hopes, I think we all know we're in good hands with our director, and I look forward to going where she leads us."

"That's very nice," said Jill. "Vincent is new in town. He's going to be a real asset to the company."

"What line of work you in, Vince?" said Mr. Santos.

"Vincent," said Vincent in his soft voice. "I'd like to open a bed-and-breakfast."

"You mean you're in the market to buy a place?" asked Mr. Santos.

"I suppose you could say that," said Vincent.

"Isn't Ingrid's mom a real-estate agent?" asked Meredith O'Malley.

Ingrid came last, after the White Rabbit, the Mock Turtle, the Duchess, and all the others. "Ingrid Levin-Hill," she said. "Alice." Just saying the word filled her with excitement, and a little pride too. As for goals or accomplishments, she hadn't been able to think of any even though she'd had the most time. "Let's have fun," she said.

That brought smiles and head bobbing from almost everyone, but not Chloe, who was looking at her funny. At her mouth, to be specific, eyeing her ... yes, braces, for sure. Ingrid, smiling too, snapped her mouth shut.

*   *   *

Jill handed out the scripts, urged them all to get off book as soon as possible. Everyone left except Ingrid, because no one was there to get her, and Jill, who had to stay behind to lock up. Jill turned off all the lights and set the security system. She handed Ingrid her cell phone.

"Mind calling them?" she said. "I'd drive you myself, but I've got be in New York tonight."

Ingrid called Mom's cell. Mom turned out to be on her way back from a meeting in Hartford, couldn't get there for an hour. "Call Dad," she said.

Ingrid called home, no answer, called Dad's cell, got his voice mail. "Hi. This is Mark Hill. I can't take your call right now, but—"

Ingrid, still listening to Dad's message, thinking, *Pick up, this is embarrassing*, followed Jill into the octagonal entrance hall. Vincent was still there, looking at the blueprints and artists' renderings again. He turned with a smile. "These are really something," he said.

Ingrid handed Jill the phone. "My mom can't be here for an hour and I can't reach my dad."

"Some problem?" said Vincent.

Jill explained the problem.

"I'm happy to drive Ingrid home," Vincent said.

"I really couldn't," said Ingrid.

"It would be my pleasure," said Vincent, "as long as you can tell me where you live – I'm still learning my way around."

"That's very nice of you, Vincent," Jill said. That settled that.

Ingrid called Mom, told her she had a ride.

164

"Thank God," Mom said. She sounded exhausted.

Vincent drove a small car – Ingrid couldn't see what kind in the darkness of the parking lot. They got in. Vincent turned the key.

"Where to?" he said.

Bzzz. At that moment, Ingrid was hit by the most amazing inspiration yet. Vincent was new in town, had no clue where she lived, would drop her anywhere. When would the chance come again?

"Three thirty-seven Packer Street," she said. "It's in the Flats." She had the key in her pocket.

sixteen

"**take** the next left," Ingrid said. "That'll be River." Wow. The town was coming together, the neighborhoods and streets taking shape in her mind, clearer and clearer every day. You just had to keep your eyes open.

Vincent glanced at her. "You know your way around," he said. She noticed he'd put on driving gloves, kind of like golf gloves with open fingers and little holes; she'd never seen anyone wear driving gloves before.

"It's a hobby of mine," she said. "Learning the town. I got the idea from Sherlock Holmes – the way he knows London."

It was dark now. The headlights of an approaching car shone on Vincent's face, sparkled on his liquid brown eyes. Ingrid was sure she could feel him thinking; she got the feeling he was pretty smart.

"You like Sherlock Holmes?" he said.

"Yeah."

"You don't find him a little cold?"

"I don't think he is cold, not underneath," Ingrid said.

He turned to her with a smile. "That's quite a gift."

"What is?"

"Being able to see what people are like underneath."

"Oh," said Ingrid, "that's not what I meant."

"What did you mean?"

"Only about Sherlock Holmes," Ingrid said. "It's not just solving puzzles for him. He cares but doesn't let on. And Watson's not smart enough to get it." Hey! She'd figured out most of that on the fly. She turned to Vincent. He was easy to talk to. She spoke the next thought that came to her mind. "What about you, Vincent? Do you have the gift?"

At that moment they came to Bridge Street. Left or right? Left, Ingrid thought, but before she could say the word, he'd done it on his own.

"Only—" he began, and then paused.

"Only what?" said Ingrid.

They stopped at a flashing red light. Vincent glanced at her, the light reddening his face, then blanking it out. "Only when I'm performing," he said, then looked both ways and drove carefully across the intersection.

Ingrid understood perfectly, or thought she did. To make sure, she said, "Meaning you find out what's inside when you're actually doing the character?"

"Something like that," he said. "Left here?"

Ingrid had lost track. She peered at the street sign: Packer. "Yes," she said, suddenly wondering whether he was saying he saw inside the character, which is what she'd meant, or saw inside himself. "I bet you've done a lot of acting," she said. Down a side street, she glimpsed the green neon glow of the Benito's Pizzeria sign.

"Some," said Vincent. "At one time."

"Where?"

"Various places," Vincent said. "Nothing to speak of."

Ingrid knew modesty when she heard it. "What are some of the plays you've been in?"

"Oh," said Vincent, "the usual."

"Like?" said Ingrid.

A moment of silence, tiny reflections of green neon in his eyeballs. "You're the curious type," he said.

"Curiouser and curiouser," said Ingrid, kind of expecting a smile if not an outright laugh. But there was neither.

"*Death of a Salesman*," he said. "*The Three Sisters. Who's Afraid of Virginia Woolf? Di*—" He stopped himself, then went on. "And others of that ilk."

Ingrid wasn't sure what ilk he meant, but they all sounded pretty heavy. "No comedies?" she said.

"No comedies."

"Oh." Comedy was the best ilk of all. "How about movies?" Ingrid said. "Jill was in *Tongue and Groove* with Will Smith and Eugene Levy."

"Missed that one," Vincent said. "I had a small role, long ago."

"Yeah? In what?"

"Nothing worth mentioning."

"Maybe it's at Blockbuster."

"No," said Vincent. "It's not." He pulled over, stopped the car. "Three thirty-seven Packer Street," he said. "Your place."

Ingrid looked out. The house, two doors down from Kate's, was dark, not one light shining inside. But all the streetlights had been fixed since the murder. They illuminated the FOR SALE sign on the scrubby patch of lawn – RIVERBEND PROPERTIES.

"Looks like no one's home," Vincent said.

"They'll be back soon," said Ingrid.

"Just the three of you?" Vincent said.

"And my brother Ty."

"How old is he?"

"Fifteen."

Vincent gazed at the house. "Have you got a key?"

"Yes."

"I see it's for sale."

"Uh-huh."

"Your mother's a real-estate agent?"

"Yes."

"So that must be her company," said Vincent. "Riverbend."

Uh-oh. Ingrid saw a possibly tricky situation lurking in the future, namely Vincent and Mom doing some bed-and-breakfast deal together. How about saying it wasn't Mom's company? Dumb, essence of. Was there ever an agent in the whole history of real estate, going back to grass huts, who'd listed her own house with someone else? "She's with Riverbend all right," Ingrid said. "But they don't do bed-and-breakfasts."

"Really?" he said, slowing the word down the same way that in the audition he'd changed the meaning of the Mad Hatter's line about not having the slightest idea. "I wonder why not."

"It's not a bed-and-breakfast kind of town."

"Funny," said Vincent, "with the falls and the jazz barge in the summer, I'd have thought ..." He turned to her. "What does your father do?"

"He's a financial adviser for Mr. Ferrand."

"Chloe's father?"

"Uh-huh."

"Small world."

Ingrid opened the door. "Thanks for the drive, Mr. Dunn."

"Vincent, please. And you're entirely welcome. I'll just watch to make sure you get in safely."

"That's all right," said Ingrid. "I'm fine."

"It's no problem," Vincent said. "The street is rather dark."

Not really, with the lights fixed, but Ingrid didn't argue. She got out of the car and walked to the front door of 337. There were three brass keys on the ring, all pretty similar, Ingrid tried one in the lock. No dice. Then the second, which also didn't work. Fumbling now for the third, she felt Vincent's eyes on her back, read the obvious thought: *How come she's having so much trouble getting into her own house?*

Key number three. Presto, like in a fairy tale, where everything came in threes. Ingrid let herself into 337 Packer Street, turned with a little wave, and closed the door. She heard the car drive off.

Other than that, nothing. The house was silent.

I'm home. A little shudder went through Ingrid when that thought popped unbidden into her mind.

Light leaked in from the street through one of those

fan-shaped windows above the door. Ingrid saw she was in a small dark-wood paneled entry, bare of decoration or furniture. Two doors faced her, both painted black, identical. *Eat me*, she thought, *drink me*, and randomly tried one of the keys in the right-hand door.

The key turned. Ingrid opened the door, saw a staircase leading down into darkness. Basement apartment. This was it. She went down, slow and silent.

At the bottom she stood and listened, heard nothing, nothing human, like breathing, sighing, snoring, nothing from the machine world, like a humming fridge, rumbling furnace, or TV talk. The apartment was cold and empty, its occupants behind bars. There was nothing to fear. She found a light switch and flicked it.

A single light went on, shining from a naked bulb in a bracket on the far wall. The main room of the basement apartment had nothing in it but a small unplugged fridge and a strange mobile suspended from the ceiling, made of balled-up and twisted audiotape and resembling a full-size hanged man. Who had made it? Why?

Off the main room was a tiny bathroom, completely empty except for a bad smell, and a narrow bedroom containing two iron bedsteads with nothing on their springs but green plastic garbage bags, one on each.

Ingrid opened them up, both packed with clothes. She dumped them out on the floor and searched through, one at a time. Albert Morales – she knew which bag was his because the first thing she saw was a Midas Muffler work shirt with ALBERT stitched on the pocket – had left behind three pairs of shoes: stinking green flip-flops, scuffed and cracked black tie shoes with worn heels, and dark yellow loafers with pointy toes and tarnished buckles. Lon Stingley had only a pair of felt slippers, very wide, probably because of his club foot. No Adidas with green paint spatters, no sneakers of any kind. Ingrid checked everywhere – under the beds, in the cabinet under the kitchen sink, behind the toilet. There was nowhere else. The apartment didn't even have closets. No Adidas sneakers, absolutely for sure. Albert Morales and Lon Stingley were innocent – innocent of the break-in, and if Chief Strade was right about the connection between the break-in and the murder, innocent of that too.

Ingrid knew she couldn't let them stay in jail. But how to get them out? It was all so convoluted now, all so twisted around. Would anyone even believe her? Would she just end up looking like a crackpot, already a convicted math cheat, totally without credibility? And it was way worse than that. Chief Strade knew there'd been tampering and believed that the tamperer could have set up Morales and Stingley or even done the murder. The truth hit her, the very dangerous truth: She had set herself up. Maybe the chief was a hard-ass after all, an unjust one like Ms. Groome. Anything could happen in a trial. Innocent people were in jail right now. And she wasn't even innocent: Tampering with evidence was a crime, crossing police lines was a crime, breaking and entering was a crime; and there were probably more. What would a jury think? A jury. A trial. Oh my God.

Who could she tell? Mom? Could Mom take it? She might actually have a heart attack. Dad? How embarrassed Dad would be in front of Mr. Ferrand, the contrast between the two daughters set in stone for all time. Ty? Forget it. Grampy? She already knew what he would say – mouth shut, head down, deny everything. Stacy? What was the point of that? Stacy was a kid, just like her, with no power in the big world. She stared at the audiotape man, hanging perfectly still. That last line of poetry Mom had recited came back to her. "I say that we are wound with mercy, round and round." Ingrid wanted to buy that idea, that she could blurt it all out and then sink into the merciful arms of others, but she just didn't believe it. It was practically babyish.

There was only one solution. She would have to—

A noise came from upstairs: a loud metal clang that shook the house. Ingrid froze and, in the heart-stopping moment that followed, made a vow to herself: *I'm never breaking in anywhere again, key or no key. My nerves just can't take it.* Then came a series of clangs, getting softer and softer and finally dying out. It was only an air bubble in the heating system, or some other technical thing like that. She started breathing again.

Ingrid repacked the plastic bags, shut off the light, went upstairs, and let herself out of 337 Packer Street. There was no one around, just a few cars parked by the curb and a raccoon scuttling through the gutter. Ingrid walked around the house, crossed the alley, and entered the woods. This time it really was just like day except for the darkness, her path clear and unambiguous all the way home. She zoomed. Griddie, the night stalker.

The garage door was open, only the TT inside. Ingrid went into the kitchen. No one there except Nigel, who saw her and thumped his tail on the floor but otherwise made no movement. She went into the mudroom, hung up her jacket. The door to the basement was open and she heard Dad: "Come on, one more, push, push, push, come on now – PUSH."

Ty let out a furious grunt.

Ingrid went downstairs. She realized she loved 99 Maple Lane, everything about it.

"Hi," she said. "What's happening?"

They both looked at her: Ty on his back on the bench press with a surprising amount of weight on the bar, Dad at the head of the bench where the safety stood.

"Bobby Moran broke his arm in practice," Dad said. "Ty's starting next game."

"Even after that flea-flicker fiasco?" Ingrid said.

They both gave her a mean look, the identical mean look, a gene Grampy probably had too, and other Hill men all the way back to some knuckle-dragging patriarch. It was kind of funny. Ingrid went upstairs, heated Ta Tung leftovers, opened an ice-cold Fresca, sat at the table.

The outside lights were off, making her reflection in the window very clear. Because of the window's angle in the nook, this wasn't her usual mirrored self but something a little different, maybe the way others saw her. She looked older, for a moment even imagined she was seeing the adult Ingrid, her face harder and determined, a formidable person. Yeah, right.

But something about her reflection prompted Ingrid to finish the thought that had been interrupted by the air bubble clang at 337 Packer Street. A big thought, probably the biggest of her life: She was going to have to solve this case – the murder of Crazy Katie – herself. There was no other way.

Mom came in, the two vertical lines on her forehead very deep.

"Oh, good," she said. "You're home. Sorry I got tied up."

"No problem."

"Is Dad here?"

"Downstairs with Ty." Mom's forehead lines got shallower, almost completely smoothing over. "He's starting," Ingrid added.

"He is?"

"The coach has Alzheimer's."

"Ingrid!" Mom said, but she was smiling at the same time. She threw her coat on the chair next to Ingrid, kicked off her shoes, slid her feet into the sheepskin slippers, wriggled her toes.

"Who drove you home?"

"Vincent."

"Who's Vincent?"

"The Mad Hatter."

"What's he like?"

"Nice."

Mom went into the pantry, started eating something crunchy, crackers or potato chips. "I hope you thanked him."

"Of course," Ingrid said. She took out the keys to 337 Packer Street and slipped them into Mom's coat pocket.

seventeen

"**ingrid.** Time to get up."

Ingrid opened her eyes and knew right away she'd had a good sleep. She didn't feel the slightest bit tired, unlike every other school morning since she couldn't remember when. What had happened last night? Ta Tung leftovers, chitchat with Mom, zip zip through her homework, of which there hadn't been much, thank the Lord, and early to bed, *Alice* script in hand. But she didn't remember reading any of it, must have gone right to sleep. She felt great.

Mom, already dressed for work, sticking a pearl earring in her earlobe, opened her door. "Ingrid? You awake?"

"I feel sick," Ingrid said.

"Sick?" said Mom, stepping into the room. "What kind of sick?"

"In general," Ingrid said, and realizing she sounded rather perky and energetic, added in a more subdued tone, "just not very well."

"How not well?" Mom said, coming to the side of the bed.

"Hard to describe," Ingrid said.

"Take off the appliance," Mom said.

My God! She'd remembered to put it on. Ingrid knew that was going to be a big help in terms of whatever happened next, even though she could see no logical connection.

Mom reached out, laid her palm on Ingrid's forehead. So gentle. Mom loved her, with a huge basic love that asked for hardly anything in return. Ingrid felt bad, tricking her like this, but what choice did she have?

"You do feel a little warm," Mom said.

Wow. The power of suggestion. Maybe everything human ended up being subjective and nothing could be known for sure. Ingrid didn't know whether that was good or bad, but Sherlock Holmes would have hated the thought, and she had to get in line. Wasn't the whole point to find out exactly what had happened to Crazy Katie, without uncertainty or subjectivity? That was number one. At the same time, she had to outmaneuver Ms. Groome till the end of the year so she could stay on the calculus track – number two; while playing soccer to win right through to the play-offs and the championship game – number three; plus give a performance of Alice that would blow them all away – number four. There: her life on a platter. And that was leaving out Joey.

"Ingrid? Are you in pain?"

"No."

"You had a strange look in your eyes."

"No pain, Mom. It's just … the fever."

Mom removed her hand. *Keep it there, Mom, a bit longer*. But Ingrid squashed that thought. She was thirteen years old, for God's sake.

"I guess you'd better stay home," Mom said.

"I guess," said Ingrid.

Ty, a towel around his waist, his chest and abs starting to look like something out of the Abercrombie catalog – although the effect was undermined by the blood seeping unnoticed from a cut on his chin – stuck his head in the room. "She's staying home?"

"The name is Ingrid," said Ingrid; the ugliest name in creation, but her own.

"How come she gets to stay home?" said Ty.

"Your sister's running a little fever," said Mom. "And you're bleeding."

"Huh?" said Ty. He touched his face, stared at the blood on his fingers. "Those blades suck," he said. "Can't you get me better blades?"

"But they're the ones your father uses," Mom said.

"They suck," said Ty, and went off down the hall.

Hey. Ty had a bunch of pimples on his back even though he'd always been one of those lucky acne-free kids. And all those muscles. Whoa.

Mom turned back to her, gave a little shudder.

Hang in there, Mom.

"I'll get you some Advil," Mom said.

"That's all right."

Mom shook her head. "Bring down that fever," she said.

Mom went off for the Advil. Ty came in, buttoning

178

his shirt, a scrap of toilet paper on his cut, white with a red circle in the center, like the flag of Japan.

"You're faking, right?" he said.

"Mister Cynic," said Ingrid.

"You're such a dork," said Ty.

Ingrid gazed at him. The punch-in-the-eye episode: She was getting new glimmerings about the cause of that, glimmerings she didn't like at all.

"Is that look supposed to scare me or something?" Ty said.

Would he do something that dumb? Probably. Anyone who'd fall for the flea-flicker twice was capable of idiocy across a broad range. The opposing coaches for the next game would be studying the films. They'd spring the flea-flicker again the moment they saw good ol' number 19 out there.

"What's that stupid smile about?" Ty said.

If only she could see her into her own future the way she could see into his.

Mom and Ty left soon after. Dad came up a little later, buttoning a button on the sleeve of his suit jacket; Dad actually had suit jackets with buttons that worked.

"On the bench today?" he said.

"I'll be fine."

He rumpled her hair. "Got a game on Saturday?"

"Yup."

"Plenty of time to get better."

"I'll be better way before that, Dad. Like tomorrow."

"Good girl."

"Dad?"

"Yeah?"

"Did you know Philip Prescott?"

"Actually know him? No. I might have seem him once or twice, but I was just a kid when he took off, like I said."

"How old was he?"

"In his twenties, I'd say."

"And he was the last one?"

"Yup."

"What happened to his parents?"

Dad rubbed his chin, a chin much like Ty's but not bleeding. In fact, Ty's face was starting to resemble Dad's, just not nearly as good-looking. "Something not good, I think," Dad said. "I don't recall. They ran out of gas, the whole family. It happens. Why do you ask?"

Ingrid shrugged. "Just curious."

Dad rumpled her hair again. "Remember that cat."

Cat! My God! What had happened to that huge cat of Kate's? And what was wrong with her, only thinking of that now?

Dad gave her a puzzled look. "Is something wrong?"

"No."

"The cat that curiosity killed, I'm talking about," Dad said. "Don't you know that expression?"

Twenty minutes later he was gone too. Ingrid got up, had a quick shower, dressed, and went into the garage, MapQuest printout tucked in her pocket. Her bike, a Univega mountain bike, red of course, with fat knobby tires and twenty-three gears, of which she used one, stood against the back wall. Ingrid brushed off a few cobwebs, got on, and pedaled down Maple Lane.

Not a bad day for biking – no wind, the sky pale blue. A little on the cold side, though. Ingrid kind of wished she'd put on gloves. She turned right on Avondale, left on Nathan Hale, right on Main. Ahead lay Starbucks – the new Starbucks, Echo Falls now having two – Harrow's Fine Men's Clothing, Championship Sports, and yes! *The Echo*. THE CENTRAL VALLEY'S SECOND OLDEST NEWSPAPER, read the gold-leaf letters on the plate-glass window: ESTABLISHED 1896 – THE WHOLE TRUTH AND NOTHING BUT. Ingrid locked her bike to a lamppost, one of those old-fashioned black ones they had on Main Street, turned toward the door of *The Echo*, and saw a dog trotting up behind her, a dog who looked something like—

Nigel.

Oh my God. He must have gotten into the garage, followed her the whole way. His tongue hung out, all floppy and absurdly big, hand-towel size, and he was panting like crazy.

"Nigel!" He pressed his head against her leg, almost knocking her down, slobbering over her clothes, moronic, loyal. What was she supposed to do with him? Through the plate-glass window, an old man watched. "You've got to be good, Nigel," Ingrid said. "Look at me. Your very best." She opened the door and went in, Nigel beside her, looking right at her as instructed, head at a strange angle and tail wagging violently.

There were lots of smells inside the *Echo* office – ink, wax, dust, mold. The walls were covered floor to ceiling by shelves of yellowed newspapers. Behind a low wooden railing stood five desks, all empty but the middle one, where the old man was now sitting. He wore a green eyeshade and a short-sleeved white shirt with a brown necktie and yellow sweater vest.

"Mr. Samuels?" Ingrid said.

"That's right," said the old man. He had a high, scratchy voice.

If there's an Echo Falls historian, it's Mr. Samuels. "Hi. I'm—"

"That your dog?"

"Yes."

"There's a leash law in this town."

"I know. See, what—"

"*The Echo* was instrumental in getting that law passed," said Mr. Samuels. "I wrote seventeen editorials."

"It's a good law," Ingrid said.

"But you're not obeying it," said Mr. Samuels.

For God's sake: She couldn't even get started. "The problem is the dogs didn't vote," Ingrid said. "So it's a constant struggle."

Mr. Samuels sat back in his chair. She saw how small he was, a tiny guy with a long nose, big ears, and alert little eyes, probably hardwired to be a reporter. "What did you say?" he said.

"It's a struggle."

"No. Before that."

"About the dogs not voting?"

"Yes. Say it again." He took out a notebook.

"The problem is the dogs didn't vote," Ingrid said. He wrote it down. "And your name?"

"You're planning to put this in the paper?"

"Be a nice kicker at the end of the Heard on Main Street column," said Mr. Samuels. "The award-winning Heard on Main Street column," he added. "Name, please?"

"Ingrid."

He wrote it down. "Last name?"

Sherlock Holmes never got into situations like this, so out of control. Why was that? On the other hand, who would know? No one read the stupid *Echo*, except her, of course; she was funny that way.

"Levin-Hill," Ingrid said.

"That hyphenated?" said Mr. Samuels.

"Yes."

He licked the tip of the pencil, paused. "Any relation to Aylmer Hill?" he said.

"He's my grandfather."

"How's he doing?"

"Good."

"Still raising hell out there?"

"I don't think so." Was Grampy a hell-raiser?

"Wouldn't mind one of those free-range chickens of his," said Mr. Samuels. "Pass that along next time you see him."

"There are no more chickens," Ingrid said. "No animals at all." She glanced down at Nigel. He was sprawled on the floor, fast asleep, drool pooling under his jaw.

"No more animals, huh?" said Mr. Samuels. "Tell me something, off the record if you want – is he ever going to sell that place?"

"I don't know."

"I hope not. He's a pigheaded old mule, but just this once it might do the town some good. The Ferrands want that land so bad they can taste it."

"Why?" said Ingrid, trying to picture a pigheaded mule.

"Why?" said Mr. Samuels. "So they can develop it, of course, make more money."

"What would they put there?"

"You name it – condos, mall, Wal-Mart, Home Depot, whatever comes along. But something's bound to come along. Look what's happening to the whole valley, going to ruination acre by God's little acre."

There were pink spots on Mr. Samuels's cheeks now, and his breath whistled in his throat.

"Is it true," Ingrid said, "that the Ferrands got rich by marrying the Prescotts?"

"Where'd you come across a fact like that?" said Mr. Samuels.

"So it's true?"

"More or less," said Mr. Samuels.

"What happened to the Prescotts, anyway?"

"The last one, Philip—" Mr. Samuels began, but Ingrid interrupted.

"How did they even get to where there was just a last one?"

Mr. Samuels did that sitting back in the chair thing again, as though getting pushed by something invisible. "You active on the student paper?" he said.

"Student paper?"

"Newspaper," said Mr. Samuels. "At your school."

"We don't have one."

"No student paper? What school?"

"Ferrand Middle."

Mr. Samuels pounded his fist on the desk, much harder than she'd have thought him capable of, hard enough to raise a puff cloud of dust. "Damn prop three," he said.

"What's prop three?"

"Prop three? You don't know prop three? That's how all the selfish empty-nesters capped property taxes in Echo Falls, why the school board's starving for cash, why there's no pool at Echo High, no gifted program, and now no paper at Ferrand Middle. It's an absolute disgrace." He scribbled furiously in his notebook. After a minute or two he looked up, blinked at her, as though he'd forgotten where they were in the conversation and who she was exactly, which suited her just fine.

"What happened to Philip Prescott's parents?" Ingrid said.

Mr. Samuels blinked again. "Perished in a boating accident."

"Where?"

"They went over the falls in a canoe."

"Our falls?"

Mr. Samuels nodded. "This was before the park rangers strung the boom across."

"So Philip was an orphan after that, all alone?"

"I suppose so, but he was grown up, in graduate school at the time."

"Where?"

"Not far – down in New Haven."

One of those top schools of Dad's was in New Haven. "At Yale?" Ingrid said.

Mr. Samuels nodded. "The School of Drama. Philip Prescott loved the theater."

"Did he start the Prescott Players?"

"No. That goes way back. But he returned from Yale and took it over. Plus the Hall and all the Prescott assets, of course."

"What assets?"

"Still considerable, at that stage of the game," said Mr. Samuels. "But it took Philip only a few years to squander most of it."

"How?"

"Time-honored method," said Mr. Samuels. "Philip loved the theater, as I said, but didn't really have a lot of talent for it. What he had was a lot of money, so he started hiring professional actors to perform at Prescott Hall, and before you knew it he was backing Broadway plays. Those Manhattan sharpies fleeced him PDQ."

"Is that why he took off for Alaska?" Ingrid said.

"Might have been part of it," said Mr. Samuels. "He wrote a letter to *The Echo*, kind of famous at the time, claiming it was about finding himself and all that hooey."

"Why didn't he take Kate Kovac with him?"

"Good question," said Mr. Samuels. "One I haven't actually considered be—" He stopped himself, his gaze narrowing on her. "You seem rather well informed on all this. I don't recall if you've explained what you're doing here."

"School report," Ingrid said.

"On what?"

"Pretty much anything."

"Figures."

"I'm doing 'The Life and Death of Kate Kovac.'"

"Well," said Mr. Samuels. "Well, well, well. And what did your teacher say about that?"

"You know teachers," Ingrid said.

"Not anymore," said Mr. Samuels. "The kind of teachers I knew are long—"

At that moment, Nigel farted, ridiculously loud, as though he had an amplifier inside him. She glanced down at him. "Nigel!" He was still totally conked out, his plump chest rising and falling peacefully. Ingrid felt herself blushing like she was the culprit. She was surprised to see that Mr. Samuels looked embarrassed too. That was kind of nice.

He cleared his throat. "So you've come for information on Katie Kovac."

"Yes."

He reached for a folder. "Your timing couldn't be better. It just so happens I'm preparing her obituary. Know your way around a copy machine?"

"Yes," said Ingrid.

"Then you can make copies of everything in here for yourself." He pointed to a copier in the corner.

Ingrid opened the little railing door and approached his desk. "Thanks, Mr. Samuels."

He handed her the folder. "She seems to have begun on a promising note. Philip Prescott met her at the drama school. Evidently she was an early experimenter with performance art."

"What's that?" said Ingrid.

"Hooey," said Mr. Samuels.

Ingrid took the folder over to the copier. There were only four clippings inside, all small and yellowed, three of them from old issues of *The Echo*, the fourth from the *New Haven Register*. The headline on the fourth clipping read BUT IS IT ART? The accompanying photograph showed a pretty young woman standing beside – what was this? – a hanged man made of balled-up and twisted audiotape. Just like – oh my God.

Ingrid scanned the article, faster and faster as she went along:

> *Katherine Kovac, first-year student ... exhibit entitled "for the record" ... audiotapes of what she calls "confessions" find "appropriate shapes" ... at the same time the confessions are played in the gallery ... sound distorted ... "like all inner thoughts in the harshness of the outside world."*

"Hey!" said Mr. Samuels. "Where are you rushing off to?"

Ingrid, clutching the copies with one hand, returning the originals with the other, heading toward the door, barely heard.

"Don't forget your dog."

She heard that. Alarm of that magnitude was hard to miss.

"Nigel!" He opened one eye, unmotivated, uninterested, unaware. A nonvoter, and with good reason.

eighteen

"that's what you call doing your best?"
Ingrid said.

Nigel, trotting along beside her, gave no sign that
he'd heard.

How did this go, exactly? She tried to relate Main
Street to the Flats in the picture of the town that was
taking shape in her mind. She was concentrating so
hard, she barely noticed Coach Ringer pop out of a deli
two doors ahead, brown bag in hand. Ingrid almost
passed him, probably would have if she hadn't caught
that hard-to-miss slogan on the back of his Towne
Hardware jacket: SCREWS FOR YOUSE SINCE 1937. She hit
the brakes, her Univega squealing to a stop. But not too
loud: Coach Ringer kept going without a pause.

So did Nigel. Ingrid watched helplessly as he followed at Coach Ringer's heels, tail wagging, bonehead
determined and why not say it? – yes – dogged. They
crossed Bridge Street. Towne Hardware stood on the
corner. Coach Ringer, still unaware of Nigel, went in.

The door closed in Nigel's face. He stood outside, one forepaw raised in that characteristic way of his, a parody of a smart, pointing dog.

Ingrid rode across the street. "Nigel!" she called to him in a stage whisper. His head swiveled around in that strange slow way he had; poised on three feet, he gazed at her without recognition.

"You moron," she said, pretty loud.

He lowered that fourth paw and trotted over.

Left on Bridge, then right on Hill, a long, gentle descent with train tracks at the bottom. The next street should be—

And it was. Packer. A minute or two later, Ingrid pulled up outside 337, Nigel panting beside her. She leaned her bike against a telephone pole.

Trash barrels lined the street. Garbage day. There was only one barrel outside 337, aluminum, with empty liquor bottles on top. The house itself was quiet and—

Oops. She no longer had the key, so cleverly put back in Mom's pocket, or so she'd thought at the time. A little late for realizing that now. Ingrid was turning over several plans for getting into 337, none too promising, when the garbage truck rumbled up. The guy hanging on at the back, who wore a pirate-style bandanna, jumped off, hoisted the trash can, and dumped its contents in the mouth of the truck. The bottles and all kinds of junk went crashing in, including—

"Hey!" Ingrid said.

The man in the bandanna turned to her. Now she

190

had a better view. Lying on top of all the trash from 337 was a big clump of audiotape, no longer in the shape of a hanged man, now just a basketball-size tangle.

"That's a mistake," Ingrid said.

"Huh?" said the man in the bandanna. He banged on the truck body. Some machine inside started up. A big metal arm began to move, squashing up all the trash.

"No," Ingrid said, rushing past the man in the bandanna, reaching in, inches ahead of that metal arm, and grabbing the audiotape.

"What the hell?" said man in the bandanna.

"This wasn't supposed to go," Ingrid said.

"Coulda got your stupid arm caught in there." The man's eyes went to the tape and his face scrunched up in a combination of puzzlement and anger. A question was forming on his lips when a voice called from the front of the truck.

"What's the holdup?"

The man in the bandanna said a word he shouldn't have in front of her and jumped up onto his narrow platform. The truck moved on.

Ingrid picked up an empty plastic shopping bag, left behind in the gutter, and got the squiggly mass of tape inside, trying not to mush it up any more. Then, the bag hanging from one handlebar, she headed for home, Nigel beside her, his pace brisk at first but falling off fast. They got about a block past Benito's Pizzeria, maybe a third of the way home by Ingrid's calculations, when a passing car slowed down, began driving along beside her, just a few feet away.

Ingrid glanced at the car. A white car with big writing on the side: ECHO FALLS POLICE: TO PROTECT AND SERVE. What was this? The driver was motioning for her to pull over. Ingrid pulled over, straddled the bike. The cruiser stopped in front of her. The driver got out. A big guy with lots of decorations on his uniform: Chief Strade.

"Any idea why I stopped you, young lady?" he said. And then, coming closer: "Ingrid?"

She knew damn well why he'd stopped her. He'd figured it out, understood everything, the whole twisted chain of events, and now she was in big, big trouble. Trial by jury.

"Sorry, Mr. Strade," Ingrid said.

He glanced at Nigel, back to her. "You're a smart girl," he said. "I'm surprised."

She hung her head. Tears were on the way. In seconds she'd be blithering, her mixed-up story flooding out.

"Our helmet law is strict for very good reasons," said the chief.

Helmet law? Ingrid actually reached up and touched the top of her head, maybe the dumbest thing she'd ever done, like a circus clown. "Oops," she said, the tide of tears ebbing fast. "I left it in the garage."

"Won't do you much good there, will it?"

She gave the right answer.

He nodded. Maybe this would turn out all right. The very moment she had that thought, Nigel got the notion to raise up all the hair on his neck and growl at Chief Strade. The chief looked at Nigel with distaste and said, "Isn't this a school day?"

"Oh, yes," said Ingrid. "I'm actually working on a project."

The chief opened the car door. "Hop in," he said. "You can tell me all about it on the way back."

"On the way back where?" Ingrid said.

"To school," said the chief. He popped the trunk and laid the bike inside, the shopping bag still on the handlebar. "Can't let you ride without a helmet."

"What about Nigel?"

"They let you take him to school?"

"He ... um," said Ingrid. "Waits outside."

"I suppose he can ride in back," the chief said.

"In the caged part?" said Ingrid. "Where the prisoners go?"

The chief opened the back door. Nigel climbed in without being asked, almost jumped in, really, except he was too fat for jumping. A model prisoner.

Dad drove with one hand on the wheel, sometimes just a finger. Chief Strade drove like Mom, both hands on the wheel in the proper ten minutes to two position, the difference being the size of the chief's hands, almost touching at the top.

"What's the project?" he said.

Yikes. "Oh," Ingrid said, "nothing worth mentioning." A handy phrase she'd heard recently. From whom?

"Try me," said the chief. "It's been a boring day so far."

"Mine's about ... littering on the bike path," Ingrid said; the best she could come up with. "Not very interesting, like I—"

"You're pretty far from the bike path," said the chief.

This was getting so hard. "Took a little pizza break," Ingrid said.

"Benito's?" said the chief.

Ingrid nodded.

"Best pizza in town," he said. "Of course Joe prefers Domino's. You know Joe."

"Yeah."

"Is he working on a project too?" said the chief.

"I don't think so."

"He didn't mention it," the chief said. "Not much of a talker, in any case. He did tell me you're quite the soccer player."

"Oh?"

He turned onto River. The driver ahead checked his rearview mirror, slowed down right away, also seemed to sit up straighter, as though the chief could ticket for bad posture. This would have been fun, except for how nervous Ingrid was feeling, that suffocating tightness in her chest.

"Which reminds me," said the chief. "Did you ever see Kate Kovac at one of your soccer games?"

"Kate Kovac?" said Ingrid. "No."

Chief Strade didn't say anything for a while, maybe only a minute or two but it seemed much longer. Ingrid felt a weight pressing in the pit of her stomach, and nervousness changed to dread.

"Reason I bring it up," said the chief, "is the red shoes I was mentioning before."

"The bowling shoes?" Ingrid said.

"Slipped up on that one," said the chief. "The tech people, meaning Ron Pina, did some high-resolution digital stuff. Turns out most likely they're soccer boots."

"Oh."

"Pumas, it looks like."

Meaning the resolution was high enough to show that leaping Puma logo at the top of the heel. Therefore – what about those soccer camp ID disks strung on the laces? Ingrid glanced at Chief Strade. He was looking straight ahead, his massive face blank. The writing on those ID disks was tiny, much smaller than the leaping Puma. On the basis of that, plus the fact that the chief hadn't said "Pumas," plain and simple, but "Pumas, it looks like," Ingrid decided that they couldn't read the disks.

"What kind do you wear?" the chief said, face still blank. A face like that – maybe it made some people think that the man behind it wasn't very bright. Ingrid was learning the truth, and fast.

"Oh, Nike, New Balance, Puma – they're all good," she said.

"I bet yours are red," said the chief.

Ingrid's heart almost stopped. "Why do you say that?"

"Your bike, your jacket," said the chief. "And weren't you wearing a red sweater when you came over to the house? No need for Holmes on this one."

"They're black," Ingrid said, although she hardly had the breath to do it. He was an observer of small things, like her. But better.

"Black it is," he said. "But if you hear anything about a connection between Kate Kovac and soccer, let me know. It's the best lead we've got."

"Lead on what?" said Ingrid.

"The third suspect," said Chief Strade.

He let them out at Ferrand Middle School; Nigel needed some urging. The chief opened the trunk, took out her bike. "That some of the litter?" he said, peering in the plastic bag.

"Yes," said Ingrid.

"Good luck with the project," he said, getting back in the car. Ingrid waved good-bye. His window slid open. "I don't want you riding that home, now," he said. "Take it on the bus."

"You can't take bikes on the bus."

"Who's your driver?"

"Mr. Sidney."

"From the battle of the Coral Sea?"

Ingrid nodded.

"Tell him I said it was okay."

"That won't work with Mr. Sidney."

The chief laughed. "Maybe not," he said. "Does he know who you are?"

"Sure."

"I mean does he know you're Aylmer Hill's grand-daughter?"

"I don't think so."

"Then just tell him."

"Why?"

"They were at Corregidor together."

"What's that?"

"Ask your granddad," said the chief. The window slid up. He drove off. Ingrid watched till he was out of sight. She realized he knew Echo Falls and the people in it backward and forward. It was scary.

She got on her bike and pedaled home, Nigel following. First thing, she had to get rid of those shoes. But where? Throwing them in the trash wasn't foolproof – she'd just learned that. *Bzzz*. It came to her, the best place on earth for losing things, guaranteed: the awesome pile on Ty's closet floor.

nineteen

ninety-nine Maple Lane had an attic, used only for storage. To get to it, you went into Mom and Dad's office, the way Ingrid was doing now, and stood on Dad's desk. From there, a tall person like Dad could reach up to the ceiling and pull on the trap-door handle. Then the trapdoor would open and a small wooden ladder would extend itself automatically. Ingrid, not so tall, used a combination of an overturned wastebasket to raise herself up a little higher and Dad's pitching wedge for getting a grip on the actual handle.

The ladder came down. Ingrid climbed up, taking her copies of the clippings Mr. Samuels had given her and the plastic bag of audiotape.

The light in the attic had a golden cast, maybe because of all the unfinished wood up there – beams, joists, studs, none of which she could identify precisely, although she knew the names. It also had a musty smell, not unpleasant, and an air of peace and stillness. Plus tons of stuff. Ingrid hadn't been up here in years, could have easily spent an hour or two examining it all – old toys, boxes of books from Mom's and Dad's college days, a steamer trunk full of God-knows-what, antiquated sports gear like wooden tennis racquets and long unshaped downhill skis, Mom's doll collection from when she'd been a kid. But only one object interested Ingrid now – a reel-to-reel tape machine, the kind they cut to in conspiracy movies when someone is being secretly recorded.

Ingrid found an outlet, lugged the machine over, and plugged it in. There was a tape already on the reels. She hit the switch and a folk song started up, all about clouds. Folk music was not Ingrid's thing. She rewound it onto one reel, which she replaced with an empty one. Then she dumped out the bag of audiotape.

She gazed down at the whole big jumbled mass. What was this? An attached Christmas sticker: TO ALBERT AND LON, MERRY XMAS, KATIE. How much more innocent could they get?

Ingrid examined the tape, all crinkly and twisted, especially, she thought, where the head of the hanged man had been. Inch-long strips of white tape appeared here and there. What was the name? Splices. The tape had lots of splices, meaning edits, different sections joined together, like scenes in a movie. Ingrid didn't know where to begin. How many ends were there? It took her a while to find just one.

She threaded it into the slot at the center of the right-hand reel, pressed fast forward. The machine whirred and started spooling up the tape. Ingrid let it slip through her fingers, hoping to smooth out the kinks. Tape wound onto the reel to a depth of about two inches. Then it snapped. Ingrid threaded the new end into the slot of the other empty reel, rewound, then hit play.

A voice spoke, deep and smoky. Ingrid recognized it right away. Crazy Katie, like she was alive. The sound made her shiver.

"... quality of mercy is not strained. It droppeth as the gentle rain from heaven upon the place beneath." What was this? Poetry, the kind Mom liked? And also about mercy? Kate said, "Oh, sure. Sure sure sure and sure." Ingrid shivered again: it was almost like Kate, from beyond the grave, was telling her to go it alone.

There was a metallic click. Ingrid had heard that sound before: cigarette lighter. Kate inhaled deeply, let out a long sigh. Ingrid could almost smell the smoke. Kate repeated those words about mercy, this time in a sarcastic voice, like an actor trying different readings. The effect was nasty and for some reason made Ingrid look around to make sure no one else was in the room. She was alone, the attic still but no longer peaceful.

A white edit zipped by with a *snick* sound. Kate said, "Sixty-three cans times five cents makes ... empty, emptier, emptiest." *Snick*. Now she was singing, harsh and raspy, "The townsfolk are renovating Prescott Hall, tra-la, tra-la." *Snick*. Her voice changed, sounded younger. "Information for Fairbanks? Philip Prescott. No address, sorry ... nothing?" *Snick*. "Information for Anchorage? Philip Prescott. No address, sorry ... nothing?" *Snick*. "Information for Juneau? Philip Prescott, no damn address ... nothing, huh? Ever think of trying a little harder?" *Snick*. Her old worn-out voice returned, now drunk as well. "Information for Planet Earth? Philip Prescott. Do you want me to spell that? K-a-t-i-e. K-o-v-a-c. Little Katie Kovac, the cutest thing you ever did see, actress extraordinaire, stardom bound, tra-la, tra-la."

Snick.

Then Kate spoke again, but sober and much younger-sounding, almost girlish. A nice voice, with lots of range and feeling. "He's very talented."

A man said: "I think you like him."

Kate said: "Don't be silly, Philip."

Philip? Had she just heard the voice of Philip Prescott? It gave Ingrid a chill.

"He sure likes you," Philip said.

"We work well together," Kate said, "that's all."

"But you're also attracted to him," said Philip.

"I admire his talent," Kate said. "That's different."

"What makes you think he's so good?" said Philip.

"Just watch him," said Kate. "Did he tell you about the movie?"

"What movie?"

"*The Accused Will Rise*."

"*The Accused Will Rise?*" said Philip. "What a ridiculous title."

"It's a major studio production."

"I'm surprised you can be fooled so easily," Philip said.

Snick of an edit.

"Are you jealous?" Kate said.

Philip laughed. "Jealous of him? That's an insult." But he was: Ingrid could hear it clearly.

"Don't be jealous, Philip," Kate said. "You know I love you."

Then came a kissing sound.

"Is that thing on?" Philip said.

"For my performance piece," said Kate. "About the whole *Dial M for Murder* production. I record over it so—"

"I hate the play," said Philip. "And how many times have I told you I can't stand that machine going all the time?"

"Sorry, Philip."

"Why can't anyone ever just simply do as I ask?" he said.

Snick.

"Say you love me," said Kate.

"I love you," Philip said.

Kissing sound, followed by the click of the recorder getting switched off. What was that all about? Ingrid had no idea. Philip Prescott sounded like a combination of snob and spoiled brat. But who was this other guy, the one they—

"Ingrid? Ingrid? Are you up there?"

Oh my God. Mom.

Ingrid snapped off the machine.

"Ingrid?"

Ingrid went over to the trapdoor, looked down. Mom, craning her neck over Dad's desk, was looking up.

"Hi, Mom," Ingrid said.

"What's going on?" Mom said. "I thought you were sick."

"I was," Ingrid said. "Then all of a sudden it went away. Like one of those twenty-four-hour flus, Mom, only shorter. And I started getting bored."

"So you went into the attic?"

"To explore around."

"What were those voices?"

Mom climbed onto the desk with surprising ease. Maybe there were athletic genes on both sides of the family. She went up two or three steps on the ladder, poked her head into the attic, glanced around.

"I was just playing with the tape recorder," Ingrid said.

Mom turned to her, feelers in action. Ingrid arranged her face in an expression of pure innocence. "Come down," Mom said. "I've brought you some soup."

"Thanks, Mom."

Mom climbed down, Ingrid behind her. Ingrid shoved the ladder back up, pushed the trapdoor closed with the pitching wedge.

Mom was watching her closely.

"Is there anything going on?" she said.

"Going on?" said Ingrid.

"Anything you want to tell me."

"Just thanks for bringing the soup, Mom. That was really nice."

Mom gave her a hug. "Miso," she said.

"From Nippon Garden?"

Mom nodded.

Nippon Garden was Ingrid's favorite restaurant. She realized she was starving, could have eaten Nippon Garden's entire family-size sushi sampler all by herself.

They went down to the kitchen. No sushi. Nothing on the table but a steaming bowl of miso soup, perfect for a sick kid at home.

Mom pulled on her leather gloves, slung her bag over her shoulder. "Client waiting in the car," she said. "See you tonight."

Even with all the business of work, Mom had taken the time for her. Ingrid felt guilty. All these – what would you call them? mental states? – seemed to have a physical feeling that went along for the ride. Guilt was dread without the tightness in the chest part, just the weight in the gut.

Ingrid walked Mom to the door. "Anything you want me to do around the house?" she said.

"Now I know you're feverish," said Mom.

Ingrid laughed. Mom opened the door, went out. The MPV was parked on the street, a client sitting in the passenger seat, gazing straight ahead. A man with a fine profile and close-cropped steel-colored hair. Ingrid recognized him right away: Vincent Dunn.

Oh my God. Vincent Dunn, out hunting for bed-and-breakfasts with Mom, despite all her efforts to stop him, to keep them apart. What had Mom told him? They would have already established that Ingrid was her daughter, of course; he'd probably mentioned that when he called the agency. So, out in the car, Mom had probably said something like "Mind a quick stop? Ingrid's home sick." And then, to his surprise, she'd parked outside 99 Maple Lane in Riverbend instead of 337 Packer Street in the Flats. And after that? Had he said, "This is where you live?" To which Mom would have said, "Yes."

But then what? If Vincent had followed that up with some remark about driving Ingrid to 337 Packer Street, then wouldn't Mom have jumped on her about that right away? But not one mention, not a hint, no signs of worry or anger dug into her forehead, just surprise to find Ingrid in the attic. And therefore? Vincent hadn't said anything about it. And therefore?

Ingrid had no idea. But it didn't mean he wouldn't rat her out her later. Ingrid was nervous the whole afternoon.

That didn't stop her from climbing back up to the attic. The first thing she did was read those clippings from *The Echo*.

Clipping one was all about how Katherine Kovac, a recent graduate of the Yale School of Drama, was now living in Echo Falls and would be giving acting lessons for all ages and abilities at the Rec Center.

Clipping two was an announcement of the engagement of Katherine Kovac to Philip Prescott. Hey! She had parents, at least had had them then, Mr. and Mrs. Charles Kovac of East Harrow, not far away. There was also a photograph of the couple. They stood on a bluff, Prescott Hall in the background. Philip Prescott turned out to be a moon-faced, chubby guy with an aggressive sort of grin that reminded her of Chris Farley. And Kate Kovac was beautiful, young, and happy. Ingrid, looking closely, couldn't see a sign of the future Crazy Katie.

Clipping three was a review of *Dial M for Murder*.
A rave review with praise for everyone, including Philip
Prescott, producer and director, actors and actresses
named R. William Grant, Bev Rooney, David Vardack,
and Marvin Sadinsky, but especially for "the radiant
Katherine Kovac" whose "slowly dawning understanding of her husband's treachery" was "wonderfully
evoked."

Sitting cross-legged up in the attic, the light starting
to fade, Ingrid went over the clippings. In *The Five
Orange Pips*, a strange story that turns out to be about
the Ku Klux Klan, Holmes tells Watson that if you
really understand one link in a series of incidents, you
will know them all, both before and after. Ingrid had
the feeling she was at one of those points of understanding right now, but just wasn't smart enough to
figure it out. Maybe she was a Watson, not a Holmes.
She was moping around like that when she was struck –
finally, you dope – by the importance of that playbill.
The *Dial M for Murder* playbill that she'd seen on
Kate's bedside table, had been dropped by the man in
the paint-spattered Adidas, and was missing after he
left.

She needed to see that playbill.

Joey called after school. Ingrid, starving, was in the
kitchen, wolfing down a peanut butter and jelly sandwich, plus Marshmallow Fluff. Plus hot chocolate for
washing it all down.

"Hi," he said.

"Hi."

"What're you eating?"

"Sandwich," Ingrid said, her tongue practically stuck to the roof of her mouth.

"You weren't in school today."

"Sick."

"Don't sound sick."

"I got better fast."

Joey laughed. "I used to try that, but there's no fooling my dad."

Oops. Joey's dad, who thought she was working on a project and had dropped her off at school. What if Joey's dad came home and said, "Saw Ingrid out on her bike today, working on her project." Or even: "What's your project, Joe?" And all kinds of things would come tumbling down, like her life, for starters. She was standing on top of a tall, rickety structure, very tall, very rickety, all her own doing. There had to be something brilliant she could say right now to keep at least this one mess-up from happening.

"Joey?"

"Yeah?" said Joey and then: "Hey. My dad's on the other line. Call you back."

But he didn't.

Mom and Ty came home not long after, Ty limping slightly, one forearm skinned from practice. He opened the fridge, guzzled orange juice right out of the carton.

"Ty!" Mom said.

He guzzled some more, put the carton back, went downstairs. The weights started clanking around.

Mom sighed, turned to Ingrid. "All better?"

"Yeah," Ingrid said. Mom was about to say something else. Ingrid got ready for Vincent Dunn and how he'd dropped her off at 337 Packer Street, another time bomb all set to blow her tall rickety thing to bits.

But all Mom said was, "How's spaghetti?"

Never a bad choice. Mom boiled the water and heated the sauce. Ingrid chopped an onion to add to it. Worry built and built inside her. She had to be sure.

"How was the showing?" she said, trying to sound casual, not easy when your face was streaming with tears, even if they were only from onions.

"I meant to tell you," Mom said.

"What?"

"He knows you from the players," Mom said. "The client, I'm talking about. Vincent Dunn."

"Oh," said Ingrid. "Him."

"A nice man," Mom said. "He thinks you're talented."

"Yeah?"

"Very. He's really looking forward to rehearsals."

Any more to come? Didn't appear to be. "What else did he say?" Ingrid asked, dumping the chopped onions into the sauce.

"Just that he hopes you get well soon," said Mom. "I told him there was nothing to worry about on that score – up in the attic like a monkey." Mom stirred in the onions, delicious smells rising up, mixing together. "That's about it. We weren't out very long. There was nothing in his price range."

Vincent had covered for her. Either that or he hadn't been paying attention on the drive to 337 Packer Street, maybe had thought he was dropping her at a friend's or something. But whatever the reason, a warm tide of relief flowed inside Ingrid. The rickety thing was still standing. She was going to be all right.

Ingrid set the table.

"Will Dad be here for dinner?"

"Supposed to be," said Mom. She checked the time. "Did he call?"

"No."

Mom gazed off into the distance. The sauce got too hot and spattered all over the stove top. "Damn," Mom said, turning it down. Ingrid set the table for four.

"Call Ty," Mom said, draining the spaghetti.

"Ty," Ingrid yelled from where she stood.

"I could have done that myself," Mom said.

Ty came up, bare chested, sweating. A vein was throbbing over one of his biceps. Mom, standing behind him, said, "I'm going to get you an appointment with Dr. Pedlosky."

"Who's he?" said Ty.

"She," said Mom. "The dermatologist. You're getting acne on your back."

"I'm fine," Ty said, pulling on his Red Raiders varsity T-shirt, probably the coolest T-shirt in town.

They sat down to dinner. Nigel entered, sniffing the air.

twenty

before the next rehearsal, Ingrid walked around Prescott Hall to see if she could find the spot where Kate Kovac and Philip Prescott had posed for their engagement picture. A long walk – she'd never realized how huge Prescott Hall was before this, with those two massive wings, each bigger than any other whole house in town, even the Ferrands'. All those towers and terraces and leaded-glass windows, pointy-tongued gargoyles sticking out here and there, and lots of architectural features she didn't know the names of: Being rich, really rich, meant you could go completely crazy, and the only result would be everyone getting so jealous they couldn't stand it. And circling around like this, Ingrid also understood how much of the place was closed off, way more than half.

At the back of Prescott Hall lay the remains of a vast garden, now one big tangle. To the right, toward the river, rose a bluff. A brick path, now in disrepair, many of the bricks broken or missing, led to the top, a flat lookout with a stone wall on three sides, little stone angels on the corners. Ingrid turned her back on the river and faced the Hall. Yes, the photograph had been taken right here, Philip and Kate standing where she now stood, the photographer by the wall.

Ingrid went to the wall, looked over. The bluff fell steeply toward the river, gliding swiftly by far below. Over to her left, just out of sight beyond the next bend, were the falls. She could just make out that boom Mr. Samuels had mentioned, the boom that hadn't been strung across when Philip's parents got swept over in a canoe. The white buoys seemed tiny, like beads on a flimsy necklace. The falls were making that sound, like a mob of people going *shhhh!* From certain spots you were supposed to be able to hear a second *shhhh!*, trailing the main one like an echo, the echo that gave the falls their name. Ingrid had never heard it before. Here, on this stone terrace on top of the bluff behind Prescott Hall, she heard it for the very first time.

Ingrid walked back down the brick path and across the tangled garden. The sun was sinking, turning all those leaded windows into gold. She climbed one side of the curving horseshoe staircase at the back of the Hall, then followed the wide second-floor terrace around to the front.

She heard voices. Looking down, she saw Jill Monteiro and Vincent Dunn crossing the parking lot. They came to the door of the octagonal entrance.

"Glad to hear it," Jill was saying. She took out her key, unlocked the door. "I'm excited too."

Vincent held it open for her, paused. "Oh, and that

reminds me, Jill," he said. "Would it be possible to get a key?"

"A key?" said Jill.

"A duplicate," said Vincent, pointing to the one in her hand. "To the Hall."

"A key to the Hall?" Jill said. "But why?"

Vincent placed one of those long saintly hands of his on Jill's shoulder, the skin so white against the black of her sleeve. "This is a little embarrassing," he said, lowering his voice, but not so low Ingrid, with her sharp ears, couldn't hear. "I've got a kind of … secret."

"Oh," said Jill, stepping back. "What's that?"

"Just about the worst thing you can imagine," Vincent said. "Stage fright."

"Stage fright?" said Jill, sounding a bit surprised. Ingrid was surprised too. She could think of lots worse secrets than stage fright.

"A horrible case," he was saying. "Really incapacitating. For years it drove me out of acting completely. I was always so calm during rehearsal – even full dress rehearsal – but the moment opening night came along, I fell apart. I tried everything, Jill – therapy, Valium, even downing two or three shots of vodka before going on." Ingrid could see the sympathetic reaction rising in Jill's big dark eyes. "All useless," Vincent went on. "Finally, by accident, I stumbled on the solution."

"Which was?" Jill said.

Vincent took a deep breath, let it out slowly. "A twist on an old story, you might say. I found I couldn't stay away from the theater. In a little town out west, I volunteered at a local company – stagehand, set building, lighting, sweeping up, you name it. I practically lived in the theater, got to know every nook and cranny, felt at home." He paused and repeated, "At home." Then another deep, sighing breath. "The play was *Death of a Salesman*. Naturally, by opening night, I knew every part." Vincent paused, seemed to be remembering. The corners of his mouth turned up in a little smile. "Five minutes before curtain, our Biff was arrested for failure to pay child support – rather ironic considering the character."

Jill laughed. Ingrid, unfamiliar with the play, didn't get it.

"Can you guess the rest?" Vincent said.

"You stepped in?" said Jill.

He nodded.

"And your stage fright disappeared?"

"Totally," said Vincent. "It was like a rebirth."

Ingrid saw Jill nod, a nod that said *I would have felt the same.*

"But," said Vincent, "the price to pay is that I have to sink into that at-home feeling for every production. That means spending hours and hours just being in the theater, puttering around, doing odd jobs, absorbing the place. My last director let me sleep in the wings during the entire production. Which is why, Jill, I'd appreciate a duplicate key."

"You want to sleep in Prescott Hall?" Jill said.

"That would be ideal."

"I have the only key," Jill said. "Except for the trustees, of course."

"We could stop by the hardware store," Vincent said.

Jill laughed. "I don't have the authority to give anyone a key," she said. "I'd have to run it by the trustees."

"I'd be very grateful," Vincent said.

Jill thought for a moment. "The only one I know is Tim Ferrand," she said. "I'll try him."

"Thank you," said Vincent, touching her shoulder again just for a second before they went inside.

Ingrid liked Prescott Hall. There was even something magical about it. But sleeping alone inside the place? What could be creepier? Stage fright must suck really bad, driving Vincent to a remedy like that. She crossed her fingers to keep it from ever siccing her.

"The Mad Hatter's table," said Jill, "will angle out toward center stage like so. The previous scene, thanks to the wizardry of Mr. Rubino—"

"Shazam," said Stacy's dad over a speaker from the booth.

"—ends with a single spot on the Cheshire Cat's smile," Jill went on, "fading, fading, fading – a grin without a cat, just as Alice says. And we come up on the tea party."

Hey! So cool, that fading grin. Jill was brilliant.

Jill peered into the darkness, up in the direction of the booth. "What do you think of a rosy, late-summer-afternoon kind of effect for the tea party, Mr. Rubino?"

"Can do," said Mr. Rubino.

Jill rubbed her hands together. "Places, then," she said. "Hatter, you'll be here." Vincent pulled a stool over to the spot, sat down. "Dormouse right beside him." Meredith O'Malley put her stool next to

Vincent's. "March Hare over here." Chloe moved into position. "And Alice enters and walks to this mark –" taping a black cross on the floor – "where the head of the table will be." Jill placed Alice's chair. "You'll have to cheat toward the audience a little, Ingrid, because of the angle. All set, everybody?"

They had a run-through. Ingrid imagined herself in a prim little Alice dress and tiny patent-leather party shoes, and made her entrance, uneasy in a strange place but putting on a brave face.

"No room, no room," they all cried, Meredith slipping into a British accent already.

"More shock than anger," said Jill.

"No room, no room."

"Better."

"There's plenty of room," Ingrid said, and flounced down on her stool, which hurt a little, stools not being good for flouncing.

Jill saw; she saw everything. "There'll be an armchair," she said.

In a sugary voice, Chloe said: "Care for some wine?"

The stage direction said "(looks around)" but Ingrid found herself gazing right at Chloe. "I don't see any wine," she said.

Chloe gave her a cold look. "There isn't any," she said, quite nasty.

"One sec," said Jill. "Dormouse? I know you're supposed to be asleep, but if you could tone down the snoring just a touch."

"Oops," said Meredith, opening her eyes. "Sorry, people." She closed them again, resumed snoring at a lesser volume. Ingrid saw Meredith had pulled a lock of hair over her mouth so that it rose and fell with her breath. A wonderful effect.

"From 'There isn't any,'" said Jill.

Chloe was waiting for Ingrid's next line, one beautiful curving eyebrow raised, sending a clear message: *Is this the best you can do?* It pissed Ingrid off. "Then it wasn't very civil to offer it," she said, and heard the pissed-offedness in her tone. Maybe too much? Jill was looking thoughtful.

"Is it civil to crash our party?" said Chloe, her voice rising; way too over-the-top, but Jill didn't say anything.

"Why is the question?" Vincent said. After a long pause, he went on: "Why is a raven like a writing desk?" His diction was precise, like typewriter keys snapping down on paper; somehow that super-educated enunciation made the line sound completely whacked.

"Oh, good," said Ingrid, going for plucky. "I love riddles."

"You think that's a riddle?" Vincent said. And then ad-libbed: "*That's* the riddle."

Everyone laughed. This was going to be great.

Ingrid waited in the octagonal room for Mom or Dad. The door opened and Chloe came back in from the parking lot.

"You're supposed to come with us," she said.

"Huh?"

Chloe shrugged and went out. Ingrid followed her across the parking lot to Mr. Ferrand's car, a Mercedes of the biggest, blackest kind. The driver's-side window slid down.

"Your father asked me to drive you home," said Mr. Ferrand.

"Uh," said Ingrid. "I can—"

"I'm in a bit of a hurry," said Mr. Ferrand. The window slid up.

Ingrid got in the back. Chloe sat up front with her father. Ingrid had never been in a car like this, so quiet, solid, powerful. It was like riding in a bank vault.

"Thanks, Mr. Ferrand," Ingrid said.

No one spoke again until they were turning onto Maple Lane and Mr. Ferrand's cell phone rang.

"Yes?" said Mr. Ferrand. He listened for a moment. "What key?" he said, and listened some more. Chloe turned to him; her profile was amazing, Ingrid had to admit. Why couldn't her father's weak chin have been passed along? A little justice would be nice from time to time.

"He wants a key to the Hall?" said Mr. Ferrand. "I don't understand."

Ingrid heard Jill's tiny voice trying to explain.

"You're not being clear," said Mr. Ferrand after maybe two seconds.

The tiny voice spoke faster.

Mr. Ferrand shook his head, a vigorous shake that reminded Ingrid of Mikey Lester, a two-year old she sometimes baby-sat over on Avondale.

"I don't think so, Jill," Mr. Ferrand said. "Bad policy."

The tiny voice didn't give up. Ingrid heard the words *stage fright*.

Mr. Ferrand interrupted. "No, I'm afraid," he said. "No is the answer." He clicked off.

"What was that?" said Chloe.

"Some nonsense," said Mr. Ferrand.

But it wasn't nonsense. The whole play depended on it. Ingrid was tempted to say something, might have in a different situation, but this situation was Mr. Ferrand, Chloe, rolling bank vault. She smoldered away in the backseat.

Mr. Ferrand slowed down. "This one?" he said. His tone implied that all the houses on Maple Lane looked the same to him, prefab hovels.

"With the stained glass in the door," Ingrid said; a small stained-glass window Mom had picked up in a junk shop for five bucks and that Ingrid didn't even like. But: *So there, all you Ferrands.*

The Mercedes glided to a silent stop. "Thanks for going out of your way," she added politely as she got out of the car.

A tiny nod from Mr. Ferrand.

"See you, Chloe."

A tinier one from her.

And if you think you're ever getting your hands on Grampy's land, forget it.

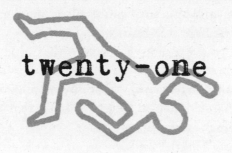

twenty-one

every fall before the weather got too cold, the whole school ran the Turkey Trot, a two-mile course across the back fields, up the hill to the filtration plant, around Schoolhouse Pond where the town's water supply came from, and back. The Turkey Trot was supposed to be a race, but years ago – no one knew when, but long before Ingrid or Ty got to Ferrand Middle – it had become uncool to win or even to try very hard. The gym teachers were always psyched about the Turkey Trot, sprinting back and forth among the kids, hopping up and down, yelling, "Pick it up, pick it up," and "C'mon – you're way faster than that." But the kids, even the fast ones like Ingrid, just loped along. To actually win and get handed the brass turkey trophy up on the auditorium stage was uncoolest of all. No surprise that Brucie Berman – one leg doing a funny sideways thing with every stride – was in the lead.

Near the back, Ingrid and Stacy trotted side by side. A cold, windy day, but way better than being inside the building, even kind of nice. Dead leaves crunched underfoot, and the sun, more silver than gold, shone between the bare tree branches.

"Hear you're doing a scene with Chloe Ferrand," Stacy said.

"Uh-huh," Ingrid said. "Got any more gum?"

Stacy handed her a stick. "What's that like?" she said. "Doing a scene with Chloe."

"Heaven," Ingrid said.

Stacy snapped her gum. "My dad's doing some work over at their house," she said. "Did you know they've got an indoor pool?"

"Yeah."

"Been in it?"

"No."

"Mrs. Ferrand swims a mile every morning. Nude."

"Your dad saw that?"

Stacy shook her head. "That's what my mom asked, first thing." Ingrid could imagine that scene. Stacy's mom had a temper and was built like a truck. "He's supposed to be installing this chandelier over the pool," Stacy said. "It comes from France or something, costs like the earth. Mrs. Ferrand told him not to come before nine because that's when she does the nudie thing."

They ran in silence for a minute or so.

"Money doesn't buy happiness," Stacy said.

"Please God let me test that out for myself," Ingrid said.

"You're rich already," Stacy said.

"Huh?"

"Living on Maple Lane," said Stacy. "And that car your dad drives."

Ingrid glanced at her oldest friend. Did Stacy really think she was rich? Maple Lane was nothing; Mr. Ferrand had made that clear. And the TT, a cool car, yes, but Ingrid remembered the fights between Mom and Dad about whether they could make the payments.

"Rich isn't having stuff," Ingrid said. "It's having the kind of stuff that brings in money, twenty-four seven."

"I guess you're right," Stacy said. "The Ferrands own a bunch of houses in the Flats. My dad's hoping that if they like the chandelier job, they'll give him more work on those."

"Houses in the Flats?" Ingrid said.

"My dad says one of them was Crazy Katie's," Stacy said.

Ingrid didn't get it. "They owned it together?"

"Huh?" said Stacy. "Crazy Katie was renting, of course. Some people rent, princess."

Ingrid gave her an elbow. Stacy gave her a harder one back. Ingrid gave her another, hardest of all. "Take that back," said.

"I take it back," Stacy said. "Your majesty."

"Listen up," said Coach Ringer at soccer practice that afternoon. "Better think again if you think Turkey Trot means I go easy today. No way, José. I know all about the trot. From way back. American kids are the fattest since the ancient Visigoths. Absolute fact. It's a disgrace. We fought wars. Big game coming up – Rocky Hill. Win, we make the play-offs. Lose, I run your tails from here to smithereens." He blew his whistle. "Three laps."

Sometimes Coach Ringer was like poetry.

The A team ran three laps around the soccer field above the hospital. Three fast laps: Assistant Coach Trimble always ran in front. Coach Ringer watched from the sidelines. Maybe you couldn't call him grossly obese, but he looked pretty lumpy in his Towne Hardware jacket. Sometimes while they ran laps, like now, he snuck a cigarette.

Coach Trimble running was a thing of beauty, and the amount of ground that flashed by with every stride – amazing. Ingrid caught up to her, churning just about her fastest.

"Coach Trimble?"

"Hi, Ingrid."

"Is that true about the Visigoths? Being fat?"

Coach Trimble gazed straight ahead. "I didn't take much history," she said.

"But they were vandals," Ingrid said. "Pillaging and stuff. They got a lot of exercise."

Coach Trimble didn't reply at first, then said, "Keep working on that left foot." Then she stepped up the pace, not by making any visible effort, more just shifting gears and letting some motor inside do the work. She was as smooth as Mr. Ferrand's Mercedes. Ingrid couldn't stay with her, not close.

Halfway through practice they had a water break. Coach Ringer came from the old school, didn't like water breaks, but league rules were strict on that. While he doled it out in paper cups, the smallest you could get, like for rinsing at the dentist, Ingrid saw Joey ride up on his bike.

Ingrid took her water, went over to him, five or ten yards from the team.

"Hi," she said.

"Hi." He was looking at her feet. "Those your soccer boots?" he said.

Uh-oh. Out of the blue, or left field, or wherever totally unexpected things came from. Ingrid glanced down to confirm what she already knew, that she was wearing the slightly too-tight black ones. "Yeah," she said, trying to keep her voice steady but aware she wasn't doing a good job. "Who else's would they be?"

Joey looked at her real funny. Something was very wrong. "How come you told my dad you were working on a project about littering on the bike path?"

"I was ditching," Ingrid said. "You knew that."

"But I thought you were ditching at home," Joey said. "What were you up to, anyway?"

"Up to?" said Ingrid. "Riding around. I got bored." Lying to Joey made her feel bad. She even felt a little nausea in her stomach. This whole rickety thing was going to make her sick. Plus he was still looking at her funny, like he was seeing her in a new way, not good. It made Ingrid afraid and angry at the same time. "And what's any of this got to do with my boots?"

"I don't know," Joey said. She could see in his eyes that he knew something. "But—"

Coach Ringer blew his whistle.

"But what?" Ingrid said.

Coach Ringer blew it again, louder. "Any interest in

being on this team, Ingrid?" he called.

She went back to practice.

"No 'I' in 'team'," Coach Ringer said as she walked by.

"But there are two of them in 'Visigoth'," Ingrid said, a remark she regretted right away.

"Take a lap," said Coach Ringer. "Make it two."

Ingrid ran two laps. Practice went bad. She lost all control over the ball. Her legs got heavier and heavier. Ingrid looked around for Joey, but he was gone.

That night Grampy came to dinner. This hardly ever happened, but whenever it did, Mom served the exact same meal – shrimp cocktail, steak with roast potatoes and a tomato-and-onion salad, and pecan pie for dessert – because that was Grampy's favorite. Ingrid's, too.

"Freshen your drink, Pop?" Dad said.

"Don't mind if you do," said Grampy. He always wore a tie when he came to dinner – even if it didn't go with his shirt, like the orange-and-green flannel one he had on now – and had his face shaved smooth and his thick snowy hair combed and wetted down.

Dad poured brandy in Grampy's glass. Mom and Dad were drinking wine, Ty milk, and Ingrid Fresca.

"What's this?" Grampy said.

"Our new dog," said Ingrid. "Nigel."

"I knew a Nigel," Grampy said.

"Who was he, Pop?" said Mom. Calling him Pop again, which she never did: Ingrid started to get an inkling of what this dinner might be about.

"Brit," said Grampy. "Spring of forty-three." They waited for more, but no more came. Grampy sliced his steak into bite-sized pieces and went after them one by one. Then he happened to see that Ty was watching him. "Better eat up, young fella," he said. That meant he and Ty would be arm wrestling after dessert, a little ritual they had that Ty hated. He never won. Ty started eating up.

Ingrid remembered something. "Hey, Grampy," she said, "do you know Mr. Sidney?"

Grampy looked up, roast potato half mushed in his mouth. "Myron Sidney?"

"I don't know his first name. He drives the school bus and wears a hat that says BATTLE OF THE CORAL SEA."

"That's Myron. What's he doing driving the school bus?"

"I think it's his job, Grampy."

Grampy looked puzzled, and for a moment not his normal strong self, more like other guys his age.

"Do you get together with him?" Mom said.

Grampy's strength returned fast. "Why would I get together with Myron Sidney?"

"But weren't you old friends?" Ingrid said. "At Corregidor?"

"Has Myron been running his mouth?" Grampy said. "Nothing changes."

Sometimes best to answer a question with a question. "What was Corregidor all about?" Ingrid said.

Grampy got a faraway look in his eyes, gone so fast you had to be watching like a hawk, and Ingrid was.

She would have bet anything he was thinking about that place beyond the point of fear. *Him or you*. Then he shook his head, had a big drink of his brandy, and went back to eating.

After dessert – Grampy had seconds – came the arm wrestling. Grampy and Ty, his face already pink and they hadn't even started, sat at one corner of the table, their sleeves rolled up. Hey! Ty's forearm was just about as big as Grampy's. That was new and should have been a good thing, but Ingrid couldn't help thinking about the acne on Ty's back.

Dad got their elbows positioned fairly and said, "One, two, three, go." Usually it took Grampy about fifteen seconds to win, but not this time. This time it went on and on, their faces purpling up, plus all these grunts and groans and bared teeth. Ty got Grampy's arm down, down, down, almost there, only two inches or so, but no more. Grampy's face got fierce. He panted. Mom opened her mouth to say something, but Dad made a little sign to shush her. Grampy's arm came up, inch by inch, back up to the top. They stayed like that for an unbearable amount of time. Ingrid saw a look in Ty's eye that said "I can beat him." Then Ty's arm started going down. And when it did, it went down faster and faster. Boom.

"Whew," said Grampy, slugging back the rest of his drink. Ty rolled down his sleeve, eyes on the floor. Grampy reached out, rumpled Ty's hair. "Last time we do that," said Grampy.

Ty looked shocked. "You're not going to give me a chance to beat you?" he said.

"What sense would that make?" Grampy said. "From now on I'll take my chances with Ingrid."

"What have you been smoking?" said Ingrid, glad, oh so glad, to be a girl.

Ingrid and Ty started cleaning up, Ingrid clearing the table, Ty loading the dishwasher. Mom and Dad stayed in the dining room with Grampy. Dad took a folder from his briefcase. As Ingrid went into the kitchen with a stack of dessert plates, Grampy reached for the brandy bottle and refilled his glass. Then she heard him say, "What's this?"

"A little proposal we printed up," Dad said. "For you to take a look at."

"In your own good time, of course," said Mom.

"Who is 'we'?" Grampy said.

"A brand-new entity," said Dad. "Still in the planning stages, depending on whether … just depending."

"Entity?" said Grampy.

Ingrid went back into the dining room for the salad bowl. Mom and Dad sat on either side of Grampy, down at Dad's end of the table.

"FHL Development Company," Dad said.

"*H* for Hill?" said Grampy.

"Yes," Dad said, with an encouraging smile.

"And *F*?" said Grampy. "What's that *F* stand for?"

Ingrid paused at the other end of the table, salad bowl in hand. No one seemed to notice her.

"It's a partnership with Tim," Dad said. "Carol knows the architect who did the Negresco condominiums in Old Saybrook."

"Understated," said Mom. "Unobtrusive."

"Didn't they win some big award?" Dad said. "The thing is, Pop—"

"Who put that *F* right beside the *H*?" said Grampy.

Mom and Dad exchanged a glance behind Grampy's back. "We could change the order," Mom said.

"Put Carol in the middle," said Dad.

Grampy was gazing at the first page of the proposal. He hadn't even opened it. Ingrid could make out what looked like a watercolor of big white buildings backed into a hillside with tennis courts and golf course down below. "Condos," Grampy said.

"Nicer than almost any houses in Echo Falls," said Dad.

"You want to put condos on my land."

"For a price," said Dad. "Enough so you won't have to worry about money anymore."

"Who says I worry about money?" said Grampy.

"For God's sake, I do the taxes on the place," Dad said, his voice rising. "If you're not worried about money, you damn well should—"

Mom interrupted, "What if you had a share, Pop?"

"A share?"

"In the partnership," said Mom. "So you'd be selling to yourself, in a way."

Mom was smart.

But it didn't do her much good, because Grampy said, "Partners with the Ferrands?"

"That's where the money comes from," said Dad. "Tim's the only one who can get the bank to back something this big."

Unobtrusive and big at the same time? Dad and Mom didn't quite have their story together, but maybe it didn't matter, because Grampy didn't seem to hear. He repeated, "Partners with the Ferrands?"

Dad banged his fist on the table, faced Grampy, took Grampy's shoulder. "Pop," he said, "listen to me. We need this."

Grampy tried to shake Dad's hand off, but Dad was a lot stronger. "You need condos on my land?"

"What you don't know," Dad said, and glanced around. He saw Ingrid. "Get in the kitchen."

Ingrid went into the kitchen. The dishwasher chugged away and Ty was gone. She lingered just beyond the archway, out of sight.

"What you don't know, Pop," said Dad, lowering his voice, but not below the threshold of Ingrid's hearing, "is that things aren't too good at work right now."

"Not good for who?"

"Me. Tim thinks I encouraged him to back this biotech start-up."

"Biotech start-up?" From Grampy's tone, Ingrid knew he had no clue what Dad was talking about.

"Some Princeton guys," Dad said. "I found them, yes, but the truth is I told Tim to go slow, even if he doesn't remember it that way."

"What are you telling me?" said Grampy. His voice sounded a little thin and scratchy.

"The drug, chemical, hormone, whatever it was," said Dad, "ended up making cancer worse. Tim lost a million bucks." There was a long silence. "Do you understand the situation, Pop?"

Maybe Grampy nodded, one way or the other, because there wasn't another word. What was the situation? Ingrid wasn't sure. How did you lose a million bucks? Was Dad's job in danger? Didn't the Ferrands have other millions, or at least the stuff to make it, twenty-four seven? She put the salad bowl in the sink.

Mom came in, those two lines deep in her forehead.

"Mom? Is it true Mr. Ferrand owns houses in the Flats?"

"Yes."

"Including the one where the woman got murdered?"

"I'm listing it tomorrow."

"So the woman rented it from him?"

"Sort of," said Mom. "She was pretty spotty about actually making the payments. Tim tried to get rid of her for years."

Upstairs, in her pajamas, the ones with the big red strawberries, Ingrid passed Ty on her way to the bathroom.

"Good job," she said. "You almost won."

"I could have," Ty said.

"I thought so too there for a while," Ingrid said.

"No," said Ty. "I mean I could have. Dad told me not to."

Ingrid was stunned. "But why?" she said. It went against the whole sporting code they'd been brought up with.

"For Grampy's pride."

"Dad said that?"

"Uh-huh."

Ingrid brushed her teeth and went to bed, more mixed up than she'd ever been. Her mind was full of questions. One rose to the top. Did Mr. Ferrand own a pair of paint-spattered Adidas sneakers? *The bigger the crime, the more obvious the motive.*

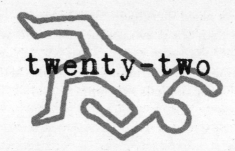

twenty-two

ingrid woke up in the night. Nigel was crowding the bed, had her jammed into the wall, her face mashed against what was left of Mister Happy.

"Move."

He wouldn't move. She pushed at him, hands, feet, both together. He didn't budge.

"You're sleeping in the basement from now on."

Still snoring, Nigel shifted over a few inches. What did that mean? Was he smarter, more obedient, better in every way, when he was unconscious?

Ingrid closed her eyes. Her own unconscious was bubbling around inside, turning things over at high speed. Shoes – red Pumas and paint-spattered Adidas; the hanged audiotape man; the good-bye letter that Philip Prescott wrote to *The Echo*; the missing *Dial M for Murder* playbill with the frightened Kate and the silhouetted actor. All that stuff spun around like one of those effects in a bad movie and kept sleep far away.

Hey.

She opened her eyes.

Who was he anyway, that silhouetted actor? So many questions. Maybe the only way to solve the case was to answer every one. Those names in *The Echo's Dial M for Murder* review, for example – R. William Grant, David Vardack, Marvin Sadinsky: Didn't the silhouetted actor have to be one of them? Philip Prescott had hired professional actors. Maybe they'd been reviewed in other places. What would Mia say at a time like this?

Google them.

Ingrid climbed over Nigel – he made a grumbling sound – and went to her computer. The house was quiet, except for the rain outside, falling softly on the roof. She Googled in alphabetical order.

J. William Grant: many, many hits for many J. William Grants, but no mention of acting, the Prescott Players, or Echo Falls.

Marvin Sadinsky: eight hits for three Marvin Sadinskys – a professor at Tulane, the head of a running club in Duluth, a scrap metal dealer in Long Beach.

David Vardack: one hit. It linked to a blog run by a fan of obscure movies. "Anybody ever see *The Accused Will Rise* with Jack Palance and Barbara Stanwyck, more than thirty years old now? Best thing in it's this one scene with a young actor named David Vardack, where he gets trapped down an old well. Whatever happened to him?" No one had replied.

Ingrid gazed at the screen, pretty sure now that the silhouetted actor was David Vardack. But what did that mean? All she'd done was add even more questions to the pile. Did any of this – Philip Prescott, David

Vardack – have to do with Kate's murder? She didn't see how; it was all so long ago. *The Accused Will Rise*, Jack Palance, Barbara Stanwyck, all complete unknowns. The only solid fact she had was Mr. Ferrand wanting to get Crazy Katie out of 341 Packer—

Someone was moving in the hall. Ingrid turned. Her door opened and Dad walked in, wearing his robe, hair mussed up.

"Ingrid," he said. "What are you doing up?"

"A little work," she said.

"It's three in the morning."

"You're up too," she said.

"I saw your light," said Dad. He leaned on her door-jamb, gazed at her. There were dark circles under his eyes. If he'd been sleeping, it hadn't been a good one. "You're a hard worker, Ingrid. Don't forget to have some fun on the way."

"I won't."

"Better get some sleep," Dad said. "What's that in your bed?"

"Nigel."

"Jesus," said Dad.

Ingrid shut off the computer. "Why does Grampy hate the Ferrands?"

"Grampy hates a lot of things," Dad said.

"Why are the Ferrands so greedy?" Ingrid said.

"They're not greedy. Tim's a good businessman, that's all."

"Do you like working for him, Dad?"

"It's a good job," Dad said. "No complaints."

Ingrid realized Dad was protecting her from worry: a

real dad. But she was protecting him from worry too. She climbed over Nigel, got back in bed. "Does Mr. Ferrand play tennis?" she said.

"That's a strange question," said Dad. "He doesn't like tennis, actually. He's played squash all his life."

That figured – mere tennis not elite enough for the Ferrands. "What kind of shoes do you wear for that?"

"Like tennis," Dad said. "Why?"

"No reason," said Ingrid. "Night, Dad. Love you."

"Night," said Dad, moving toward the door. He stopped. "Heard about the backward poet?" he said.

"Backward poet?"

"Who always wrote in verse," Dad said.

"Please," said Ingrid.

Friday night. The visitors wore black and silver, very cool uniforms. They did a lot of yelling during warm-up, yelling that drifted over to the parking lot where Ingrid was grilling burgers for the Boosters.

Stacy and her brother, Sean, came over, their faces painted red. Sean had his shirt off too, even though it was cold, or maybe because it was cold, and on his chest in big red letters was the word KILL. Was that about the game or something else? The problem with Sean – lots of problems with Sean, actually – was that you never knew.

"Want me to paint your face?" said Stacy.

"No, thanks."

"How about just the tip of your nose?" Stacy said.

That struck Sean as pretty funny. "Yeah," he said. "Like Rudolph." Which was kind of immature coming from a seventeen-year-old of DUI fame. He uncapped a paint stick and leaned across the grill.

"I said no," Ingrid said.

"Lay a burger on me, then," said Sean.

"I'll sell you a burger," said Ingrid. "Fifty cents."

He turned to Stacy. "Got fifty cents?"

Stacy fished two quarters from her pocket. She wasn't the same around her brother. Ingrid stuck a patty in a bun and was handing it over to Sean when she saw a police cruiser pull into the parking lot, park on the far side. Not unusual; two or three cops came to every football game, but—

But when the door opened, Chief Strade got out. Ingrid didn't remember him at any games.

"You gonna let go of that?" Sean said.

Ingrid let go of the burger. A taxi parked beside the cruiser. The driver got out. An unshaven guy chewing on a toothpick? Too far away for Ingrid to tell, but how many taxi drivers could there be in Echo Falls?

"Stacy," she said, "I changed my mind."

"About what?"

"Paint my face," Ingrid said.

"Yeah?" said Stacy. "Maybe I'll have a burger too. That one in the bottom—"

"Now," said Ingrid.

"Huh?"

Ingrid grabbed Sean's paint stick, smeared red paint all over her face.

"You're doing a terrible job," Stacy said.

Ingrid smeared more – forehead, nose, cheeks, upper lip, chin, neck, ears. Sean started laughing.

"Shut your stupid mouth," Ingrid said.

"What did you say?" said Sean. Then he saw Chief Strade approaching and backed away a little.

The chief came over with the taxi driver trailing along. Yes, unshaven and chewing on a toothpick, although Ingrid, busily flipping burgers, took that in from the corner of her eye.

"Ingrid," said the chief. "That you under the war paint?"

Ingrid looked up. "Oh, hi, Mr. Strade. Ready for some football?"

The taxi driver was looking at her closely. Chief Strade glanced at him. The taxi driver shrugged.

The chief's eyes went to her, Stacy, Sean. "Do you always—" he said, gesturing at their faces, all painted. And just at that moment, proving there was a God and he could be kind and just, a whole bunch of kids went by, every one with a painted face. Kids united!

"It's a big game," Ingrid said.

The chief nodded. "Keeping your nose clean, Sean Rubino?" he said, not looking at him.

Sean jerked a little, like a startled baby. "Yeah," he said.

"Squeaky clean?" said the chief. "I've been to too many funerals."

"Squeaky clean," said Sean, recovering his poise fast, fast enough to add the slightest edge of mimicry to his answer. He drifted over toward the condiments, squirted ketchup on what was left of his burger, kept drifting.

"Murad?" said Chief Strade. "Mind stepping forward so Ingrid can get a good look at you?"

The taxi driver stepped forward.

"Have you ever seen this gentleman before, Ingrid?" the chief said.

"Never," said Ingrid.

"You've never ridden in his taxi?" said the chief.

"Ridden in a taxi?" Ingrid said, as though that was just about the most outlandish thing an Echo Falls girl could do. All those years with Jill Monteiro paying off. She remembered Watson saying somewhere that the stage lost a fine actor when Holmes went into detection. He was also – oh my God – a master of disguise.

The chief's penetrating eyes met hers for a moment, but their penetrating power was weakened by all that diabolical red. "Okay," he said. "Just checking."

"Care for a burger?" Ingrid said.

"No, thanks," said the chief.

"How about you, sir?" Ingrid said, then thought, uh-oh, maybe Murad had dietary laws and she'd just screwed up.

"Burger," said Murad. "Two."

Ingrid selected two of the juiciest. Murad reached for his wallet. "Compliments of the Boosters," Ingrid said, stopping herself, with some difficulty, from adding "Welcome to America."

"Just checking?" said Stacy after they'd gone. "Checking what? He's such a jerk."

Over on the field the band was playing "The Star-Spangled Banner".

"Game time," said Ingrid, shutting off the gas. Chief Strade scared her, but she didn't think he was a jerk. More like the opposite, in fact. She realized she didn't want to disappoint him, and not just because he was Joey's dad. Somehow this had to come out right.

The black-and-silvers tried the flea-flicker on their second play. Ty started to come forward, started to take the bait like everyone else, and then – yes! – saw what was really happening. Blessed miracle. He backpedaled, found the receiver, matched him stride for stride. Ball in the air. They both leaped, hands outstretched, a frozen moment under the lights. And – 19 came down with it! Ty! He turned upfield, dodged a tackler—

"Run! Run!" Dad was jumping up and down, beside himself. They all were.

And dodged another tackler and shifted into a gear Ingrid hadn't known he had. Maybe Ty hadn't known either. He just blazed, right down the sideline, maybe not graceful like Assistant Coach Trimble but even faster. Crowd on their feet. Touchdown. He raised the ball high but didn't do any embarrassing dancing or stuff like that. The best moment of his life, Ingrid just knew it. She almost cried, which was so weird.

Back at home alone – Mom and Dad at a fund-raising party for the Heritage Committee, Ty out celebrating with the team – Ingrid had another look at the engagement announcement from *The Echo*. She found that line about Katie's parents, Mr. and Mrs. Charles Kovac of East Harrow.

Bzzz. Did the Echo Falls phone book include East Harrow? Ingrid checked. It did not. She tried information.

"No Charles Kovac," said the information woman. "The only Kovac's an Eleanor on Moodus Road. Do you want that?"

"I don't know."

"Up to you."

"Okay."

The information woman transferred her over to some electronic voice that gave the number and dialed it automatically for fifty cents. It rang a bunch of times and Ingrid was just about to hang up when a woman answered.

"Hello?" she said. An old woman, kind of shaky. "Hello? Hello? Who is it?"

Ingrid hung up.

twenty-three

ingrid awoke on Saturday morning and remembered that she still hadn't handed in her topic for the science fair. Being in the science fair wasn't compulsory, but anyone who entered got thirty automatic bonus points in science on the next report card, points that could come in very handy. Last year Ingrid had done planaria worms, a gross and disgusting project about cutting off their heads and seeing how fast they grew back in different environments. Jammed against her bedroom wall, Ingrid decided that this year's experiment would involve Nigel.

Still lying in bed, she called Joey.

"Hello?" he answered, sounding sleepy, his voice all clogged and deep.

Ingrid got a funny physical feeling, sort of all over her body, her voice clogging up a little too. "Hi Joey. Did I wake you?"

"No."

"Hi."

"Hi."

"What's happening?"

"Not much," he said. He cleared his throat and his voice returned to normal, more like a boy than a man. "How about you?"

"Gotta come up with a science project," Ingrid said. "I was thinking of something with Nigel."

"Nigel?"

"My dog."

"I know," said Joey. "But like what?"

"That's why I called you," Ingrid said.

Silence. It went on for a long time. Was Joey planning some knockout Nigel experiment, a real prize-winner? She waited patiently, letting him think. At last he said, "You were at the game last night." Kind of weird the way there was no question mark at the end.

"Yeah," said Ingrid. "Were you?"

"Yeah."

"I didn't see you."

"Your brother played good."

"Where were you sitting?"

Another silence. What was taking him so long? Where had he sat? It wasn't a tough one.

"Ingrid?" he said.

"Yeah?"

"Your soccer shoes are black, right?"

Oh my God. It wouldn't go away. "You saw them," Ingrid said. "Why?"

"No reason."

"No reason? C'mon, Joey."

"They're black, that's the main point," Joey said.

An innocent person would now say "What's this all about?" Ingrid said it.

"It's kind of crazy," Joey said. "About the murder. My dad thinks there might have been a witness, or even ..."

"Even what?"

"An accomplice," said Joey. "Some girl soccer player with red boots."

"Really."

"But say it's a witness," Joey said. "That would be important, because the D.A.'s going to have trouble making the case against those two guys without one."

Good, Ingrid thought. What if she now said "If your dad wants to solve the case, he should take a look at Mr. Ferrand's squash shoes." Then everything would come flooding down like after a dam bursts, and there'd be action, big-time. But what kind? She couldn't see into that future. It was chaos. This, so messed up in many ways but in her hands, was still better. Besides, she could feel patterns forming deep in her mind. Out of sight, yes, but she sensed the beginning of understanding. "Really," she said again.

"Nothing to do with you," Joey said, "since yours are black." Silence. "But," he said, "do you know anybody who wears red ones?"

"Are you asking me to rat people out?" Ingrid said.

"No. Where'd you get that idea?"

"Because I don't do that," Ingrid said. That was true, part of her code: Kids didn't rat out kids, and those who did were just that, rats. "And half the soccer players in town, maybe more, wear red boots. Red Raiders rule, in case you hadn't heard."

"Hey," said Joey. "Sorry."

Another silence, real long. Ingrid was about to say good-bye and hang up when he said, "Maybe something with a maze."

"Huh?"

"Nigel," said Joey. "We could test his smelling skills by putting him in a maze."

"Mazes aren't going to be his thing," Ingrid said.

"We could use different foods," Joey said. "As variables."

"Hey," Ingrid said. Variables – that was pure science. The idea grew on her fast; also the way he'd said *we* – that grew on her too. Nigel, still sleeping, opened his mouth very wide, the way dogs sometimes do – yawning even as he slept, not a care in the world, no idea that science was about to fall on him like a ton of bricks. *Dream on.*

That afternoon at rehearsal – finishing up the tea-party scene – Vincent didn't seem like his usual self. He stumbled over his lines a few times, and even when he didn't, they were flat. Ingrid knew what that was all about: Jill must have told him that Mr. Ferrand had said no to the duplicate key idea. There'd be no sleeping in Prescott Hall, no getting comfortable with the place. Vincent's stage fright was waiting in the wings.

"Let's take a break," Jill said, after fifteen or twenty minutes. She came over to the tea-party table – an ornate heavy thing, the first prop to arrive – and smiled, but her big dark eyes were thoughtful. "I know you've all had a long week," she said. "Here's where we can shake it off."

Mr. Santos, sitting front row center and sewing his caterpillar costume, did that shaking thing of his, for when he slid into character.

"Yes," said Jill. "Like that. Everybody now."

They all shook themselves, except for Vincent and Chloe. A button popped off Meredith O'Malley's blouse and flew off the stage.

"Five minutes," Jill said.

Ingrid went to the backstage vending machine. Hey! Fresca. That was new. Jill's doing, had to be, must have noticed that Fresca was her drink. Jill was amazing – an artist and a leader too.

Ingrid got Fresca from the machine. Chloe appeared; she stuck in a dollar and bottled water tumbled out.

"How's it going?" Ingrid said.

Chloe shrugged.

"Playing much squash these days?" Ingrid said.

"Excuse me?" said Chloe.

"Like tennis," Ingrid said, "only more so."

Chloe's face got all suspicious, like she was being made fun of. Who could make a face like that without looking at least a little ugly? Chloe, for one. "I don't play squash," she said.

"But your dad does," said Ingrid.

"So?"

"I hear he's pretty good."

Chloe shrugged again. Ingrid understood why police were sometimes tempted to take suspects out back.

"What kind of shoes do you wear for that?" Ingrid said.

"Excuse me?"

"For playing squash."

"Squash shoes."

"Are they like tennis?" Ingrid said.

"Only more so," said Chloe.

Zing. That one hurt.

"What kind of squash shoes does your dad like?" Ingrid said.

"You want to know what squash shoes he likes?"

"Adidas, Puma, Nike, New Balance – you know," said Ingrid, guiding her along.

"Why?" said Chloe.

Ingrid shrugged, as close to Chloe's shrug as she could get, like Marie Antoinette hearing about the starving peasants. Being Chloe would be fun, no doubt about that. "Just curious," she said. "I'm into shoes."

Chloe glanced down at Ingrid's feet. She was wearing beat-up Skechers, one of the laces broken and knotted in the middle. Chloe, on the other hand, was wearing – oh my God, really? – Manolo Blahniks.

"He wears his own kind," Chloe said.

"What do you mean?" Ingrid said.

"Of squash shoes," said Chloe. "Isn't that what you're asking about? He wears his own kind, of all shoes, for that matter."

"I don't understand."

"It's not complicated," Chloe said. "My father's shoes are custom made for him in London."

"Oh," Ingrid said, could do no better than that, just a plain little off-the-shelf *oh*.

She went back onto the set. Only Jill and Vincent

were around, standing in the wings beside the upright piano. The stage was dark except for an orangey-red glow shining on the tea-party table. It grew more purple as Ingrid watched: Mr. Rubino, up in the booth, trying things out.

So Mr. Ferrand turned out to be a red herring. He might have wanted Crazy Katie out of 341 Packer Street, but did he own a pair of Adidas sneakers? Far, far beneath him. He was off the hook.

Ingrid started to uncap her drink. So who was on the hook? Who else had a motive? Her mind spun around uselessly, getting nowhere. She barely heard the rumble of the rolling piano; then she turned and saw Jill and Vincent pushing it across the stage. At that moment, Mr. Rubino cranked up the strobe; he loved the strobe, but Jill never let him use it in actual productions. Vincent's eyes, looking right at Ingrid, seemed to flash at her. *His flashing eyes*, she thought, remembering Mom's poetry session in the kitchen. That one was the coolest of all: *Beware! Beware!* What other poems did Mom—

Yikes. Fresca came spurting out of the bottle, a stop-action spill under the flashing strobe, making a little puddle on the stage floor.

"Mind giving us a hand, Ingrid?" Jill said. "Vincent's going to try the 'Twinkle Twinkle' song."

Good idea, Ingrid thought, *that'll get us going*. She set her drink on a stool, went to the keyboard, took her place pushing between Vincent and Jill. Jill moved around to the other side, gave them directions.

"A little more this way," she said, appearing and

disappearing under the strobe, leading them toward the Mad Hatter's place at the tea-party table.

Vincent started pushing more to the left.

"No," said Jill, peering over the piano, "to your right."

"My right?" said Vincent, steering even more to the left, "or your right?"

"Yours," said Jill, but he never got a chance to change course, what happened next coming so fast. All of a sudden his legs flew out from under him – oh my God, the spilled Fresca – and he lunged forward, fully outstretched, losing his grip on the piano. Ingrid lost her grip on it too, the huge heavy thing shooting forward. Jill looked up, her eyes widening jerkily in the strobe flash. Then came a thud as the piano barreled into her. Jill, so light, flew through the air, straight at a corner of the tea-party table. Her head struck it with a sickening crack. She fell to the stage and lay still. The house lights came up.

Mr. Rubino knew CPR, but it wasn't necessary. Jill's heart was beating and she was breathing fine. "A good sign," said Mr. Rubino, kneeling beside her, his finger on the inside of her wrist. But she was still unconscious, her glossy black hair clotting with blood, when the paramedics arrived minutes later and took her to the hospital, sirens blaring.

The Prescott Players stood around the spot where she'd lain, marked now by a bloodstain, bright red under the house lights. Vincent rubbed his forehead. His face was white; all their faces were.

"I don't know what happened," he said, sounding close to tears; they trembled in his dark liquid eyes. "I must have slipped on something."

Ingrid, who was in tears, said, "The Fresca. It's all my fault."

All heads swiveled toward her.

"What do you mean?" said Vincent.

Ingrid pointed to a glistening liquid patch on the stage floor, the skid marks of Vincent's feet clearly visible. "I spilled my drink," she said, coming close to a wail. "It's my fault." She forced herself not to wail, not to cry. Making herself the center of attention at a time like this, sucking up sympathy – disgusting.

Mr. Santos found a mop and cleaned up the Fresca.

Meredith O'Malley gave Ingrid a hug. "It was an accident, dear," she said.

"Yes," said Vincent. "An accident. Don't blame yourself."

"And I'm sure she's going to be just fine," said Meredith.

Mr. Santos stepped over and mopped up the bloodstain. They all looked at each other. "I think I'll head over to the hospital," Vincent said.

Ingrid wiped her face on the back of her sleeve. "Can I go with you?"

"Of course," said Vincent. He patted her on the back.

They all ended up going together in a convoy that stuck close together, winding along River Road and up the hill to the hospital. Ingrid rode in Vincent's car, her feet resting on a bag of kitty litter. Silence grew. The feeling of dread – suffocation plus a heavy weight in the stomach, like an anvil – also grew, feeding on the silence.

"You've got a cat?" Ingrid said, just to hear some sound.

He nodded.

More silence. It was like a third person, too big for the car.

"Was Barbara Stanwyck a big star?" Ingrid said.

His eyes shifted toward her for a second, a quick flash. "Barbara Stanwyck?"

"Like Ingrid Bergman," said Ingrid. "That kind of star."

Vincent smiled. "I forgot you're a movie buff," he said. "Yes, she was a big star. But different from Ingrid Bergman. Better, in my opinion."

"How?" said Ingrid.

"Hard to describe," Vincent said. She could feel him thinking. Then he laughed, a little laugh, to himself. "The way she spooned honey into her tea, practically the whole jar."

"What movie was that in?" Ingrid said.

"Movie?" he said. His hands – he was wearing those driving gloves again – tightened on the wheel. The oppressive silence fell again. "I forget," Vincent said. "She made so many."

They pulled into the visitors' lot at the hospital.

The Prescott Players sat in the admissions waiting room, taking almost every chair. Rain started falling outside, harder and harder. There was college football on TV and nothing to read except old people's magazines. Ingrid leafed through one, full of white-haired people laughing their heads off and ads for every medicine known to man. After a while Mr. Ferrand arrived. He had a few words with Chloe, then spoke to the nurse at the desk, who led him through a door marked NO ADMISSION BEYOND THIS POINT. On the way he had time for a quick glare at Ingrid.

Lots of people around, but Ingrid was all alone with the dread. She went over the accident a million times, thinking of all the things she could have done differently. Like not taking her drink onstage, which was against the rules. And why, greedy pig, did she need a Fresca so badly in the first place? And how about opening it with more care? And once it had spilled, she should have said, "Stop, it's slippery." But no. How could you call what could have been prevented so easily an accident? All at once she remembered Sergeant Pina, on crutches for six weeks, hunting trip ruined. She was a danger to the community.

Some time later, the no-admission door opened and Mr. Ferrand and a doctor in blue scrubs came out, dabbing his forehead with his little blue hat.

"This is Dr. Washington," said Mr. Ferrand.

The Prescott Players were on their feet, gathering around.

"She's going to be all right," Dr. Washington said.

Everyone went *whew* all at once, like a soft breeze, and through the windows the sky seemed brighter. There was even some clapping.

"Skull fracture," said Dr. Washington, "but she's

regained consciousness and there's no internal bleeding."

Ingrid raised her hand. "Can we see her?"

"Maybe in a day or two," said Dr. Washington. "We'll be keeping her here for a few days, and after that she'll have to take it easy for a month or so. Any questions?"

"Thanks, Doc," said Mr. Rubino. More applause.

Dr. Washington smiled and went back through the door.

Mr. Ferrand ran his eyes over the Players. "I assume you'll be shutting down the production?" he said.

Lots of foot shuffling. Mr. Ferrand moved things along so fast, Ingrid realized. But it made sense. Six weeks till opening night. How could they possibly do it on their own? She didn't even want to.

But then came a surprise. Meredith O'Malley put her hand over her heart and said, "I don't think Jill would want us to quit."

Heads nodded.

"How about Vince?" Mr. Santos said. "He could take over."

"Vince?" said Mr. Ferrand, not sure whom Mr. Santos was talking about, although Ingrid remembered Mr. Ferrand and Vincent shaking hands in the octagonal entrance hall.

"Vincent, here," said Mr. Santos.

"Oh, yes," said Mr. Ferrand, gazing at Vincent with maybe a glimmer of recognition.

"Vince's got a lot of experience – anybody with eyes can see that," said Mr. Santos.

"How about it?" said Mr. Ferrand.

Vincent shook his head. "I really couldn't," he said. "It's Jill's vision, and besides—"

"Try it for a week or so," said Mr. Ferrand. "How can that hurt?"

"Makes sense," said Mr. Rubino.

"What do you say?" said Meredith.

"Da show must go on," said Mr. Santos in his thickest wiseguy accent.

Everyone's eyes were on Vincent. He took a deep breath. "You flatter me," he said. "I'm touched."

"Meaning yes?" said Mr. Ferrand.

Vincent nodded. "I'll need a key," he said.

twenty-four

sunday morning. The note on the fridge read:

> *Hi Ingrid! I've got an open house till four, Dad's out with the Sandblasters, and Ty stayed over at Greg's. Waffles in the freezer. Have a nice relaxing day. Plus homework. Love, Mom.*

Ingrid toasted waffles. Waffles, such a great invention, and all because of those little squares, like rice paddies, perfect for filling up with a melted butter and maple syrup combo. Another example of what made America great – the nation that turned plain old rice paddies into syrupy butter paddies. As for a suitable drink – how about hot cocoa?

Ingrid sat in the breakfast nook, gazing out at the backyard and the town woods beyond. A clear blue day, the treetops still; but not warm-looking. Cold didn't stop the Sandblasters, a group of fanatical golfers at Dad's club who'd sworn a blood oath or something to keep playing all year long. She'd been forced to take lessons one summer. The outfits, the lingo, the tedium: Ingrid had never laughed so hard in her life, actually rolling around on the practice green one day – her last at the club, as it turned out.

She called Stacy.

"What are you eating?" Stacy said.

"Waffles."

"With that butter syrup thing?"

"Yeah. Any news about Jill?"

"My dad called this morning. She's doing good."

"Did he speak to her?"

"Hey, Dad," Stacy yelled. "Did you speak to Jill?"

Ingrid heard Mr. Rubino in the background. "Just the nurse," he said. "Jill's got a bad headache but she's eating solid food."

"She's eating solid food," Stacy said. "Wanna come over? Sean got a new video game where the whole earth is just a blood cell in the body of the galactic monster."

"Sounds good," Ingrid said. "I'll—"

The doorbell rang.

"Just a sec." Ingrid went to the front door, opened it. Grampy.

"Call you back," Ingrid said.

"Later," said Stacy.

Ingrid clicked off. "Hi, Grampy." Grampy looked perky. Despite the cold, he wore just a T-shirt, plus baggy corduroys and filthy work boots.

"Hi, kid," he said. "Need some help with the chores."

"No one's home," said Ingrid.

"You are."

"Me?" said Ingrid. "What chores?"

"You'll see," Grampy said.

Mystery chores with Grampy versus blood cells in the body of the galactic monster? Maybe Grampy sensed her reluctance. "After that we'll do some shooting," he said. "You can try out my new gun."

"You got a new gun?"

"Wait till you see this baby," said Grampy.

The barn door opened and out came the tractor, Grampy at the wheel. "Hop on," he said.

Ingrid hopped on.

"Ever driven one of these?" he said.

"No."

Grampy looked surprised. "Nothing to it," he said. "Just like driving a car."

"I've never driven a car," Ingrid said. "I'm thirteen."

"Did I remember your birthday?"

"Fifty bucks," said Ingrid.

"No flies on me," said Grampy. He brought the tractor to a stop. "Guess how old I was when I learned to drive," he said.

"I don't know," said Ingrid. The wind was picking up. She could have been warm and cozy in Stacy's entertainment center. Instead she was out on the tundra, playing guessing games with Grampy.

"Go on, guess," he said.

"You took lessons from Henry Ford."

Grampy laughed. "Just about. Tenth birthday. Drove

my friends down to the picnic grounds in the Studebaker."

"Below the falls?"

"What other picnic grounds are there?"

Ingrid had been to the picnic grounds a few times on class trips late in the spring, on those warm days when school had already ended, except on the calendar. They played Frisbee, ate their lunches, watched the water roaring over that long drop to the rocks below.

"Course the moment I got home, my daddy took the belt to me," said Grampy. "Real good. Here, change places."

Ingrid changed places.

"What was your daddy like?" she said.

"Long time ago," said Grampy. "Lower that seat a couple notches. Now turn the key. Gas on the right, brake on the left. Got it?"

"Not really, Grampy, I—"

"This thing here's the shift. Stick it in gear like so. And – we're off."

The tractor shot forward. "GRAMPY!"

"Ease off the gas a touch," said Grampy. "Now we're in business. Nothing to it."

There wasn't.

Ingrid drove the tractor across Grampy's fields. Every so often he'd point out the direction he wanted to go and Ingrid would make a slight change in course. At first she drove in that Mom/Chief Strade style, both hands on the wheel, ten minutes to two; but soon she was experimenting with Dad's two-finger grip. What was more fun than this? Let freedom ring!

"Round the orchard," Grampy said.

Ingrid steered onto the cart path that circled Grampy's apple trees, headed toward the back road. At the top of a rise, the wind rattling some old cornstalks, stiff and brown, he said, "Whoa."

Ingrid stepped on the brake and they came to a stop, maybe a little abrupt. Grampy said, "Look down there and tell me what you see."

Ingrid gazed down a long, gradual slope. "An old falling-down shed. Fields. The back road."

"What about that little sinkhole at the bottom?"

Ingrid saw a small circular depression not far from the road. "What about it?" she said.

"Important environmental feature," said Grampy.

"It is?"

"Not now," said Grampy. "But in the near future."

He climbed down from the tractor, took a wooden crate off the back.

"Grab that cooler," he said.

Ingrid grabbed the cooler, a medium-size one, not heavy. They walked down the slope.

"Is this the land they want for the condos?" she said.

"Soon see about that," said Grampy. "Know how close the water table comes to the surface, down in that sinkhole? Two inches. Now suppose that sinkhole sank some more, got filled up with water permanently. Then what?"

"You could swim in it?" said Ingrid.

"Why'd I want to do a thing like that?" said Grampy. "No circulation. It's gonna be a scum bath."

At the edge of the sinkhole Grampy set down the crate, opened the top.

"What's that?" Ingrid said.

"Dynamite, kid," said Grampy. "Gonna just re-arrange the surface level the teensiest bit."

"But why?"

"Bring that water level up, like I just told you," said Grampy. "Make a nice little pond."

"I still don't get it."

Grampy looked down at her, smiled. "Open the cooler," he said.

Ingrid opened the cooler. Inside lay some freezer bags, maybe a dozen, filled with water, and in the water floated these long strings of tiny round balls, jellylike and almost see-through.

"What are these?"

"Toad eggs," said Grampy. "And not just any toad eggs, but good old –" Grampy dug a scrap of paper from his pocket – "*Scaphiopus holbrooki*, otherwise known as the eastern spadefoot toad." Grampy looked up in triumph.

Ingrid was lost.

"The *endangered* eastern spadefoot toad," Grampy said. "One hundred percent officially endangered, certi-fied Grade A, signed, sealed, and delivered. See where I'm headed with this?"

Ingrid caught the first glimmerings.

Grampy reached into the crate. "What do you think?" he said. "Two sticks or three?"

"You know about dynamite, Grampy?"

His eyes darkened; she guessed he was thinking

about the war. "Hardly a newfangled invention," he said.

In the end Grampy settled on four sticks of dynamite. He and Ingrid huddled behind a big tree, partway up the slope. Grampy pointed a remote – not too different from an ordinary TV remote – and pressed a button. *KABOOM!* A mud cloud rose in the air, real high, for some reason better than any Fourth of July Ingrid could remember, and came splattering back to earth.

"Grampy!" She was jumping up and down.

"Maybe three would have done," said Grampy. But he was smiling, kind of a savage smile if you looked from a certain angle.

It got very quiet, as if all nature was stunned. Water was rising in the sinkhole now, the bottom wet already. Ingrid took off her shoes and socks, rolled up her sweatpants, and went into the hole, planting toad eggs in hollowed-out nests of mud. Endangered-toad eggs – more powerful than any developer, even Donald Trump.

The water rose and rose. It was two feet high by the time they climbed back on the tractor.

"I'm an environmentalist," Grampy said. "That kind of gets lost in the shuffle."

Ingrid dropped Grampy off at the kitchen door, drove back to the barn by herself. She parked next to Grampy's old Caddy, which mostly just sat there ever since he'd got his pickup two years back. A cool car, creamy on the outside, red leather within. Ingrid opened the door: like the tractor, as Grampy said – gas, brake; shift. She noticed that the keys were in the ignition.

She went up to the house. "Grampy? Are we going to do some shooting now?"

No answer. The phone started ringing.

"Phone, Grampy."

It kept ringing. She picked it up.

"Aylmer?" said a man; he sounded old.

"This is his granddaughter," said Ingrid.

"Oh, right," said the man. "Bob Borum here, over on Robinson Road. You people hear sort of a boom a while back? Thought it was a transformer, but we've got electricity."

"So do we," said Ingrid. Absolute truth.

There was a little silence and then he said, "Well, not to worry then."

"'Bye, Mr. Borum."

Ingrid found Grampy lying on the couch in the living room, fast asleep. He looked happy. She covered him up with a threadbare old blanket she found on his rocker by the fireplace.

The thing about Route 392 – the road that went by Grampy's place – was that East Harrow lay on that very same road, ten or twelve miles south. Ten or twelve miles was out of the question for walking, just about out of the question for biking, but a snap in a car. A wild idea, but some of the best ideas were wild – she'd learned that in history. And she had to know.

Ingrid took it one step at a time. Or rather, the steps took her. Step one: back to the barn. Step two: behind the wheel of the Caddy. Step three: adjust the seat. Step four: turn the key.

Vroom. A nice sound. Ingrid checked the shift. *P* for park, *R* for reverse, *N* for God-knows-what, *D* for drive, some other *D*s – one, two, and three for when things got fancy. She wouldn't need them. Nothing was going to get fancy. Ingrid shifted into *D* and drove slowly out of the barn.

Nothing to driving, really, just as Grampy said. The driving age should be lowered at once. Probably all sorts of other things, too – drinking, voting, serving on juries. Kids could handle it. The whole country was missing out on—

This arrow, pointing to 50. Could that be the speed thing? Maybe – those broken white lines were whipping by pretty fast. And the way they were passing right under the car, dead center, seemed a bit off. You were supposed to drive on the … right side of the road, just like with her bike. What a dummy. Ingrid steered over to the right, easing off the gas pedal. Getting a ticket would not be good. She looked around, realized she hadn't been doing much looking around, checking the traffic, driving defensively, as Dad told Ty, ad nauseum, whenever he gave him a lesson. But she had the road to herself – no police cars, no cars at all, nothing to be defensive about. This was meant to be. A minute or two later, the East Harrow sign went by. A minute or two: This was the only way to get around. Her first Caddy.

And then to her right, so soon she almost missed it: MOODUS ROAD. DEAD END. Ingrid turned onto it, remembering the turn signal too late. Moodus Road entered some woods. It got narrower and bumpier, and ended in a circle, like the bulb of a thermometer. On the far side of the circle stood the only dwelling she'd seen, a silver trailer set back in the trees.

Ingrid parked at the bottom of the circle. Oops. What was that? Not a tree, really, more like a little sapling – would probably spring back in no time. She got out of the car and checked the name on the mailbox: KOVAC. Ingrid walked up the pine-needly path to the trailer and knocked on the door.

An old woman opened it, but only as far as the chain allowed, about four inches. She peered out at Ingrid. A real old woman, maybe the oldest person she'd ever seen. Old, old people like this creeped Ingrid out; she couldn't help it.

"I just bought some," the woman said, her voice thin and wavery but angry too. "Not two days ago."

"Bought some?" said Ingrid.

"Girl Scout cookies," said the woman. "One whole box I didn't need."

"I'm not a Girl Scout," Ingrid said. "I'm working on a school project."

The old woman gazed at her. She wore a frayed pink nightgown, open at the neck. Her skin was all wrinkles and green veins and those liver spot things. Plus she had only a few wisps of hair on her head and was missing some teeth. But if you just looked at her eyes, not the sockets around them but right in the center of the eyes, they were actually quite beautiful, a kind of golden brown, and could have been almost any age.

"My project's about the Prescott Players," Ingrid said.

"Good luck to you," said the old woman.

"You're Mrs. Kovac, right?"

The woman nodded, pulling her nightgown closed at the neck.

"The whole ... history, Mrs. Kovac," Ingrid went on, doing some improvising. "With bios and stuff on all the actors. I heard your daughter Kate was one of them."

"I have no daughter Kate," said Mrs. Kovac.

"I'm sorry," said Ingrid. "I read about ..."

"I never had a daughter Kate," said Mrs. Kovac.

"But—"

"She was my granddaughter."

"Oh."

"So you've got a long way to go," said Mrs. Kovac. The golden brown eyes studied Ingrid through the four-inch gap. "Are those braces on your teeth?" she said.

"Yes."

Mrs. Kovac closed the door. Then came the metallic chink of the chain falling free. The door opened.

"Come in," said Mrs. Kovac. "And be quick. Can't you feel the cold?"

Ingrid stepped into a tiny living room with two armchairs and a footstool, covered in a floral print. The chairs also had those – what was the word? doilies – actual doilies, which she'd read about but never seen.

"Sit down," said Mrs. Kovac. "My daughter is dead too, even if that's not part of your project." She went down a narrow corridor.

Ingrid sat in the chair without the footstool. She sat down slowly – those last words of Mrs. Kovac's had chilled her – and looked around. No other furniture in the room but a TV and a floor lamp; the footstool was piled with mail and a few packages, all unopened.

Mrs. Kovac returned. She handed Ingrid a framed black-and-white photo of a girl about her own age. "Katie," she said.

Ingrid gazed at the photo. Not just the same age, but there was a bit of a physical resemblance between them, Katie and Ingrid. Katie had braces on her teeth, for one thing. Hey. Two granddaughters who wore braces. Wore braces and loved acting. Ingrid got a weird feeling, not nervousness, not dread, more like some forces were in the air.

"Pretty, wasn't she?" said Mrs. Kovac.

"Yes."

Mrs. Kovac took the picture, sat in the other chair with a wince, as though something hurt. She stared at the photo. For a moment her voice grew gentle. "A free spirit, as anyone can plainly see." Then she turned the frame facedown in her lap. "What else do you want to know?" she asked, back to her previous tone, a tone that made Ingrid think of the Queen of Hearts.

"Well," said Ingrid. And a question popped out. "What happened to her?"

"Off the rails," said Mrs. Kovac. "It all went off the rails. Topsy-turvy." She closed her eyes. The circles under them were deep and purple-black, the color of the sky after sunset but just before full night. "Is it too much to ask for my reading glasses?"

"Where are they?" said Ingrid.

"If I knew, would I be asking?" said Mrs. Kovac. "They've been missing for days. Why do you think I haven't been opening the mail?"

Ingrid didn't answer.

Mrs. Kovac opened her eyes, turned them on Ingrid. "Because I can't read without my glasses. Couldn't you have figured that out?"

"Where should I look?" said Ingrid. She glanced around, didn't see any glasses.

"It's not important," said Mrs. Kovac.

"Do you want me to go through the mail for you?"

"That's better."

Ingrid knelt by the footstool, went through the mail – mostly junk except for a few bills and one package that had come recorded.

"What's that?" said Mrs. Kovac.

Ingrid read the label. "It's from the Norwich National Bank."

"I don't have an account there," she said, very suspicious.

"It's addressed to you."

"Open it then," said Mrs. Kovac. "Is that what you want me to say?"

Ingrid opened the package. Inside was a letter, a sealed manila envelope, and a box wrapped in white tissue paper and tied with a bow.

"Is that a letter?" said Mrs. Kovac.

"Yes."

"Read it."

Ingrid read the letter aloud, "'Dear Mrs. Kovac, As discussed, we are hereby forwarding the contents of your late granddaughter's safe deposit box. In deepest sympathy, Evelyn White, assistant manager.'"

Mrs. Kovac blinked a few times. "As discussed?" she said. "When in God's name ..." Her voice trailed off. She closed her eyes again, or maybe the eyelids closed on their own, unstoppable. "What's in the box?"

"Do you want me to open it?"

"Is it going to open itself?" said Mrs. Kovac.

Ingrid took off the bow, careful not to damage it, then removed and folded the tissue paper. Inside was a small turquoise gift box. "It's from Tiffany's," she said.

Mrs. Kovac's eyes opened with surprising speed. She held out her hand. Ingrid laid the Tiffany box on her bone-white palm.

"You know what this is, don't you?" asked Mrs. Kovac.

"No," said Ingrid, but if she'd had to bet money –

"The engagement ring Philip Prescott gave her," said Mrs. Kovac.

– she would have won.

Mrs. Kovac opened the box, took out the ring. She held it up to her eyes, very close. "Diamonds," she said. "Worth a pretty penny." She looked across the footstool at Ingrid. "I'll thank you to close the door on your way out."

"But we haven't talked about—"

"I'm asking nicely," said Mrs. Kovac, thrusting the ring deep in the pocket of her nightgown and keeping her hand there. "Why make this unpleasant?"

Ingrid started to rise. "Thanks for showing me the picture, Mrs. Kovac."

"Yes, yes," said Mrs. Kovac. "Nice and tight. The door."

At that moment, Ingrid did something terrible. Rising like that, right by the footstool, it wasn't hard to do. That sealed manila envelope practically slid into her hand. Terrible. But: She and Katie shared things, little things like braces and big ones like love of acting and doubts about mercy being all around. Katie deserved to have her murder solved. Maybe that was a kind of mercy. Ingrid closed the door nice and tight on her way out.

She turned back, listening for movement, a shout, anything, but it was quiet in the trailer. On top of an earth-filled flowerpot by the door, she saw a pair of glasses. They had one of those bands for wearing around the neck. Ingrid hung them on Mrs. Kovac's doorknob.

twenty-five

ingrid drove back down Moodus Road, toward the junction of Route 392. But after a few hundred yards, she couldn't wait any longer. She stopped the car and tore open the manila envelope. Maybe she should have steered over to the side first and then stopped, but—

What was this? Another envelope inside the manila one, an ordinary-size white letter envelope, although the paper had gone slightly yellow, the way paper did with age. Thick, heavy paper, and in the top left-hand corner was a return address, the letters in blue, bumpy to the touch, expensive-looking: Philip Prescott, Prescott Hall, Echo Falls, Connecticut. In the center of the envelope was one typed word: Katie. Ingrid opened it with care.

"My darling Katie," it read, the whole thing type-written:

> *I'm leaving this where I know you'll find it.*
> *Soon there will be a letter from me in that*

ridiculous rag, The Echo, *but I want you to know the truth. Something horrible happened last night. David came up from New York to see me. He asked for money to back some play he's written. Naturally I said no. Finances aren't great right now, as you know, and my record as an angel on Broadway hasn't been stellar. David got very angry. He said outrageous things, the kind no man can let pass. The worst was that I've used my money to buy your love. He can't believe you prefer me to him. This all goes back to when you turned him down, that time he approached you in the wine cellar. He got incensed. He believes you actually do prefer him but are blinded by my (supposed) money. Well, that was a disgusting thing to say about you. I pushed him. It wasn't even a particularly hard push, and besides, he's bigger than I am and – and anyway, Katie, he fell. And somehow he hit his head on a corner of one of those brass radiators – this was in the theater – and oh God he just lay there. Dead. He was dead. Is this really happening? All I know is I can't go to jail. Murder, Katie, or some kind of manslaughter at the very least. It's unimaginable. No one will ever find the body and maybe he won't be missed – just another wandering actor – but I'm leaving before dawn. I don't know where, and anyway the information would be too dangerous for you*

to have, Katie. I don't know what's going to
become of me, so there's nothing I can prom-
ise you. Best to forget about me and go on
with your beautiful and talented life. Please
burn this letter. I'm so sorry.

Philip

Ingrid sat in Grampy's Caddy, stopped in the middle of
Moodus Road, Philip Prescott's letter in her hand. The
sky was darkening. Grampy would be waking up soon,
if he wasn't up already. But her mind was busy – too
busy to allow her to do anything else – connecting the
dots. Philip Prescott killed David Vardack and ran
away, maybe to Alaska, as the letter to *The Echo* said,
maybe not. David Vardack stopped appearing in
movies long ago because he'd been dead all these years.
And now Katie Kovac was dead too, also murdered.
What did Holmes say? When you have eliminated the
impossible, whatever remains, however improbable,
must be the truth. The impossible suspects were Albert
Morales, Lon Stingley, and Mr. Ferrand. Was this the
remaining truth, then: that Philip Prescott was a murderer, that he'd returned and met up with Katie, that
Katie, now half crazy or more and blaming him for her
lost life, had threatened to turn him in – and so he
killed her too? It made sense, linked two murders
neatly, like one of those division problems that came
out evenly.

If so, where was he? What would Philip Prescott look
like today? All she had to go on was that engagement
photo. Back then he'd looked like Chris Farley. Also, he

wasn't tall, about the same height as Katie. A short Chris Farley, but thirty years down the line. Had she seen anyone like that around? No. And – wait a minute. One more thing. Was it possible that Katie would have had trouble recognizing him too?

She began to fit two things together. That footstep she'd heard upstairs the first time she'd been in Katie's house was one. The other was the way Katie had gone all weird when Ingrid mentioned the Prescott Players. At the time it had just been part of Katie's craziness. But ... but could it have been a bulb lighting up in Katie's head? Ingrid had heard her climbing the stairs, just as Murad the taxi driver honked outside. Oh my God.

Ingrid folded the letter, put it back in the manila envelope. She found the headlights switch and turned them on. Then she shifted from *P* to *D* and started driving. This time, turning left on Route 392, she even remembered the turn signal. But she was no longer having fun. Her hands were in the proper ten to two position, locked to the wheel. The river blinked at her through the trees, electric blue, holding on to the dying light.

When Ingrid walked into the kitchen, the Caddy safely back in the barn, Grampy was at the table eating peanuts, shells all over the place.

"A little nap," he said. "Had it up to here with naps. Manage to keep yourself amused?"

"Yes," Ingrid said. "Mr. Borum called. He said he heard a boom."

From the expression on Grampy's face, she could tell

he wasn't pals with Mr. Borum. "What did you tell him?" he asked.

"That we still had electricity."

"Good girl," said Grampy. "And honest, too. Peanuts?"

"No, thanks, Grampy. I better be getting home."

"Take the pickup," Grampy said.

Oh my God. "What did you say?"

Grampy laughed. "Just a little joke," he said, rising. "Driving the tractor around the farm's a lot different from a car on the open road. Don't have to tell you that. You're one of those kids with natural-born good judgment."

Ingrid laughed too.

He drove her home in the pickup. Night had fallen. Grampy was quiet. The headlights bored a long tunnel in the darkness. Ingrid felt very safe there in the cab with Grampy, which was kind of crazy.

For no reason at all, she said, "You're lucky, Grampy."

"Hell, I know that," said Grampy. "I've got you."

He parked in front of 99 Maple Lane. Lights were on inside and the MPV was in the driveway. Ingrid opened the door, the manila envelope under her jacket.

"That little Greenpeace episode?" said Grampy. "Let's keep it between you and me."

Ingrid knew that wouldn't be a problem. Secrets had different weights. The Greenpeace secret was a light one, easy to bear. Other secrets, she was learning, were much, much heavier.

"Night," said Ingrid.

Grampy coughed. "Night," he said, then coughed a few more times, the last one with a little wheeze at the end.

"Grampy, you all right?"

"One hundred and ten percent," said Grampy.

"Chores?" said Mom. "What kind of chores?"

"You know," said Ingrid. "Chores."

"And aren't you supposed to be grounded?" Mom said.

"But Grampy's family. That's still grounded."

A tricky point of family law. Mom gazed at her, then nodded. "How was he?"

"In a pretty good mood," said Ingrid.

"Really?" said Mom. "Did he talk about … the real estate thing at all?"

"Talk about it?" said Ingrid. "No." Strictly true.

Dad came in, golf clubs over his shoulder.

"Hi everybody." He leaned the clubs against the mudroom wall.

"Did you return those movies to Blockbuster?" Mom asked.

"Damn," Dad said, snapping his fingers.

"They're overdue already," Mom said. She glared at Dad.

"I'm sorry," Dad said. "Geez."

Yeah, c'mon Mom – it's only a late fee. Sometimes Mom went way over the top about the littlest things.

The glare faded from Mom's eyes and she sighed. "I'll do it."

"I will," said Dad.

274

"I have to go in anyway," said Mom.

Bzzz. Inspiration zap. "I'll go with you," Ingrid said.

"Have you done your homework?" Mom said.

"Uh-huh," said Ingrid, meaning not exactly done if you meant actually finished and completed, more like it was going to get done, nothing to worry about.

"All right," said Mom.

"The Accused Will Rise?" said the clerk at Blockbuster, gazing at his monitor. "Nope. Try Wally's."

Ingrid turned to Mom. "Can we go to Wally's?"

Mom wrinkled her nose. Wally's was a grubby little video place in the Flats, with an adults-only room at the back.

"What's *The Accused Will Rise?"* Mom said.

"This old movie," said Ingrid.

"Ever seen *The African Queen?"* Mom said. "That's old too. You'd like it. Humphrey Bogart and Katharine Hepburn sail down a—"

"Don't have it either," said the clerk.

Mom drove her to Wally's. It was closed.

Back in her room, Ingrid did her homework. She found herself doing a first-class job, checking all the algebra problems twice, answering every question in the Declaration of Independence packet in whole sentences complete with punctuation, reading the required first three chapters of *To Kill a Mockingbird* with care, absorbing every word. When the homework was all done, another funny thing happened: She wished there were more.

Her door banged open. "Phone," said Ty, tossing it to her.

"Hello?" Ingrid said.

"This is Vincent. How are you doing?"

"I feel bad about Jill."

"As do I," said Vincent. "My clumsiness was the cause, if you want the honest truth."

"I spilled the drink," said Ingrid. "It was my fault."

"Not at all," said Vincent. "Let's call it an accident. Accidents happen. Jill's exact words, by the way. I spoke to her this afternoon and she's doing fine, specifically said she didn't want you to fret."

"She did?"

"Why would I make that up?" said Vincent, his soft voice rising slightly. "But it's not the purpose of my call. I've scheduled an extra rehearsal for tomorrow at seven."

"I'll be there," Ingrid said. "Oh, and Vincent?"

"Yes?"

"Ever heard of an actor named David Vardack?"

Something seemed to change in the phone wire, or wireless wire or whatever it was, like more electricity was pulsing through. Maybe Vincent heard it too, because he was silent for a moment. Then he said, "How are you spelling that?"

Ingrid spelled Vardack.

"Doesn't ring a bell," said Vincent. "Why do you ask?"

"He was in this movie called *The Accused Will Rise*. With Barbara Stanwyck."

"Oh?" said Vincent. "What's it about?"

"I don't really know," Ingrid said. "But David Vardack was a Prescott Player, a long time ago."

The electric pulsing speeded up. "Have you seen the movie?" Vincent said.

"No," Ingrid said. "It wasn't at Blockbuster."

"How did you hear about it?" Vincent said.

"On the Internet."

"Oh dear," said Vincent. "Can't believe everything you see on the Internet. Hardly anything, in fact."

"You don't think it's a real movie? I was going to try Wally's."

"Wally's?"

"The only other video place. It's in the Flats."

"Ah," said Vincent. "The Flats."

Uh-oh. Was he referring to how he'd dropped her there, how she'd fooled him about where she really lived? What else could it be? Maybe it was time to clear the air. "Vincent, I—"

"Must run," said Vincent. The electric pulsing faded fast, down to nothing in an instant. "See you tomorrow night."

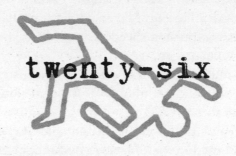

twenty-six

"**welcome,** one and all," said Vincent. "Here are new scripts. You'll notice some little changes."

He passed out the scripts. They sat around the Mad Hatter's table onstage in Prescott Hall – Meredith O'Malley, Vincent, Chloe, Ingrid – a few filtered lights shining down on them.

"Tonight I wanted to nail down the tea-party scene," Vincent said. "We'll begin the croquet match on Wednesday."

Ingrid checked the title page of her script. In place of what had been written there before – "*Alice's Adventures in Wonderland*, by Lewis Carroll. Adapted for the stage by Jill Monteiro" – it now read "*Alice's Adventures in Wonderland*, a play by Vincent Dunn (story by Lewis Carroll)." She opened it to her first line, the opening line of the play. Jill had thought of a really cool beginning: The stage is dark and you hear Alice's long clattering fall down the rabbit hole. Then a spot comes up on her, and she says, "Oh my goodness, where am I?"

The clattering fall was still the same, but – hey. There was a new opening line: ALICE: If I ever lay my hands on that rabbit, he'll be sorry.

Ingrid looked up. Chloe and Meredith were leafing through their scripts; Vincent was watching her. He smiled. "I thought it lacked a little edge," he said.

Meredith blinked. She wore new eyelashes, big enough to make a breeze. "Edge?" she said.

"We're in the twenty-first century," said Chloe.

"Precisely," said Vincent. "Now let's turn to the tea-party scene, page twenty-nine, and do a read-through from Alice's entrance."

After a moment or two Ingrid realized they were all waiting for her.

"Ingrid," said Vincent, "if you please – your mark."

"But Vincent," Ingrid said, moving to the black cross Jill had taped to the stage.

"Yes?" he said.

"I don't understand."

"Understand what, Ingrid?" he said in that soft voice of his.

"My new first line," Ingrid said.

"Of the play?" said Vincent.

She nodded.

"Not strictly speaking the subject of this rehearsal," he said. "No one's fault, but we really don't have a lot of time. Jill was running a little behind schedule."

Meredith and Chloe were turning to the first page, reading the new opening line. Meredith blinked again.

Chloe said, "Pretty cool."

"What's cool about it?" said Ingrid. The words came popping out on their own. Chloe got under her skin like nobody else.

Chloe shrugged. "The old line was so wussy. This gives her some spunk."

"She already had spunk," Ingrid said.

Chloe raised an eyebrow, so maddening.

"There's a difference between being spunky and being mean," Ingrid said. "Like wanting to kill rabbits, for example." Oops. This could be taken as dissing Vincent's work, not nice, and besides, he knew way more about the theater than she did. Maybe he was right. Was Jill's way a little boring, basically the same old thing? She shouldn't have shot her mouth off so fast.

"How interesting," Vincent said, shifting on his stool, changing the angle of the light from above. His face seemed to have gotten a little thinner; he was brilliant, all right. You could see it in his eyes. "Exactly the kind of discussion we can only hope to set off among our audience," he went on. Jill had never mentioned setting off discussions. But so what? Vincent had different goals – nothing wrong with that. "Shall we get to work?" he said.

He, Chloe, Meredith moved their stools closer together – Mad Hatter, March Hare, Dormouse. Ingrid crossed to her mark.

"No room, no room," they all cried.

Vincent held up his hand. "Meredith? Chloe? Try to project a little fear."

"Fear?" said Meredith.

Fear of Alice? Ingrid thought.

"Alice's presentation will be a little different from before," Vincent said. "It will all make sense."

"Different?" said Ingrid.

"Mostly costume and makeup changes, more or less a punk effect," Vincent said. "Plus she'll be armed."

"Armed?" said Ingrid.

"With a croquet mallet," said Vincent.

Chloe laughed.

"In this vision of the material," Vincent said, "Alice appears more as an intruder in a magical world."

"Cool," said Chloe.

"Does that help you at all, Ingrid?" Vincent said.

Ingrid thought about it. Alice *was* sort of an intruder in a magical world, but not in a threatening way. Wasn't it supposed to be a fun story? On the other hand, he might be right. There were times, when Alice got so big, for example – "all persons more than a mile high to leave the court" – that the others clearly thought of her as a threat. Yes, this might work. She even started to feel some excitement. Maybe this was what it was like to work with a really great artist. "It does help," she said.

"Excellent," said Vincent. "Then from 'No room, no room.'"

"No room, no room," they said, Meredith shrinking back this time with her arms raised, like one of those virgins in a Dracula movie.

Ingrid checked her line, "There's plenty of room," in Jill's script. Now it read: "Are you all blind?" She spoke the words: "Are you all blind?"

"A little more feeling," said Vincent.

"Are you all blind?" Ingrid said again.

"Not louder," Vincent said, "so much as … contemptuous."

"Contemptuous?" said Ingrid.

"Sorry," said Vincent. "It means when you feel superior to other people."

Ingrid knew what contemptuous meant. But how did it fit Alice? An intruder and maybe unwelcome, but didn't Alice kind of enjoy all these characters – Hatter, Hare, Dormouse, Caterpillar, White Rabbit, even the out-and-out crazies like the Queen of Hearts? More like a friendly unwelcome intruder. Plus for some reason Ingrid really didn't know how to do contemptuous.

"Try again," said Vincent.

"Are you all blind?"

Vincent sighed. "Think of someone you don't like," he said, "or have problems with."

Chloe, of course. Mr. Ferrand, too. And Ms. Groome. But was not liking someone the same as looking down on them? Was there anyone else, anyone she actually looked down on? No one came to mind.

Ingrid did the next best thing. She thought of Chloe, looked right at her, and tried again. Was that really her voice, so sharp and grating? But contemptuous? She wasn't sure.

Vincent made a note in his script. "Let's move on," he said. "Alice sits down and—" He cued Chloe.

Chloe said: "Care for some wine?" Just as before, in Jill's script.

Ingrid checked her next line, no longer "I don't see any wine," but "In a clean glass." She said it.

"Not so much fussy," said Vincent, "as snobbish."

"Like you know the glasses will be dirty," said Chloe.

"That's it," said Vincent.

Ingrid didn't want any help from Chloe. It pissed her off, and this was no time for that because she needed to focus. Alice was getting away from her. She'd felt so inside Alice at the last rehearsal, just the way acting was supposed to work; now she was starting to feel naked.

She tried the line again, trying to be really nasty, curling her lip. Better? Impossible to tell from the expression on Vincent's face. He made another note on his script.

"Did the lip curling work, Vincent?" Ingrid said.

"Ah, lip curling," said Vincent. "I see. Perhaps some homework in front of the mirror." He turned the page. "Now I – the Hatter – say: 'A clean glass? Then let's all move one place down.'" His voice was suddenly full of charm and at the same time half whacked. Vincent was really very good.

Chloe read her line: "I can't. The Dormouse is asleep."

"Meredith?" said Vincent.

Meredith stopped snoring – a low snore she'd adopted, following Jill's direction – but kept her eyes closed. "Yes?"

"Try whimpering," Vincent said.

"Whimpering?"

"As though you were having a nightmare."

Meredith whimpered.

"Perfect," said Vincent.

She opened her eyes. "Really?"

"Couldn't be better."

Meredith smiled a big moony smile.

"Then comes a bit of stage business for Ingrid," Vincent said.

Ingrid looked down at the script: "(Alice roughly elbows the Dormouse awake.)"

"But—" Ingrid said.

"Can I fall off my chair?" said Meredith.

"Wonderful," said Vincent. "The scene's much too static as is."

What was going on? Why was everyone getting this except her? Ingrid got the crazy feeling that this was turning into *Alice in Wonderland* for real.

"Let's try it now," said Vincent. "Minus the falling, Meredith – we'll have landing pillows for that. Just the elbowing, if Ingrid is ready."

But she wasn't ready. "Do you really think Alice is capable of something like that?" she said.

"Something like what?" said Vincent.

"Violence."

"Isn't everyone capable of violence at one time or another?" Vincent said.

Ingrid didn't know. And anyway, weren't there different kinds of violence, some worse than others?

Vincent waited for a reply, his liquid eyes reflecting a green-filtered light from above. When no reply came, he said, "Shall we?"

Ingrid leaned across the table and elbowed Meredith's upper arm.

"Can we be just a teensy bit more convincing than that?" Vincent said.

"But Vincent."

"What is it?"

Ingrid put her finger on it. "Isn't this supposed to be comedy?" Then she thought of Vincent telling her the plays he'd been in and remembered he didn't do comedy.

"It's my belief, as director," said Vincent, "that there's a little more to it than that."

"A lot more," said Chloe. "It's satire."

Vincent gave Chloe a long look; Ingrid could see how impressed he was. "Satire of the most savage sort," he said.

Chloe smiled.

Something happened in Ingrid at that moment, a hot-red something, rising so fast she was hardly aware of it. The next moment she elbowed Meredith good, and maybe more in the neck than the upper arm this time.

"Ow," said Meredith. "That really, really hurt. What's wrong with you, Ingrid?"

Ingrid started crying, couldn't help it.

"Perhaps that's a wrap," Vincent said.

Ingrid hurried off the stage, up the red-carpeted aisle, into the lobby outside the theater. The *Alice's Adventures in Wonderland* posters – "directed by Jill Monteiro" – had all been taken down. Two doors led out of the lobby – one to the octagonal entrance hall, the other, which was always closed and had a NO ENTRY sign, into the shut-off part of the building. She was probably too upset to notice that the NO ENTRY door was slightly ajar, would not have noticed if a huge cat hadn't suddenly run across the marble floor, a rat in its mouth, and disappeared in the opening.

She went outside. Dad was already there, parked by the door. Practically a first, but thank God, because she heard Chloe and Meredith coming up behind her, didn't want to see them. She got in the car. Dad, punching numbers on a calculator, glanced at her.

"Something wrong?" he said.

Ingrid came really close to spewing out a whole mess of things. But she got a grip, dabbed at her eyes, and just said, "Rehearsal didn't go so well."

"You'll get 'em next time," Dad said, patting her knee.

What a stupid thing to say, like it was football. Ingrid sat stone-faced, arms across her chest. But halfway home, the moon higher in the sky now, no longer lemon yellow but now outlining all the trees and houses in silver, she realized he was right, had confidence in her. She'd get 'em next time.

"Thanks, Dad," she said.

"Huh?" said Dad. "For what?"

Back home, in her room, Ingrid started rereading *Alice's Adventures in Wonderland*, looking for signs of the mean Alice. But the words swam around and soon she could hardly breathe, the feeling of dread so strong inside her. After a while she got up and practiced lip curling in the mirror. She looked like a fool.

Her door opened.

"Phone," said Ty.

"I don't want—"

But the thing came flying in and Ty was gone.

"Hello?" Ingrid said.

"This is Vincent. I sense you're having some slight problem with the new vision."

"A little bit, Vincent. I was looking at the book and—"

"What book?"

"*Alice.*"

"The novel is just the starting point," Vincent said. "The play is completely different, a work of art on its own."

"I know, but I still think it's meant to be a fun thing."

"A fun thing?"

"The whole story of Alice," said Ingrid. "Falling down the rabbit hole, having all these adventures."

"Not all adventures are *fun*, to borrow your little word, and—"

"But in this case—"

"In this case," said Vincent, "as in all cases having to do with the theater, actors must take direction."

Ingrid was silent.

"Perhaps you'd be better off waiting for a production more suited to your capabilities," Vincent said.

Ingrid wasn't sure what that meant. "You're not saying I should quit?" she said.

"That's such a harsh word," said Vincent. "We could

call it a withdrawal, for illness, say."

"Oh, no," Ingrid said. This was her passion, no doubt about it. "I could never quit."

Silence. The strange electric pulse started up in the phone wire again.

"Then perhaps an extra rehearsal might help," Vincent said.

"Oh, yes," said Ingrid. "Thanks."

"Shall we say tomorrow, the regular time?"

"I'll be there," said Ingrid. "Do you want help making the calls?"

"No," said Vincent. "And in the meantime, rethink your approach to this darker Alice. I suggest you work from within."

twenty-seven

the wind rose and the waves rose with them, whipped into a frenzy. At first the snug little boat did what it always did, bobbed snugly along, staying warm and dry. Then a worm crawled up from the space between two deck planks. It started mouthing at the wood. Another worm wriggled up, and another and another. Soon there were hundreds, thousands, millions of worms, chewing and chewing, the worms in a frenzy too, eating the boat out from under her. Ingrid awoke. Nigel was whimpering beside her.

Brucie Berman got on the bus, did what he must have thought of as a cool King Tut dance down the aisle. No one looked at him. He stopped by Ingrid's seat.

"Way cool," he said, "that thing in *The Echo*."

"Huh?" said Ingrid.

"About dogs not voting."

"Guy," called Mr. Sidney from the front. "Zip it."

"Thing in *The Echo*?" said Mia, sitting beside her.

"No one reads *The Echo*," said Ingrid.

"I do," said Mia. "What thing?"

It turned out that lots of people read *The Echo*, including Mr. Porterhouse, a dodgeball lover who taught gym and was also Ingrid's homeroom teacher, which meant taking attendance and recording tardies before letting them loose.

"Our friend Ingrid here made the paper," he said, standing under the basketball hoop and holding up *The Echo*. He took reading glasses from the pocket of his warm-ups – Mr. Porterhouse always wore warm-ups, the colors always intense – and read aloud: "Heard on Main Street. Best quote yet on the widespread and much-to-be-lamented disobedience of the town's leash law comes from the mouth of thirteen-year-old Ingrid Levin-Hill, eighth grader at Ferrand Middle. According to young Miss Levin-Hill, 'The problem is that the dogs didn't vote.'"

No one laughed except Mr. Porterhouse.

"Get it, kids?" said Mr. Porterhouse, looking at them over the rims of his glasses. "Town meeting voted in this leash law thing – but *the dogs didn't vote!*"

Silence, unless all the blood flowing into Ingrid's face made a noise.

Mr. Porterhouse cleared his throat and read on: "We had the pleasure of making Miss Levin-Hill's acquaintance when she dropped by *The Echo* office while researching a school project about 'pretty much anything.' Our intrepid middle-schooler, who has chosen 'The Life and Death of Kate Kovac,' is a young lady to watch indeed."

More silence. Ingrid's embarrassment deepened, got all mixed together with the dread.

"Enough culture," said Mr. Porterhouse. "Choose up for dodgeball."

Mia was a captain. She chose Ingrid first. "What school project?" she said.

Who else was going to be asking that same question?

At lunchtime Ingrid hung out by the swings with Mia and Stacy. No one actually ever swung on the swings, but they stood in a corner of the yard farthest from the school and partially screened off by trees. Clouds were thickening overhead, growing darker and darker, and the wind was blowing across the grounds, scattering dead leaves and the shouts of a bunch of boys playing touch football.

"You sick?" Stacy said.

"No," said Ingrid.

"Does Ingrid look sick to you?" said Stacy.

"Maybe a little," said Mia.

"I'm fine," said Ingrid.

A football came bouncing their way, end over end, and landed in the sand. A boy ran over, picked it up, turned to run back. Joey. Ingrid hadn't recognized him at first, partly because he wore a wool ski hat that hid his blunt-feather thing, but mainly because she'd never seen him run before, hadn't realized he was pretty fast. He saw her.

"Hi," he said.

Joey threw the ball back to the other boys, stayed where he was.

"Hi," said Ingrid.

Stacy and Mia kind of melted away. *What the hell?* Ingrid thought.

"How's it going?" Joey said. His face was getting unpudgier by the day, or maybe it was the ski hat.

"Good," Ingrid said. "You?"

"Good," said Joey. "Um. You know the Rec Center?"

"Do I know it?"

"I mean more like ... ever go there?"

"No."

"Me either," said Joey.

Silence.

"The thing is," he said, "they're gonna start having dances."

"Yeah?"

"Yeah." He kicked at the sand. "Like there's one next Saturday. With a DJ from Hartford."

"Yeah?"

"Yeah. Um. He brings his own sound system. It's supposed to be awesome. The sound."

The school bell rang, lunchtime over. Joey had dug a pretty big hole in the sand with his foot.

"Maybe we could ... go," he said.

"Sure," said Ingrid, and at the same time had a strange thought: *I'd rather go over to your place and have another look at the catapult.* She came very close to saying it – the words were forming on her tongue. Yikes. That would have been so out there, so brazen. Catapult. Oh my God. They'd learned about metaphors. She was losing her mind.

"Sure?" said Joey. "Like yes?"

"Yes."

"Oh," he said. "Good."

They walked back toward the school. Ingrid noticed a police car pulling up to the front door.

"Do you read *The Echo*, Joey?" she said.

"No."

"Do you get it at home?"

"Uh-uh. My dad hates *The Echo*. Why?"

"No reason," Ingrid said. In the distance a man in uniform got out of the cruiser. Too far away to tell if it was Chief Strade, but Ingrid had a feeling. Joey didn't seem aware of any of this.

"I read the *Hartford Courant*," he said.

"Yeah?" Maybe Chief Strade hated *The Echo*, but that didn't mean it wasn't delivered to the station, where someone might point out the Heard on Main Street column. And what then? Chief Strade would find out pretty soon that there was no school project. What was her answer to that? I was misquoted? She'd seen a million interrogations on TV and in the movies. Once you started giving any answers at all, they had you, would uncover every secret, especially when there were secrets like a stolen murder confession lurking around. How many laws had she broken by now? Beyond count. She'd become a career criminal. *A young lady to watch indeed.*

"Just the sports," Joey was saying. "And *Dilbert*. You like *Dilbert*?"

Ingrid stopped. "I forgot something," she said. "Go on ahead."

293

"Forgot something?" said Joey.

"My gloves. I'll catch up."

"Gloves?"

Almost all the kids were filing back into the school. Joey hesitated. Ingrid gave him a little push. He went off.

Ingrid returned to the swings. She glanced back. Joey had almost reached the school, seemed to have his head pointed in the direction of the cruiser, spotting it at last. Ingrid kept going. She got to the chain-link fence that surrounded the school, not high, maybe four feet or so, a symbolic sort of fence. Ingrid climbed it and hurried away.

Cold and blowy. Ingrid wished the madeup gloves were real. She stuck her hands in the pockets of her jacket, bright red, the only bit of color in the whole darkening town. Wally's 99¢ Video Heaven stood at the bottom of Foundry Street across from the empty wasteland where the railroad yards had been. Ingrid didn't get lost on the way – School Street to Bridge, Bridge to Hill, Hill to Foundry. She was learning Echo Falls.

Ingrid opened the door and went inside. One of the reasons people avoided Wally's was the mildewy smell. Another was the gloom, getting darker and darker toward the back of the store, empty now except for Wally, avoidance reason number three, sitting behind the cash register at the front. He wore a tank top and had big flabby arms, a Freddy Krueger tattoo on one and a big WALLY – festooned with razor wire, blood dripping from the tail of the Y – on the other. One of the tattooed blood drops had a hairy mole growing in the center. When you noticed little things, the world could sometimes be a nasty place.

Wally looked up from what he was doing, which happened to be cleaning his fingernails with a penknife.

"Help you?" he said.

"I'm looking for a movie called *The Accused Will Rise*," said Ingrid.

"Jack Palance and Barbara Stanwyck?" said Wally.

"I think so."

"Where he says 'I'm getting on that train' and she says 'If you do it'll be in a box'?" said Wally.

"I don't know," said Ingrid. "I haven't seen it."

"And then Jack Palance throws the city boy down the well, and just when you think he's drowned for sure, his head bobs up one more time like a curse?" said Wally.

"That sounds right," Ingrid said, remembering the details of the blog. "Have you got it?"

"What a question," said Wally. "This is Wally's." He tapped his keyboard, peered at the monitor, nodded to himself. "Here we go – A419, way at the back. Hasn't been rented in five years." Wally folded the knife. "Now what was the name of that actor, the one who played the city boy?"

"David Vardack?" Ingrid said.

Wally looked at her in surprise. "Movie buff, huh?" he said. "I got a discount club here, but you need a driver's license to join. Got one, by any chance?"

"No," said Ingrid. "Was he in any other movies?"

Wally closed his eyes tightly, his face scrunching up

in a really repulsive way. "Drawing a blank on that one," he said. "Which means no, ninety-nine point nine percent guaranteed."

"What became of him?" Ingrid said.

"Showbiz," said Wally with a shrug. "Tell me about it." Did Wally think he was in showbiz? He pushed himself to his feet. "Anything else you want while I'm back there?" he said.

"Is *The Accused Will Rise* the one with the honey scene?" Ingrid said.

"Honey scene?" asked Wally.

"Where Barbara Stanwyck keeps spooning honey into her tea."

Wally shook his head. "Nothing like that in *The Accused Will Rise*," he said.

"It must be in another one of her movies," Ingrid said.

"Nope," said Wally.

"Nope?"

"She never did a scene like that. You're looking at her number-one fan. Name me a Barbara Stanwyck movie and I've seen it a dozen times." Wally started naming them himself. "*Forbidden, Baby Face, Woman in Red, Double Indemnity, Witness to Murder ...*" The list went on and on. He waddled toward the back of the store, disappearing in the shadows. Ingrid heard rummaging, grunting, muttering, more rummaging. The phone rang on the counter beside her.

"Wanna get that?" Wally called.

Ingrid picked up the phone. "Wally's Ninety-nine Cent Video Heaven," she said.

"You open?" asked a man in a low whispery voice that wouldn't have been out of place on a Freddy Krueger soundtrack.

"No," Ingrid said, in case he lived around the corner.

Wally came back empty-handed. "That's weird," he said.

"What?" said Ingrid.

"*The Accused Will Rise*," said Wally. "I know I had it."

"You mean—"

"It's not there," said Wally.

"Maybe it got put on the wrong shelf," Ingrid said.

Wally shook his head. "The backups to my backup systems have backups," he said. "It's gone."

twenty-eight

ingrid lay on her bed. Lying on the bed in the middle of the day – not her at all. Plus it was a school day and she'd just cut for the very first time. She actually wanted to be back in school – even though she'd be in math at this very moment with Ms. Groome – back with the other kids, bored out of her mind and itching to get out of there.

Also, she was feeling weird. Or at least everything around her felt weird. It was hard to describe. All the colors had a brownish tint, like she was trapped in one of those old sepia photos. Maybe that was a result of the day being so dark, but how to explain the fuzziness in the air, how all sound seemed muted and faraway, as though she were wrapped in insulation? At the same time, her hearing was sharp, maybe sharper than ever. Right now, for example, she could hear Nigel down in the kitchen, lapping water from his bowl. How could sound be muted and clear at the same time? *Does she look sick to you?*

Ingrid rose, crossed the hall, went into the bathroom, looked in the mirror to see if she looked sick. Oh my God. Maybe not sick, but something: face pale, lips without color, the only color being those sunken purple half-moons under her eyes. And the eyes themselves? They looked scared. *Get a grip*, she told herself, willing strength and confidence back into her eyes.

How about a cup of tea? She started downstairs. And why not with honey, since it was on her mind. A little strange, Vincent remembering Barbara Stanwyck spooning honey into tea and Wally saying it hadn't happened. Both of them movie buffs, so—

There was a knock at the front door. Ingrid, in the front hall, turning toward the kitchen, froze. Another knock, harder. A voice called from the other side of the door.

"Ingrid?"

It was Chief Strade.

She stayed where she was, silent, motionless.

He knocked again. The door vibrated. "Are you in there, Ingrid?"

She said nothing, hardly breathed.

"Open up, please. I want to talk to you."

She didn't move.

"Can you hear me, Ingrid?" He paused, waiting for a reply. "Are you scared, is that it? If you just tell me what's going on, what kind of trouble you're in, I can help." He knocked again. This time the whole house vibrated, scaring her even more. "Say something."

She kept her mouth shut.

"I know some kids don't like cops," he said. "I

understand that. I'll be fair, whatever happens. I promise you."

Would he be fair? What did that even mean, especially after she told him all her crimes? Fair might just mean she'd get a fair trial. And no matter what, he'd be disappointed when he heard. That went for everyone: Everyone she knew would be disappointed, at the very least, and no one would ever forget or see her the same – the way the DUI had changed how people looked at Sean Rubino. Ingrid didn't say a thing. She had to solve this case, quickly and on her own.

Chief Strade knocked once more, softly this time. His footsteps faded down the walk. A car door opened and closed. The car drove off. Ingrid stayed where she was, just breathing.

Then the phone started ringing. She let the answering machine pick up.

"This message is from the guidance department at Ferrand Middle School. It appears that Ingrid left during school hours without authorization. This infraction automatically puts her at Level Two, meaning a week of detention, and requires parental notification. If there are any questions, please call the office."

Ingrid pressed the delete button.

But what good would that do? Just give her a little extra time, no more than that. Time was closing in, crushing her. She could sense it, sense it in the way the colors were getting squeezed out, in the way sound was getting flattened.

Ingrid looked outside. The school bus was going by, her bus. It was so dark now that Mr. Sidney had the interior lights on. Brucie was tracing the letter *F* on the dusty window, maybe for Ferrand, although Ingrid doubted it.

The phone rang again a few minutes later.

"Hey, Ingrid, you there? It's Mia."

Ingrid didn't pick up, didn't want to start lying to Mia.

"You feeling all right?" Mia said. "Call me."

Mia sounded really worried. Ingrid felt bad. Mia had enough to worry about.

Ingrid went back to her room, closed the door. The day got darker and darker. Time closed in. Her once-snug little boat, now full of worms, took shape around her.

"Ingrid?" Mom's voice, very soft. "Are you all right?"

Mom stood in the doorway, silhouetted in the hall light.

"Yeah," Ingrid said. Had the school – or worse, Chief Strade – gotten in touch with her?

"Just tired?" Mom said; meaning that they hadn't.

"Uh-huh," said Ingrid.

"Wasn't there an extra rehearsal tonight?"

Oh my God. "What time is it?"

"Quarter of seven."

She bolted up.

Mom dropped her in front of Prescott Hall. The wind was blowing hard now, driving the clouds away, exposing the night sky. Across the river, the moon had risen, hung just above the horizon, It was huge, huge and yellow, not the golden yellow of the sun but paler, like lemon sherbet. She'd never seen the moon this big, had trouble accepting it for the real thing. Then that huge cat, almost bobcat size – like everything was growing out of proportion – glided across the parking lot into the shadows of the Hall and disappeared. The moon, the cat: everything growing out of proportion, or … or was she getting smaller, Alice style? This was turning into the weirdest day of her life, and why would tomorrow be any better? She had good reason to believe it was going to be worse.

Ingrid walked up to the front door, opened it, went inside. It was quiet. She walked through the octagonal entrance hall and into the theater. Except for a single spotlight shining on the Mad Hatter's table, the theater was dark and no one was there. Had she gotten the time wrong?

"Hello?" she called.

Vincent's voice floated down from the balcony. "Up here, Ingrid," he said.

Ingrid turned, looked up. In the dim glow of the exit signs and the aisle lights, Ingrid saw him sitting behind the balcony railing, front row center.

"Where is everybody?" Ingrid said.

"No need for the full cast," Vincent said. "A one-on-one will be more efficient. Come on up."

"To the balcony?"

"Sometimes a fresh perspective is all it takes."

That made sense. This new vision of the play was all about perspective; Ingrid saw that. She went back out to the lobby and up the balcony stairs.

"Should I turn on the lights?" Ingrid said.

"If you like."

Ingrid switched on the balcony lights, went down to the front row, sat two seats from Vincent. His driving gloves were curled over the railing.

"Sometimes it's good for actor and director to get better acquainted," he said.

"Thanks for taking the time, Vincent," she said. "But I'm not sure how we're going to do this."

"Do what?"

"The tea-party scene," Ingrid said. "Without the others. We're going to try it again, aren't we? I've been thinking that maybe if Alice is actually frightened inside, her behavior might seem kind of mean but it's only because she's scared."

"Interesting," said Vincent. "And what would she be scared of?"

"Being in such a strange situation," Ingrid said.

"Is that always scary?"

"Maybe at first," Ingrid said. "I don't know."

"I can see you've thought about this," said Vincent. "Like one familiar with strange situations."

She didn't quite get that.

Vincent saw that she hadn't and raised something from his lap. Ingrid had assumed it was a copy of the script, but it was *The Echo*, open to Mr. Samuels's Heard on Main Street column, the part about her circled in red.

"Isn't this a strange situation?" he said. "A schoolgirl getting so interested in a murder?" He glanced down.

"'The Life and Death of Kate Kovac.'" He read that dramatically, like an announcer.

Ingrid didn't like being called a schoolgirl. Vincent was smart and talented, but did that give him the right to be so ... contemptuous? He did contemptuous very well. She didn't say that, of course. But her voice rose a little. "It's not so strange. She was an actress, a Prescott Player on this very same stage."

"Is that a fact?" Vincent said. "What else do you know about her?"

"She was engaged to marry Philip Prescott, the last of the Prescotts, who owned this place. You wouldn't know, being a newcomer, but he broke the engagement and ran away to Alaska, supposedly, which was what started all her problems."

"Supposedly?"

"That's what people say."

"Based on what?"

"He wrote a letter to *The Echo*. I saw a copy."

"Where?"

She was about to say "At the *Echo* office" when she remembered that in fact Chief Strade had shown it to her. But she didn't want to bring him up, so she said, "In my research."

Vincent was watching her closely, liquid eyes yellow under the balcony lights. "But you doubted the letter?"

"Not at first."

"But now?"

Now, having read Philip Prescott's letter to Katie, which made no mention of Alaska, she had her doubts, but how could she say that without exposing everything?

Vincent spoke again, his voice as soft as she'd ever heard it. "Why do you doubt he went to Alaska?"

"It's just a feeling," Ingrid said.

"Just a feeling?" Still soft, the voice, but the contemptuous part was back.

She nodded.

"I assume that drive we took to the Flats was part of your research," Vincent said.

"I'm sorry about that, Vincent. I didn't mean—"

He raised one of his long, saintly hands. "We all have our little secrets," he said.

At that moment – irony, essence of – Ingrid was suddenly tempted to spill the whole thing, every secret she had, crimes and all. Did she know anyone smarter than Vincent? Probably not. Plus he was sophisticated and unconventional, might come up with an answer no one else would, the same way he had an original vision for Alice. But there was that contemptuous tone. Maybe it went along with being so brilliant, but she didn't like it.

"Having deep thoughts?" he said.

"Not really," said Ingrid. "Should we get started?"

"Started?"

"On the play."

"Oh, that. So much less interesting than your little project. Tell me what else you've discovered."

"Barbara Stanwyck didn't spoon honey into her tea," Ingrid said. "At least according to Wally at Wally's Video, and he's seen all her movies."

Vincent went still. Maybe he didn't like being corrected. And why, of all things, had she brought that up? It wasn't connected to anything, except perhaps very distantly to the David Vardack thing, and Vincent had already told her he'd never heard of him.

"I must have been mistaken," he said. "But how does that fit into your research?"

"It doesn't, really," Ingrid said. "Should we try the tea-party scene or something else?"

Vincent reached for his driving gloves. "I'm afraid I have some unpleasant news. For the good of the play, especially in light of the new vision, I've decided that Chloe will take over the role of Alice."

Ingrid actually felt faint, the theater turning white around her. "But we haven't even worked on it yet, Vincent. I know if I had another chance—"

"Time is against us," Vincent said.

It came out of nowhere. She was stunned. "Then you … you'd already made up your mind. Why did you bring me here?"

"To get better acquainted, as I said. But in doing so, I'm more convinced than ever that your talents lie in the comic vein, as I suspect you know yourself."

Was he right about that? Even if he was, it didn't make this fair. She wanted to cry but was too damn angry.

"You should have just told me on the phone."

"The personal touch is always preferable," Vincent said, "although perhaps you're right in this case. But in the end, the play's the thing, the only thing."

So unfair. But maybe Dad was right, maybe it was like sports, and that made Vincent a sort of coach. Ingrid remembered what had happened to Stacy when she'd gotten into a battle of wills with Coach Ringer, how she'd been sent down to the Bs even though she had the strongest foot on the team. No *I* in team. And this wasn't like being cut, more like switching positions. Come on, step up.

"When's the next rehearsal?" Ingrid said.

"I beg your pardon?" said Vincent.

"I'll need to learn the March Hare, won't I?"

"Ah," said Vincent. "The March Hare is now in the hands of Mrs. Breen."

Mrs. Breen, the bank teller who could cry on cue? Ingrid barely heard what came next.

"It's best that you sit this one out," Vincent was saying. "You'll come back to the next production rested and refreshed, like a rebirth. That's how we learn in the theater. Trust me."

Ingrid jumped up. "No," she said. "It's not right."

Vincent rose too, one hand on the railing. Somewhere along the way, he'd put his gloves on. "An actor must take direction," he said, "or—"

"Hey, Ingrid!" a voice called from down in the orchestra. Ty. "Didn't you hear the horn?" She – and Vincent – looked down. Ty was looking up. He wore his red varsity jacket, and from this angle his shoulders looked huge. "Mom's been honking for five minutes."

"We can't have that," said Vincent.

They rode home in the MPV, Ingrid crying a little in back.

"Acting's for losers anyway," said Ty. "Besides, you're okay at soccer."

twenty-nine

no i in team, but two I's in
Ingrid. Or two eyes. Two eyes in Ingrid, but she still
couldn't see. She lay in bed, weird, useless thoughts zipping through her mind. And always questions: If Philip
Prescott, already a murderer once, had indeed returned
and killed Katie, where was he? What had happened to
the body of David Vardack? Why had Philip been so
sure that the body would never be found? And why had
Vincent wanted to get better acquainted if he'd already
made up his mind? Why Chloe? And even Mrs. Breen
ahead of her, with those big fat tears and total inability
to memorize lines.

The house was quiet, the moonlight shining on
Mister Happy. Sleep would have been bliss, but not the
kind of stormy sleep that awaited Ingrid. Every time she
got close, her wormy boat started going under. After a
while, she climbed over Nigel, got out of bed, and went
to her computer.

She Googled Philip Prescott and again got only the

one relevant hit. She tried David Vardack, got that one link to a movie lover's blog. Her fingers lay on the keys, tapping lightly, not making anything appear on the screen. Then they pressed a little harder and typed in Vincent Dunn.

Three hits. The first took her to whitehorseplay.org, which sounded like one of those sites she wasn't supposed to go to but turned out to be the Web page for the Whitehorse Community Theater. Their upcoming production was *The Glass Menagerie*, Vincent Dunn directing.

The second link was a year-old review of a *Death of a Salesman* production in the *Whitehorse Weekly News*. Vincent's name appeared in the middle: "... and the very talented Vincent Dunn, longtime stalwart in local theater circles, gave a riveting performance as Biff." Biff – the role Vincent mentioned when he was telling Jill about his stage fright – but not a word in this review about him stepping in at the last minute. Was it the same Vincent Dunn?

She tried the third link, also to the *Whitehorse Weekly News*, but this time ten years old. It was a short column called Arctic Artmakers, with single-paragraph write-ups of a sculptor, a poet, two candle makers, and Vincent, down at the bottom.

> And what a joy to have the gifted Vincent
> Dunn in our community. When asked why
> he never made a grab for the "big time" of
> Hollywood or Broadway, the soft-spoken Mr.
> Dunn replied he was happy with life "just as

*it is." To which this columnist can only say,
"Bravo!"*

Soft-spoken. Had to be the same Vincent Dunn. But where was this Whitehorse place? Ingrid Googled that too. Turned out to be in the Yukon, part of Canada. She went to maps.com. Hey. A part of Canada, all right, the part right next to Alaska. In that farewell letter to *The Echo*, the one full of lies, Philip Prescott had written about maybe going to Alaska. Meaning? Ingrid didn't know, felt confused. A neat solution to everything would be if Vincent Dunn resembled Philip Prescott, but he didn't – too tall, too thin, too dark, things thirty years going by wouldn't change. But was it possible they knew each other? Two guys into the theater, stuck in some frozen God-knows-where? And if they did, so what? Ingrid had no answers, but while all this thinking was going on, she was also getting dressed. She had to know.

Not a sound. That was very important. Ingrid crept downstairs, put on her red jacket, plus her pom-pom ski hat and wool gloves. She went into the kitchen, opened the door to the garage, went inside. Her bike leaned against the back wall, moonlight gleaming on the handle-bars. Ingrid wheeled it out the side door, hopped on, and pedaled away.

She knew the town now, had been paying attention whenever Mom or Dad drove her someplace. No traffic, like all of Echo Falls lay in a deep sleep. Maple Lane to Avondale, Avondale to Bridge, Bridge to—

A car was coming the other way. Ingrid pulled to the side trying to get in the shadows, out of the headlight glare. The car sped by, the sign on its roof lit up: TAXI. Ingrid pedaled on. Bridge to the other side of the river, then right on Upper Falls Road.

The moon hung high overhead now, at the very top of the sky, and so bright. The coldest night of the year so far: Ingrid could see her breath, and frost coated the ground, the first frost, shining in the moonlight like the whole world was turning silver, beautiful and scary at the same time. And she was already scared, big-time. She took a deep breath and kept pedaling.

Upper Falls wound through some trees, climbed a hill. Ingrid heard that *shhhh* sound of the falls, somewhere to her right. She rounded a bend, and there at the top of the hill stood Prescott Hall, huge and dark, darker than the sky, except for moonlight sparkling on all those windowpanes.

Ingrid rode through the gates, up the long drive, into the parking lot. Vincent's car was parked near the door. He was director now, had a key, would be sleeping backstage, overcoming his stage fright. Did he look like the stage fright type? Not to her.

She laid her bike against the stone steps, climbed them to the front door, tried it. Locked, of course. She glanced around. Maybe by circling the Hall, she might find a—

What was that? Something came gliding out of the night; not something but a cat, that big cat, bobcat size. It crossed the lowest stone step, tail high, and ran alongside the left-hand wing of the Hall. Then it disappeared, in a flash, as though swallowed up by the brick wall.

Ingrid went down the stairs, walked through the empty flower beds beside the left-hand wing, following the cat's path. Something about that cat was bothering her, but she couldn't think what. At the spot where the cat had disappeared, she knelt and examined the wall. Not all brick: down at ground level was a small square made of wood. She pushed and it gave. A cat flap. This one was big enough for a real big cat, maybe even big enough for a girl Ingrid's size. She tried it – yes, just big enough. She wriggled through to the other side: down the rabbit hole.

Ingrid stood up. Moonlight came through tall leaded windows. She was in a big room, empty except for a billiard table in the center and delicate spiderwebs glinting here and there. A faint sound came from far away, like scraping, maybe. Moving toward it, she stepped into a spiderweb right away, getting it all over her face. She felt the spider itself on her cheek, brushed it away with a little cry, couldn't help herself. The next second it got very quiet; silent, in fact, no scraping sound.

Ingrid crossed the room, running her fingers over the billiard table on her way – dust an inch thick. On the other side stood a heavy wooden door with metal studs in it, open a foot or so. She stepped into a corridor, dark and windowless. Which way? She was in the closed-off part of the Hall, unfamiliar territory.

Something brushed her leg, something soft and strong at the same time, also intelligent: the cat's tail. It moved off, like a flowing shadow, down the corridor to her right. The feeling of cat tail brushing her leg: When had she felt that before? It dawned on her, and with that dawning came what had been bothering her about this big cat: Katie Kovac had had a bobcat-size cat too, a cat that had brushed against Ingrid this very same way in the purple-and-gold parlor at 341 Packer Street. Ingrid even remembered wondering what had happened to it. Couldn't be dumber if she tried. And don't leave out that bag of kitty litter in Vincent's car. Griddie the dunce. She followed the flowing cat shadow down the unlit corridor, somewhere in the closed-off part of Prescott Hall.

Ingrid followed. The cat led. Katie Kovac's cat, and Ingrid got the feeling it really was leading, not going too fast, staying in sight: along the corridor, then up one of those circular staircases, like climbing in a shaft of total darkness. But there was light at the top, dazzling moonlight, flooding in through a glass ceiling. She was in an enormous room with a grand piano and music stands at one end, cobwebs everywhere. The cat's paws left shallow depressions in the dust on the parquet floor.

An easy trail to follow. Ingrid followed it down a grand white marble staircase, like from some palace. The cat lay curled up on the bottom step, eyes closed.

Ingrid looked around. To her right a wide hall led into darkness. Straight ahead two tall glass doors opened onto a terrace; a stone planter, big enough to hold a small tree, had fallen on the terrace and cracked in two. To her left lay a narrow corridor, also dark, but at the very end glowed something faint and blue. Ingrid went left, leaving the sleeping cat behind.

Ingrid walked down the dark corridor, her feet silent on the wooden floor. She heard the scraping sound again, louder now, coming from somewhere below. Several doors opened off the corridor, ignored by Ingrid. She moved toward that blue light.

End of the corridor, door partly open. Ingrid peeked around the edge. She saw a big square room – a library, for sure, with floor-to-ceiling shelves, all empty. No one there. In the center of the room – dark and windowless – stood three things: an iron bedstead she recognized from the props department; an open suitcase lying on the bed; a laptop computer, also open, sitting on the floor, the source of that blue glow. A movie was playing on the computer screen, some sort of Western, the voices of the characters too soft to drown out the scraping sound from below, louder now, and metallic.

Ingrid moved into the room, real quiet, except for her heartbeat of course, probably audible for miles. She stood over the bed, looked into the suitcase. On top of some clothes, neatly folded, lay two things. The sight of them took her breath away; she really couldn't breathe for ten or twenty seconds.

The two things in the suitcase. One, the Prescott Players playbill for the *Dial M for Murder* production. Two, a DVD box – *The Accused Will Rise*, starring Jack Palance and Barbara Stanwyck. A sticker on the box read WALLY'S 99¢ VIDEO HEAVEN.

Ingrid picked up the playbill, gazed at Katie Kovac's frightened face and the silhouette of the man who was frightening her. She opened it, found cast pictures.

314

Another photo of Katie, smiling now, her hair loose, very pretty. David Vardack's photo was right below. And in the margin, written in ink: "Katie, it's been a treat. Hope to do this many many more times. Love, David."

Scrape, scrape.

Ingrid stared for the first time at the face of David Vardack. A very handsome face, maybe even movie-star handsome, with big dark eyes, long dark wavy hair, good bones. Was it possible? He looked so young. She didn't know, couldn't tell, wasn't getting this at all.

The DVD box was empty. Ingrid turned to the laptop. A beautiful woman with spitfire eyes slammed a door in a man's face. Barbara Stanwyck and Jack Palance: She knew from the picture on the box. Then came one of those fades and Jack Palance was peering down a well. He sees another man – David Vardack – down at the bottom of the well, treading water in dusky light. Jack Palance smiles a nasty smile – a little over the top in Ingrid's view; she registered that, despite everything. Then the camera closes in on David Vardack. He says something. Ingrid bent closer so she could hear.

David Vardack spoke his line: "I'll be in your dreams every night for the rest of your life."

That voice. Ingrid knew. For absolute sure. David Vardack and Vincent Dunn were one and the same. Barbara Stanwyck had never spooned honey into tea in a movie. Vincent had seen her doing it for real, on the set or in a restaurant. He'd made a mistake, an absolute giveaway. She'd been so dumb.

Jack Palance laughed an evil laugh but looked a bit

worried. He covered the well with a piece of sheet metal.

Ingrid had a sudden thought, a really amazing one, maybe the kind Sherlock Holmes would have had, if he'd lived to see laptop computers. She clicked online. That bar came up at the top, the one with Favorites in it. Click on Favorites. Vincent Dunn had only one: prescottrevival.org, the site all about the renovation project, the site she'd scanned in the visuals for. Ingrid checked History. He'd been to prescottrevival.org dozens of times, going back for months. Why?

A vibration came through the floorboards, like a far-off trembling. Scrape, scrape.

Ingrid rose. There were two doors in the library, the one she'd come in through and a second at the other end. That was the one she took. She was so close to knowing everything.

The second door led to a wooden staircase, going down, a fancy, carpeted staircase with dark banisters and an oval window in the wall. The moon was still out there, a little lower now.

At the bottom of the stairs she came to a closed door. She opened it, slow and soundless. Right away the scraping got louder. More stairs, crude now, the wood rough and unfinished; but dust free and cobweb free, she found as she started down into darkness. She came to a landing, made a U-turn, descended another flight, then one more, each step careful, silent. She said to herself: *Don't take any chances*.

A light glowed at the bottom, not blue this time, but yellow. Something thumped. A man grunted. Ingrid kept going, down to the last step.

She was in a basement or sub-basement, lit by one of those workmen's lights, the kind with a caged bulb, hanging over a chair. The chair stood at the edge of a deep pit in the brick floor. At the other side of the pit rose a mound of bricks and earth. And in the pit, stripped to the waist, sweat dripping off his face, was Vincent Dunn. He was turned sideways to her, digging with a long wood-handled spade, his chest and arms, dirt smeared and sweaty, much stronger-looking than she would have thought.

Vincent dug up a spadeful of earth, tossed it on the pile, then another and another, working fast. Five or six spadefuls later, the blade clanged on something hard. Vincent grunted again. He bent down, out of Ingrid's sight, then rose with something in his hands. A typewriter, covered with dirt. He opened a heavy-duty green plastic garbage bag folded by the mound of bricks and earth and stuck the typewriter inside.

A typewriter? Ingrid made a connection. Philip Prescott's farewell note to Katie, the one where he confessed to killing the man now digging this hole, was typewritten, right down to the signature. And therefore?

Vincent started working even faster, flinging the dirt up out of the hole, panting with effort. The blade struck something else down in there, not with a clang this time, more of a crack. Vincent laid the spade aside, bent down again. This time when he rose, he had a human skull in his hands.

He climbed up out of the hole. Wearing sneakers, yes, Adidas sneakers, with green paint spatters. He held up the skull, gazed at it. Philip Prescott hadn't made it to Alaska or anywhere else. He'd never even left home.

It was all clear to Ingrid, pretty much explained by the farewell note, if you just changed things around a little, like who killed who. Then, thirty years later, up in Whitehorse, Vincent Dunn, formerly David Vardack, surfing the net – or maybe checking up on things back in Echo Falls, maybe he'd been worried the whole time – discovers the renovation plans, realizes that big changes are coming to Prescott Hall. Changes like walls coming down and floors getting dug up. Ingrid remembered now that a whole new heating system was going in – furnace, boiler, all that, way down here someplace. So he had to come back, had to get inside Prescott Hall and remove the evidence when no one was around. And Katie? Ingrid was starting to get an idea about what had happened with her, but there'd be plenty of time to piece that together. She had all she needed. Now was the moment to run silently back up, get out of Prescott Hall, and tell Chief Strade everything. Ingrid turned to go, and as she did, she felt the soft, strong, intelligent brush of cat tail against her leg. Then came a meow, maybe not very loud, but it sounded like a scream down there under Prescott Hall.

Vincent's head snapped around. He saw her, looked stunned. Then his face changed, came close not only to looking normal but to making the whole scene somehow look normal. He was a great actor.

"What brings you here?" he said; that soft voice not quite at its softest; there was something like barbed wire underneath.

"You didn't have to kill Katie," Ingrid said. She couldn't help herself.

There was a long pause. Vincent's eyes, dark, liquid, picked up the yellow light from the caged bulb, reflected it at her. He took a deep, regretful breath. "So I thought," he said. "She didn't even recognize me. And the irony is she'd completely lost her appeal, the way she turned out. You wouldn't know about irony, too young." His lips quivered up in a fleeting little smile. "And now you'll never know."

Ingrid backed up one step. "But Katie finally figured out who you were," she said. Ingrid had seen it happen, had even been the cause of it, bringing up the Prescott Players; she just hadn't understood.

"Unfortunate for her," said Vincent. "But a just ending, when you consider."

"Consider what?" Ingrid said.

The soft surface of his voice cracked completely, like an eggshell when some baby reptile breaks through. "Don't you realize what I could have been? Brando, Olivier, even better. A towering figure. A paragon. A legend." Philip Prescott's skull trembled in his hands.

But he couldn't be in the movies as long as Katie thought he was dead. How many thousands of times had he watched that well scene? "You kind of trapped yourself with that good-bye letter," Ingrid said.

He didn't like that at all. His face got savage. A vein throbbed in his neck, green and twisted. And then he was after her, springing across the pit, the skull hanging in midair for an instant before falling back down with a thud.

Ingrid turned up the stairs and ran. She could run, had always been able to run, but never like this, flying. To the landing, up to the next flight, and the next, banging through the half-closed door that led up to the fancy staircase and the library. But had there been windows in the library? No. She needed windows, a door, a way out, something. At the base of the fancy stairs she saw another door and tried that.

It led to another corridor, this one almost completely dark, but what was that? A moonbeam glow at the end. She raced down the corridor, burst into a big room, walls and ceiling all glass. What was this? The greenhouse, conservatory, whatever they called it, lit up by the moon. She'd seen it from the outside, knew its placement – ground level at the back of Prescott Hall. The door. She ran to it, her footsteps echoing on the flagstone floor.

Locked. Locked, but made of glass. She kicked at it, kicked at it again. Glass shattered all over the place. She kicked once more, bending back the metal framework, then leaped through.

Ingrid ran along the back of Prescott Hall. She had to round the corner of the building, not far, ten or fifteen yards more, and then get herself down the long slope to Upper Falls Road. There were houses on Upper Falls Road. She'd be safe.

Faster, Griddie. To her right the falls were going *shhhh*. Up ahead lay one of those bulkhead door things built against the side of the Hall, and right after that came the corner. Ingrid dodged around the bulkhead doors, and as she did, they burst open and Vincent came hurtling out with a wild cry that almost killed her all by itself.

He crashed into her, knocked her down, grabbed her. They rolled across the frost-coated grass. Ingrid squirmed out of his hands, sprang up, ran from him, toward the river, trying to make a wide turn, but she slipped on all that frost and went sprawling. And he was on her again, with one of those grunts of his. They rolled and rolled and then, with a sudden lurch, went hurtling down the steep drop-off, down, down, and splash. Into the river.

The cold made her gasp. She heard Vincent gasp too. Then the river swept her away, so strong, so fast. She tried to kick, to swim, could do nothing, her whole body freezing up. The water soaked her clothes, weighing her down, but the current was so swift, she stayed on the surface. The *shhhh* of the falls grew into a roar, two echoing roars, crazier and crazier. Then crack. Her head struck something hard and she came to a halt.

The boom – that line of buoys strung across the river just above the falls. She grabbed hold of a buoy, clung to it. The river tore past her, trying to rip her free. Ingrid held on with all her might, the roar of the falls so close.

And there, just a few feet away, also hanging on to the boom, was Vincent Dunn. He was shivering. So was she. Moonlight sparkled in his eyes, on his forehead and cheekbones; the rest of his face was shadow. *Those flashing eyes.* She'd seen them before. What had happened to Jill was no accident. *Beware! Beware!* He was a great improviser.

That vein throbbed again in Vincent's neck, black now in the moonlight. "This can still work," he said.

Then he came toward her, hand over hand along the buoys. Ingrid tried to back away, tried to move toward shore, but her hands seemed to be stuck to the boom. He raised himself up, got one hand on top of her head, forcing her underwater, down under the buoy line. The river ripped at her. She was going to die. She started going out of her mind with fear. Then she remembered Grampy. This was way past the point of fear. This was him or you.

Vincent pushed and pushed. Ingrid's job was to hold on. Hold on no matter what. Hold on to the boom and hold on to her breath. Him or you. She held on. She kicked. She wriggled. She kicked again and suddenly Vincent lost his grip on the buoy, and then he was underwater with her, both those long thin hands slipping down her body, then clamping tight around her legs. She kicked at him, kicked and kicked with all her strength. Him or you. He slid down farther, now had her just around the ankles. The force of the river tugged her body way out under the boom, toward the falls, and his even more. She held on to the buoy – death grip, yes – and did a writhing thing, trying to snap her legs. Her shoes came off in his hands. The river tore him loose at once.

Ingrid pulled herself up, gasped in a huge lungful of air. She hung on. Vincent bobbed up to the surface. He tried to swim, got nowhere, helpless in the torrent. The river rushed him along, closer and closer to the edge. His head turned toward her, the color of bone in the moonlight, mouth opening in a round black zero. And then he was gone, as though jerked from sight by a chain.

The falls grew quieter, closer to their normal *shhhh*. Ingrid hung on to the boom, or maybe she was simply frozen to it. She shivered uncontrollably. She tried to say, "It's all about shoes," but couldn't make the muscles of her mouth do a thing.

Then the moon got very weird, kind of doubling up. Moon one kept shining down in the usual way, cold, distant, incurious. But moon two was different, poking around here and there in the river, a narrow, probing kind of moonbeam. It shone on her for a second, went away, came back.

Another noise started up, not a *shhhh* but a motor. It grew louder. Then came voices. A wave splashed over her. Just great. Now waves. She turned to see what could possibly be making waves and saw a boat standing alongside her, the word POLICE on the hull.

Then strong arms were around her, lifting her out of the river. She looked up, saw Chief Strade. He wrapped her in a blanket. She felt a little guilty. He deserved an explanation.

"It's all about shoes," she said. But total garble, teeth chattering, face numb. She saw he didn't understand and tried again. Uh-uh.

"You can explain later," said Chief Strade.

"Now you're talking my language," Ingrid said.

He didn't get that either.

thirty

nigel ended up being the hero. He'd woken up during the night – hungry? thirsty? sufficiently rested? – and noticed that Ingrid wasn't there. That had led to a lot of whining, barking, and clawing at closed bedroom doors until the whole house was up. They'd phoned the police. Not too long before that, the police had taken a call from Murad the taxi driver, best hero in a supporting role. Murad had noticed a kid biking across the bridge in the middle of the night, a kid way too young to be out at a time like that. Only two dots to connect. The dispatcher had done it herself, although she let Chief Strade think it was all him.

Ingrid stayed in the hospital overnight for observation but didn't observe anything, just slept a deep sleep, Mom sitting in a chair beside her, Dad out in the hall with Chief Strade. In the morning she went home. Dad carried her upstairs, entirely unnecessary. "What did the duck say to the horse?" he asked, and answered it. "Why the long face?"

"Please," said Ingrid.

She slept some more. Nigel kept licking her face and had to be sent from the room. Ingrid hardly noticed. She didn't wake up until late afternoon, when Mr. Sidney tooted the school bus horn on the way by.

Albert Morales and Lon Stingley were released from jail. They hired a lawyer to sue the town. Mr. Santos stepped into the role of the Mad Hatter as well as directing the play. He began preparing yet another script, this one more of a *Goodfellas* meets *Alice* kind of thing, but Jill Monteiro made a sudden rapid turn for the better, checked herself out of the hospital, and took over, putting Ingrid back in the Alice role. The Ferrands flew off on an impromptu breather to St. Barts, and Chloe resigned from the production.

On Friday, Ingrid's first day back, Ms. Groome sprang a pop quiz and she got forty-seven percent, her all-time lowest. She remembered the different branches of arithmetic, as defined by the Mock Turtle – ambition, distraction, uglification, and derision. The Mock Turtle had gotten it right.

After school, Chief Strade came over to the house for a long talk, off the record. They sat in the dining room. He was very gentle, promised that nothing she said would leave the room. She knew she owed him. On the other hand, he was going to be disappointed. She was still going back and forth when Ty poked his head into the room and said, "What were these doing in my closet?" He held up her red Pumas, the ones with the ID disks from soccer camp. Ingrid made a full confession. The chief was silent for a minute or so afterward.

Then he rose, shook her hand, and left.

Saturday morning Vincent Dunn's body was found snagged on a public pier way downstream, twenty miles or so.

Saturday night Ingrid went to the Rec Center dance with Joey. He turned out not to be much of a dancer. Also, the DJ played a lot of classic rock, which Ingrid despised. After a while they went to the side table for some punch and pizza. Joey's face was very red.

"I'm building a telescope," he said.

"Yeah?"

"Not grinding my own lenses or anything like that," he said. "Don't get me wrong."

Ingrid sipped her punch – delicious.

"I'll be able to see the moons of Jupiter," Joey said.

"Jupiter has moons?"

"A ton," said Joey. Long silence. "Jupiter's in the sky right now," he said. "If you want to take a look."

"Okay."

They went out the back of the Rec Center, across the tennis courts. The sky was cloudy, completely covered over, which was just fine with Ingrid – she wasn't in the mood for moonglow.

Joey looked up in chagrin. "How did that happen?" he said.

Ingrid laughed. Joey could be pretty funny.

He reached for her hand, a sudden movement that went awry, ended up as a kind of karate chop to her elbow. Then he tried again and got it right. They went for a walk.

*   *   *

From the Arts, Entertainment, and Things to Do page of *The Echo*:

> *Run, do not walk, to catch the Prescott Players'* *energetic new production of* Alice's Adventures in Wonderland, *directed by Echo Falls' very own Broadway star, Ms. Jill Monteiro. Old Prescott Hall rocks with laughter and merriment as the Lewis Carroll classic is brought noisily to life. Kudos to the whole wonderful cast, but special mention must be made of Sylvia Breen, for her surprising performance as a teary-eyed duchess; Harvey Santos as the most menacing caterpillar this reporter has ever encountered; and finally young Ingrid Levin-Hill in the title role, for her witty portrayal of a girl struggling to inject some sanity into a world gone mad.*

Ingrid's investigations
continue in ...

BEHIND THE
CURTAIN

Turn the page to read
the first chapter.

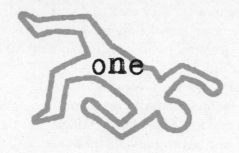

one

ingrid Levin-Hill sat in math class, her mind wandering pleasantly. She had the best seat in the house – very back of the outside row by the windows, about as far as could be from the teacher, Ms. Groome. Ferrand Middle School stood on a hill overlooking the river, about a mile upstream from the falls. There was always something interesting to see on the river, especially if, like Ingrid, you were in the habit of noticing little details. Little details like how the water ruffled up as it flowed around a rock, and a big black bird drifting on the current, wings tucked under its chin, and—

"Ingrid? I trust I have your attention?"

Ingrid whipped around. Ms. Groome was watching her through narrowed eyes – and her eyes were narrow to begin with.

"One hundred percent," said Ingrid, in the faint hope of pacifying her teacher with math talk.

"Then I'm sure you're excited about MathFest."

MathFest? What was Ms. Groome talking about?

The word didn't even make sense, one of those contradictions in terms. "Very excited," said Ingrid.

"Just in case Ingrid happened to miss any of this," said Ms. Groome, "who wants to sum up MathFest?"

No one did.

"Bruce?" said Ms. Groome.

Brucie Berman, middle row, front seat, class clown. His leg was doing that twitchy thing.

"MathFest be my guest," said Brucie.

"I beg your pardon?"

Brucie tried to look innocent, but he'd been born with a guilty face. "Three lucky kids from this class get to go to MathFest," he said.

"And MathFest is?"

"This big fat fun math blowout they're having tomorrow," said Brucie.

"Not tomorrow," said Ms. Groome. "Saturday morning, eight thirty, at the high school."

"Even better," said Brucie.

Ms. Groome pursed her lips, totally focused now on Brucie. There was a lot to be said for having Brucie in class. Ingrid tuned out, just in time to catch that big black bird disappear around a bend in the river. No way this had anything to do with her, no way she'd be one of the chosen three. She shouldn't even be in this section, algebra two. There were four math classes in eighth grade – algebra one for the geniuses, algebra two for good math students who didn't rise to the genius level, pre-algebra, where Ingrid should have been and would have been happily if her parents hadn't crawled on their knees to Ms. Groome, and math one, formerly remedial math, for the kids out on parole.

Math blowouts on Saturday morning. Who thinks these things up? Grown-ups, of course, the kind with a sense of humor like that warden in *Escape From Alcatraz*. Ingrid was half aware of Ms. Groome scrawling long chains of numbers on the blackboard, all dim and fuzzy. She wrote a note – *What's the word for stuff like giant midget or MathFest?* – balled it up and tossed it discreetly over to Mia's desk across the aisle. Mia was the smartest kid in the class, should have been in algebra one, but she and her mom had moved from New York last year and the school had messed up.

Mia flattened out the note, read it, wrote an answer. The sun, one of those little late fall suns, more silver than gold, shone on Mia's hand – her fingers, skin, everything about her, so delicate. She rolled the note back up, flicked it underhanded across the aisle. Ingrid reached for it, but all at once, so sudden she wasn't sure for a moment that it had really happened, another hand darted into the picture and snatched the note out of the air. Nothing delicate about this hand, skin scaly, knuckles all swollen.

"What could be so important?" said Ms. Groome, unfolding the note. "I'm dying to find out." The sun glared off fingerprints on her glasses, hiding her eyes. She read the note, stuck it in her pocket, returned to the front of the class. Her mouth opened, just a thin shark-like slit. Some withering remark was on the way, but at that very moment, like a message from above, the bell rang.

Class over! Saved by the bell! Chairs started scraping

all over the room as the kids got up. Hubbub, and lots of it. Thanksgiving couldn't come soon enough.

"Just a second," said Ms. Groome, not so much raising her voice over the bedlam as cutting through it like an icepick. Everyone froze. "We still haven't chosen our MathFest team."

Brucie raised his hand.

"Thank you, Bruce. Congratulations."

"Oh, no," said Brucie. "Wait. I was just going to say let's do it tomorrow."

Ms. Groome didn't seem to hear. "Any volunteers for the other two spots?"

There were none.

"Then the pleasure will be mine," said Ms. Groome. She smiled, if smiling meant the corners of the mouth twisting up and teeth making a brief appearance. "Mia. Ingrid. Everybody wish our team good luck."

"Go team," said everybody, glad it wasn't them.

"But wait..." said Brucie.

"I could get sick," Brucie said on the bus ride home.

Someone snickered.

"What if I forged a note?" Brucie said. "With Adobe Photoshop I could make it look like a doctor's—"

"Zip it, guy," said the driver, Mr. Sidney, his BATTLE OF THE CORAL SEA cap slanted low over his eyes, like a ship captain in rough seas. Brucie zipped it: the other choice was walking the rest of the way, as Brucie had learned on the first day of school last year and then had to relearn again just last week.

Mr. Sidney stopped in front of Ingrid's house.

"See you, petunia," he said. Girls were "petunia" to Mr. Sidney, guys "guy". Things must have been a lot different when he was growing up.

Ingrid stepped off the bus, started up the brick path to her house. Ninety-nine Maple Lane was the only place she'd ever lived. Not the biggest, newest or fanciest house in the neighborhood, Riverbend, but there were lots of good things about it. Such as the breakfast nook in the kitchen with windows on three sides, where the family – Mom, Dad, Ingrid and her brother, Ty, a freshman at Echo Falls High (home of the Red Raiders) – ate just about all their meals; and the living-room fireplace, the bricks set in zigzags that matched the brick patterns in the chimney and front walk, a nice touch in Ingrid's opinion; and maybe most of all her bedroom at the back, overlooking the town woods – the smallest room in the house, excluding bathrooms, and the most peaceful.

Ingrid went around to the side, unlocked the mud-room door. Nigel ambled out.

"Hey, boy," said Ingrid, reaching down to pat him.

Nigel loved to be patted, maybe his second favorite thing, next to food. But now he changed course, making a kind of slow-motion swerve that took him just out of reach of her hand.

"Nigel?"

Nigel, crossing the lawn, swiveled his head around in her direction, walking one way, looking another. He had a jowly face and tweedy sort of coat, just like Nigel Bruce who'd played Dr. Watson in the old black-and-white Sherlock Holmes movies; Ingrid, a lover of

335

Sherlock Holmes, had them all on video. Her Nigel, like Dr. Watson, could be slow on the uptake. Unlike Dr. Watson, he wasn't always reliable.

For example, the way he was now avoiding eye contact and had resumed his course, headed for the road. Nigel wasn't allowed on the road. Ingrid, with a book in hand called *Training Even the Dumbest Dog*, had spent hours with Nigel, teaching him not to leave the property, rewarding his eventual success with a pig-out of Hebrew Nationals, his hot dog of choice.

Nigel paused at the edge of the lawn, right forepaw raised in the attitude of one of those clever pointing dogs that understands commands in several languages. Was he remembering those hot dogs, even maybe just a little bit?

"Nigel?"

He stepped onto the street, a dainty little movement – like Zero Mostel in the *Producers* movie, one of Ingrid's favorites – that still surprised her and always meant no good. The next moment he was picking up the pace, pushing himself into that waddling trot, his top speed.

"Nigel!"

Ingrid dropped her backpack, hurried after him. Nigel tried to go faster – she could tell from the furious way his scruffy tail was wagging, slowing him down if anything. He reached the other side of Maple Lane, sniffed at the Grunellos' grass and then made a beeline for the stone angel birdbath that stood by their front door.

"Don't you dare," said Ingrid, running across the lawn.

Too late. Nigel raised his leg against the birdbath.

Ingrid grabbed his collar, dragged him away, trailing a golden arc all the way back to the road. Nigel didn't like the Grunellos, a quiet middle-aged couple who were kind to animals, never bothered anybody and spent a lot of time away. Like now, please God. At the edge of the driveway, he snatched up the Grunellos' copy of *The Echo*.

"Put that down."

But he clung to the rolled-up newspaper with all his might until they were back at the mudroom door. Then he dropped it in a casual sort of way and scrambled inside.

"Kiss those hot dogs goodbye," Ingrid said. She could hear him panting in the kitchen as though he'd just performed some incredible feat.

Ingrid picked up *The Echo*, kind of drooly and tattered now. She'd have to make a trade, dropping their own copy back on the Grunellos' lawn. But the delivery kid seemed to have missed them today.

Ingrid went inside, glancing at the front page. The big story was SENIOR CENTER OPENS WITH A BANG, accompanied by a photo of some white-haired people laughing around a flower pot. Below that was something about new rules from the Conservation Commission, pretty much chewed through, and below that, under a headline that read ECHO FALLS NEWCOMER, was a photo of a striking woman who looked to be a little younger than Mom. She actually resembled Mom – dark hair, big, almond-shaped eyes – but although Mom was beautiful you couldn't call her striking.

Ingrid gazed more closely, saw the prominent cheek-bones, the fine shape of the lips, everything perfect, if a bit severe; maybe not like Mom after all.

> *Ms. Julia LeCaine, formerly of Manhattan, has moved to Echo Falls to take the position of Vice President of Operations for the Ferrand Group.*

Hey. Dad worked for the Ferrand Group. And he was a vice president, too.

> *Ms. LeCaine, a graduate of Princeton University with an MBA from the Wharton School of Business, later founded an Internet company. A former outstanding soccer player, she was a Team USA alternate in 1992. Welcome to Echo Falls, Ms. LeCaine!*

Ingrid went into the kitchen, took a Fresca from the fridge. Bliss, essence of. Whoever invented Fresca was a genius. Could that be an actual job, inventing sodas? A whole new career possibility arose, handy backup in case her number one choice, acting and directing on stage and screen, didn't pan out.

Ingrid drained the can to the last drop, opened the trash cupboard under the sink.

"That's funny," she said.

At the top of the trash bag – which needed to be replaced, Ty's job – lay *The Echo*, today's *Echo*, still rolled up. How could that be? Mom and Dad were at work, wouldn't be home for a couple hours at least, and Ty was at football practice, the only freshman on the varsity. Ingrid glanced over at Nigel, lying by the water bowl with one paw over his eyes in that way he had, as if warding off the light. Nigel – getting out of the locked house, retrieving the paper, depositing it in the trash, locking himself back in? Only in an upside-down universe.

Ingrid heard a footstep, somewhere upstairs. Oh my God. She recalled a moment like this once before, when she'd helped Chief Strade solve the Crazy Katie case. A creepy moment that led to all sorts of scary things. She stood motionless by the kitchen sink. Another footstep, right overhead. That would be Mom and Dad's office, the extra bedroom on the second floor. And was there something familiar about that footstep? Did footsteps have a sound unique to every person, like fingerprints but much harder to distinguish? Ingrid didn't know; but she thought she recognized that footstep.

She went into the front hall, up the stairs, turned left toward the office. The door was half open. Ingrid peeked in.

Dad was at the desk, his back to her. The computer was on and he wore a suit – all Dad's suits were really nice, with sleeve buttons that you could actually unbutton – but he wasn't working. Instead he was slumped forward, his head on the desk.

"Dad? Are you all right?"

He sat up quickly and swiveled around. Ingrid caught one glimpse of his face as she rarely saw it – pale and anxious. Then came a smile and in a second he looked more like himself, the handsomest dad in Echo Falls.

"Hi, cutie," he said. "What are you doing here?"

"Me?" said Ingrid. "I'm home from school."

"Oh," said Dad. "Right."

"Everything okay, Dad?"

"Sure," said Dad. He glanced at the computer, switched it off. "Just punched out a little early. All work and no play –" He paused, waiting for her to finish.

"Makes Dad a dull boy," Ingrid said.

He laughed.

The computer was blank now, but Ingrid had quick eyes and they'd grabbed that last fading screen: Jobs.com.

BEHIND THE CURTAIN

PETER ABRAHAMS

In Echo Falls everyone has a secret…

Too many things are amiss at 99 Maple Lane. What's bothering Ingrid's dad? Why has her brother Ty turned so moody? And when will everyone get off Grampy's back about selling his farm?

Meanwhile Ingrid stumbles upon some suspicious goings-on at the high school. Inspired by her hero Sherlock Holmes, she begins fishing around to find out who's really pulling the strings in Echo Falls.

And then she gets kidnapped.

Venice, Italy, 1592. Donata Mocenigo, daughter to one of the city's noble families, leads a life of wealthy privilege. But constrained by the strict rules of etiquette a young noblewoman must observe, she longs to throw off her veil and wander freely around the vibrant city she can see only from her balcony. So Donata comes up with a daring plan to escape the palazzo and explore – a plan that will change her own and her family's lives for ever.

"Full of fascinating historical details which bring Renaissance Venice to vibrant life."
Celia Rees, author of Witch Child

"Napoli writes with vigour and compassion ... *Daughter of Venice* thrums with historical detail and feminist ardour."
The Independent on Sunday

"Don't cry. We won't be parted, I promise."

It is 1662 and England is reeling from the after-effects of civil war, with its clashes of faith and culture.

Seventeen-year-old Will returns home after completing his studies, to begin an apprenticeship arranged by his wealthy father.

Susanna, a young Quaker girl, leaves her family to become a servant in the same town.

Theirs is a story that speaks across the centuries, telling of love and the struggle to stay true to what is most important – in spite of parents, society and even the law.

But is the love between Will and Susanna strong enough to survive – no matter what?

"Here is a novel that needs a trumpet to be blown for it... " *The Guardian*

In a newspaper office, Paul Faustino, South America's top football writer, sits opposite the man they call El Gato – the Cat – the world's greatest goalkeeper.

On the table between them stands the World Cup...

In the hours that follow, El Gato tells his incredible life story – how he, a poor logger's son, learns to become a World Cup-winning goalkeeper so good he is almost unbeatable. And the most remarkable part of this story is the man who teaches him – the mysterious Keeper, who haunts a football pitch at the heart of the claustrophobic forest.

This extraordinary, gripping tale pulses with the rhythms of football and the rainforest.

"This is a tremendous book, profoundly moving, dizzyingly conceived." *School Librarian*

Mary Elizabeth (or Lola, as she prefers to be called) longs to be in the spotlight. But when she moves to New Jersey with her family, Lola discovers that the role of resident drama queen at Dellwood "Deadwood" High has already been filled – by the Born-to-Win, Born-to-Run-Everything Carla Santini. Once the curtain goes up on the school play, which drama queen will take centre stage?

"Lola will rightfully take her place among the unforgettable and lively female characters of young adult novels. Like its heroine, the story is off-beat, outrageous and utterly charming."
School Library Journal

"High school has always been this stressful, but rarely this hilarious."
Booklist